THE
OCTOBER
KILLINGS

THE OCTOBER KILLINGS

WESSEL EBERSOHN

Minotaur Books

New York

This is a work of fiction. All of the characters, organizations, and events portrayed in this novel are either products of the author's imagination or are used fictitiously.

www.minotaurbooks.com

Library of Congress Cataloging-in-Publication Data

Ebersohn, Wessel.
    The October killings / Wessel Ebersohn.—1st U.S. ed.
        p. cm.
    ISBN 978-0-312-65595-2 (alk. paper)
    1. Anti-apartheid activists—South Africa—Fiction.   2. South Africa—
Politics and government—20th century—Fiction.   I. Title.
    PR9369.3.E24O3 2011
    823'.914—dc22

                                                              2010037509

First published in South Africa by Umuzi, an imprint of Random House Struik (Pty) Ltd.

First U.S. Edition: January 2011

10   9   8   7   6   5   4   3   2   1

For Harry, Jenny, and Timothy—
You are always close.

THE
OCTOBER
KILLINGS

1

October 21, 1985

The convoy stayed in the shadow of the hillside until after darkness had fallen. By the time the ten armored personnel carriers started moving, the trees on the far side of the valley had long since faded into poorly defined shadows.

The route they were to travel had been carefully planned to raise as little interest as possible. Much of the way would be on dirt roads. They would pass through no towns and were likely to be seen only by the sort of rural people who would watch them with no more than the vaguest interest. According to the planning, the distance of almost two hundred kilometers to the border was going to take a little over three hours.

Each vehicle carried the driver and ten men, seated back-to-back, facing outward in two rows of five. In the leading vehicle, Leon Lourens, nineteen years old, broad in the shoulders, but lean after six months of intensive training, was sitting slightly forward on the thinly padded seat, his hands clasped together between his thighs. His rifle was stacked under the seat along with those of the nine other men.

Like most nineteen-year-olds of his time and culture, Leon was a patriot. He knew that, if need be, he was willing to die to defend his country. Tonight was to be his first commando raid. He did not fully understand the risks he would be facing, but he was confident that he was ready to meet them.

Most of the men were under thirty, but all of the others had seen action along the country's borders. Leon was the youngest and he was excited at having been chosen for so important a mission. He was going to show his comrades and his family, if word ever got back to them, that he was worthy of being selected.

He was aware that his breath was coming in the brief snatches of the overawed and tried consciously to control it. His excitement could not have been greater if he had been on the way to a willing young woman, any young woman, anywhere. It had taken concentration, but his hands were still and he had controlled the tremor in his left knee that he sometimes felt at times of great excitement. Slowly his breathing started to return to something more normal. He had gone through the instructions Captain van Jaarsveld had given them many times in his mind. Now he was fully prepared.

The captain himself was sitting next to Leon and directly behind the driver. Like his men, he too was silent. Leon had never spoken to the captain and the captain had only ever spoken to him in direct military commands. But he was Leon's senior officer and Leon knew that he would follow wherever he led.

According to the briefing the captain had given them, there were between ten and twenty terrorists in the house, which was on a fairly isolated stretch of road a few hundred meters from the nearest neighbor. They expected to reach the track that would take them to the border fence just after midnight. They would approach the fence in darkness, the engines at little more than idling speed. Two men from their vehicle would cut the fence two kilometers from the house. At that point they would be joined by a uniformed scout who would ensure that they got the right house. The six rear vehicles, two of which were empty to accommodate prisoners, would seal off the road on either side. The soldiers from the first two would go straight into the house. They were to shoot only if there were signs of resistance.

Leon's was an almost perfect shot, but he had never before

aimed a firearm at another human being. Now there was some-thing he had to know and only the captain could give him the answer. He looked at van Jaarsveld's face, but could read no ex-pression there. "Permission to speak," he said.

"What is it, soldier?"

"Do you expect resistance, captain?" He had turned his head toward the captain and tried to keep his voice low enough that no one else would hear his question.

Now it was van Jaarsveld's turn to examine his face. "There's always resistance."

"Always, captain. When they see they're outnumbered . . ."

"They're terrorists. They always resist."

That answered the question. They were going to resist and he would have to fire. But that was all right. That was what he had been chosen and trained for.

By the time the lights of Ficksburg came into view they were half an hour ahead of schedule and had to stop. The men were allowed to get down and loosen up, taking their rifles with them. It also gave them the opportunity to load. The R4 rifle's magazine took twelve shells. Another twelve were kept in the side pocket of each man's fatigues.

The night sky was clear and cloudless. There was no moon, but the brightness of the stars in the dry Highveld air was enough for the men to recognize one another. The lights of Ficksburg were a thin and distant line. "This is it," Leon told himself. "Just another hour. This is what I've been training for. This is the mo-ment." The weight of the rifle felt good. He knew that he was not only an excellent shot, but he was also a quick one. Aim-ing, even at a distant target, took only seconds. At close range he took almost no time. He was as sure with a rifle as any man in the company, and better than any in the squad.

It took a while to reach the border from the place where they had stopped, but to Leon it felt like the descent of a large aircraft after a long flight. Even if it took half an hour, you felt that the journey was over and you were already there.

The convoy approached the border fence in darkness, up a narrow gully, digging tracks in the crisp veld grass. The two men whose job it was cut quickly through the wire. As it came loose, Leon and the others rolled back a section on either side. In less than a minute they were moving again. The scout who had been waiting at the fence climbed up next to the driver.

At the top of a rise they left the grass and followed a dirt road. Up ahead, Leon could see the first house. In the glow of a yard light two figures dashed away, boys of perhaps ten or eleven, barefoot and in short pants. Their skinny legs and bare feet were vaguely disturbing. In his nineteen years he had seen so many like them and played with them as a child. They were too ordinary to be here. Leon looked at Captain van Jaarsveld, but the captain's face was in darkness. He was leaning forward in readiness to rise.

There were only two houses in the first block. They rolled past them without raising any obvious interest. The next block held three houses, two on the left and one on the right. Leon knew that the house they were aiming for was the one on the right. The first time he saw it, it was some fifty meters ahead and in complete darkness. It was an old corrugated-iron-roofed house, an unevenly supported veranda running down two sides. Even in the darkness it was clear that it had been a long time since the house had last been painted. The captain rose and was opening the hatch on the roof. It was time to go.

2

Abigail Bukula was late for the meeting. Being late was not unusual for her, but it was unusual for her to be late when the minister was expected. She had gotten to know him fairly well in the three years she had been with the Justice Department. He had been good to her in the way that powerful older men can be good to intelligent and attractive young women, without expecting anything in return. She did not want ever to disappoint him.

Abigail had run the length of the long uphill arcade from the parking garage to the pedestrian crossing in front of the department's offices. She stopped on the curb, hot and out of breath, hoping that her makeup had survived the exertion. She was wearing a light gray trouser suit that was intended to make her look at least her thirty-five years. She was all too aware that she looked years younger than her actual age and that this was not a good quality when seeking promotion in her country's civil service. As for the trousers, Abigail remembered owning a skirt once, but that was long ago and it had been a gift from an aunt. She had worn it only once and that had been to please the aunt.

It was almost twelve years since the country's first democratic elections, but the names of Pretorius Street, where her car was parked, and Schoeman Street, where she now waited for a pause in the traffic, had survived the attention of government and bureaucracy so far. Both streets still carried the names of pioneering white settlers.

Pretoria was a city in which white anxiety and black frustration wrestled each other with almost equal determination. The anxiety in the suburbs was based on unknowable strictures that the black majority may yet inflict upon them, while the frustration in the black townships rose from a political victory that for many seemed to be in name only. The suburbs were still white and wealthy and the townships were still black and poor.

It was not so for Abigail though. Brought up in exile during the apartheid years, she had been educated at University College, London, and Harvard. The combination of her own ability and the shortage of skills among black South Africans, especially women, had seen her rise from senior professional officer to chief director in just three years. She was just two steps away from the director-generalship of the department. With both the current director-general and most deputy directors-general on three-year contracts, it was not impossible to imagine her in the top position in the department within a few years. Most women in government would applaud the idea. At least as many men, still subscribing to the African notion of male superiority and despite government policy to the contrary, would do what they could to keep her out.

Ahead of her and to her left as she crossed Schoeman Street was the nondescript building that housed the department's offices. As the government machinery had grown over the last thirty years, one department after another had been moved out of the Union Buildings that still housed the presidency, and were now scattered around the city. The modest buildings they occupied belied the standard notion of excessive government spending.

As she came through the checkpoint at the entrance to the building, she flashed her card at two uninterested guards from a private security company. Both had seen her many times, but the system insisted that every card, including that of the minister himself, be shown whenever the holder entered the building.

It was only in the lift, on the way to the fourth floor where the meeting was being held, that Abigail was able to be still. The opportunity lasted only a few seconds, but it gave her that long to compose herself. All day she had tried to keep herself even busier than usual. The busier you are, her barely conscious thinking told her, the less chance you have to remember. And remembering was to be avoided if that were at all possible.

He was going to be there. More than that, honoring him was the reason for the meeting. She had always known that sooner or later this day would come. Now it was upon her.

She had worked out a strategy for dealing with the meeting. She would leave her car downtown as an excuse for coming late, telling anyone who asked that it had developed a fault. She would make sure that she was seen by some of the department's senior people, but would try to stay shielded from the minister, slip away as soon as the main formalities were completed and avoid the socializing afterward.

Already her plan was falling apart. She had left the car downtown and timed her leaving it to get to the meeting late, but despite her intentions, she had found herself running up the arcade. Hot and flustered, she would probably not be as unobtrusive as she had hoped.

Johanna, her desperately busy personal assistant, met Abigail in a passage that was crowded with the overflow from the meeting. "You look like you've been running," the younger woman said.

"My car broke down," Abigail told Johanna. "I hope the meeting's not over yet."

"It hasn't even started . . ." Johanna began.

Oh, Christ, she thought. All this for nothing.

"The minister has just arrived, but Michael Bishop is not yet here."

That was his name. It was only the second time she had come across it in twenty years. The first time had been just the day before, when she had received an e-mail instructing her to be at the meeting.

They had reached the door of the meeting room. "I'll wait out here for a moment," she said.

"No–o." Johanna's eyes had grown wide at the idea. "The minister's been asking after you."

"What did you tell him?"

"I said you'd been held up in court." Johanna was a township girl and life on the township streets had taught her to think on her feet. Her parents were schoolteachers, who had insisted on her spending her afternoons studying and had been present to enforce their ruling. Right now, she was aiming for her second degree. She was in her mid-twenties, some ten years younger than her boss, almost as ambitious and unconsciously modeling herself on Abigail. "I said that being held up in court was the only possible reason that you were not yet here. I said I'd tell you that he wanted to see you the moment you got here. I said you wouldn't miss this for anything."

Johanna was out of breath from telling Abigail all the things she had said to the minister. She stopped to breathe. "What did he say?" Abigail asked.

"He said, please. Please bring her to me the moment she arrives."

"The guest of honor's not here yet?"

"No." Johanna's eyes were wide again. "I can't wait. He's so mysterious."

There must have been more than one hundred people in the meeting room. Most were senior government functionaries from the justice department, the men in dark suits and ties, and the women in muted colors. They were the new government elite. Most were under forty, African and looking for better paid options in the corporate world. Here and there a white or Asian face, often belonging to a former trade unionist who had found this new place in which to stay out of the rain, dotted the confined landscape. The only casually dressed people were to be found among the handful of reliable journalists, the kind who knew to be careful about the questions they asked, or perhaps to whom the difficult questions never occurred.

The gathering had split into small, chattering groups, one of which now gathered around the minister. He had spotted Abigail and was gesturing for to her to come closer. "Here she is," he was saying. Around the minister were two directors-general, three deputy directors–general and one chief director who, given his relatively modest rank, was lucky to be included in the company. The minister turned to Abigail and smiled. The other men all smiled too. Whatever they thought about ambitious young women who may yet overtake them could keep for a more appropriate moment. "How are you getting on?" the minister asked. "I've told these gentlemen not to crowd you, that they must give you room to move." He paused only a moment. "Well, Abigail, are they giving you room to move?"

All except my own deputy DG, she thought. She saw the object of her thoughts looking directly at her, lips pursed, like a schoolmaster observing an unreliable pupil. "Of course they are, Mr. Minister. You instructed them to," she said.

The minister laughed. "If only life were that simple." He turned to the men around him. "Do you gentlemen always do as I instruct you?" He led the laughter that followed and nodded with real amusement at the protestations of absolute obedience.

The minister was speaking to the group as a whole now. "This occasion is overdue," he said. "It is astonishing that this hero of the liberation struggle has gone so long without recognition." There were murmurs of agreement from the other men. He turned again to Abigail. "Did you ever meet him during the exile years?" he asked.

How do I answer this? Abigail asked herself. Had I ever met him?

"Did you ever meet Michael Bishop?" the minister asked again.

"I think so," she said. "Perhaps." Oh God, she thought.

"Of course that was long ago. You would have been very young."

Not that young, she thought. "Yes," she said. "I was very young."

"Yes," the minister said, "a genuine hero of the struggle. While the rest of us were getting educated at international universities, he was in the front lines, risking his life. It just shows how sound our nonracial policies are." The last reference was to the fact that Bishop was white. Again, all those around the minister were nodding in agreement. "Now, gentlemen, if you will excuse me for a moment, I need to venture down the passage."

Abigail took the opportunity to extricate herself from the group and joined Johanna on the other side of the room. "There's no word from him," Johanna said. "He's already half an hour late, but we've heard nothing."

Abigail had only ever seen Bishop once and that one occasion would be with her as long as she lived. In all the many party meetings and public occasions she had attended she had never been aware of his presence at any of them. She had never heard of an invitation to speak at a meeting being issued to him or even any public acknowledgment of his existence—until now.

"He may not come," she told Johanna, the words issuing forth unplanned, almost surprising herself.

"But everyone is here, even two cabinet ministers."

"I know."

"Do you know him?"

"No."

None of this satisfied Johanna, but there was something in the tone of Abigail's answers that forbade further questions.

"I do hope he comes," Johanna said.

The minister waited another half hour, then, trying hard to conceal his irritation, made his speech about the power of selfless devotion to the cause and how Michael Bishop's life confirmed this. The recognition of his part in the liberation struggle would not be confined to this day and the country would never forget the sacrifices he had made.

The minister's speech continued for some thirty minutes, but Abigail stopped listening after only a minute or two. She had found a place at the back of the room and, resting against the wall, barely took in the content of the minister's speech. There were times when a blank mind was its best possible state.

3

Abigail was still hurrying. Her evening function followed so close behind her afternoon one that she barely had time to shower and change before leaving.

As was her way, she had paused only briefly before the mirror before leaving. Abigail knew that her face and figure were pleasing to men. She also knew that a little more weight in the bosom would have further improved matters, but she was perfectly content with the way things were. For the occasion she had dressed in a plain black pants suit, broken only by a single string of pearls, the first present Robert had ever given her. The thought that this would be very simple attire compared to that worn by most of the ladies had not entered her mind.

Robert Mokoapi, her husband, had been putting the day's edition of his newspaper to bed and would shower and change at work, meeting her at the home where the function was being held. Abigail had no clear idea of the reason for this evening's occasion, except that Robert wanted her to strengthen her relationship with the controlling shareholders of the company he worked for.

At night the run from their apartment on the Groenkloof hillside overlooking eastern Pretoria to Johannesburg's northern suburbs took no more than thirty minutes. Now, with the evening commuter rush not quite over, the drive from city to city could take more than twice as long.

Following the directions Robert had given her, she found the high-walled multimillion-rand house at the end of a short street of other high-walled multimillion-rand houses. In much of South Africa, and especially in Johannesburg, if your lifestyle revealed that you had money, you needed to take precautions to safeguard it and your family. Every house in the street had electrified fencing along the tops of its walls, closed-circuit television cameras at the gates, electronic alarm systems and rapid-response armed guards on call. Abigail's own home too was protected by all of these devices.

A uniformed guard compared her name to those on a list before opening the gate. She drove into a garden that did not seem to contain a house at all. It was surrounded by five acres of garden and was not visible from the garden walls. As she followed the drive, the house came into view through a network of jacaranda, palm and plane tree branches. The parking area alone, to which she was guided by another uniformed guard, covered half an acre.

There were perhaps twenty cars in the parking lot. Among them was Robert's Mercedes, a perk on which the company had insisted. Robert always said that the symbols of status meant nothing to him. He was after the real thing, he said, not just the appearance of power.

As she opened the car door she could hear the sound of many animated voices against the background of Beethoven's *Pathétique* sonata. She smoothed down the pants of her suit. The glass sliding doors were open and the guests had flooded out onto a broad patio, paved with Italian tiles and fringed with tiny, stunted palms. The pianist, a young blond woman in tuxedo and bow tie, was working a grand piano that had been positioned under a yellow canvas awning on the edge of the patio. To Abigail's ears, she was adding little floral bits that would have surprised the composer had he been present.

A middle-aged man, whose receding hair was so black that

to Abigail it had to be dyed, was scurrying around the patio giving orders to waiters and others. He came forward to meet her. His public relations company had sent out the invitations. "Abigail," he said, in a tone that suggested that her presence had made the evening for him.

"Martin," she said, trying to capture in her voice some of his enthusiasm. "How good of you to invite me."

"I always invite the really important people, my dear." They laughed, both knowing that he had nothing to do with the invitation list. "Robert has been asking after you," he said. "He's over there with the bigwigs."

She recognized the man with her husband as the controlling shareholder and chairman of Robert's company. Nearly as tall as Robert and in his late sixties, but lean and tanned, in immaculately tailored slacks and turtleneck sweater, he looked like an advertisement for a luxury cruise line. He was, in fact, the third-generation custodian of his family's gold-mining money. During the apartheid years, when sanctions kept his company confined by South Africa's borders, he had invested in many nonmining activities, from shoe stores to real estate. He had since rid himself of all non-core businesses, excepting Robert's newspaper.

"The food tonight is something really special." Martin was still next to her, no new guests having followed her from the parking area. Abigail raised an eyebrow in a feigned attempt at curiosity. "Fried mopani worms and locusts for starters."

Since she had left home she had been aware that some irritant had been at work, just below the surface of full consciousness. Now that she gave the matter her attention for the first time, she realized that it was the label on her suit that had been scratching the back of her neck. Over the last half hour it had been tearing persistently at her skin and was now almost impossible to ignore.

"Say again . . . ?" she said to Martin.

"Followed by crocodile steaks with phutu porridge, and then fermented Amarula fruit with sour cream for dessert. To drink we have KwaZulu palm wine, distilled in their kraals by Zulu peasants."

"Are you serious?"

Martin was indeed serious. "We decided to go all-African tonight. What do you think?"

"Astonishing," was all Abigail could manage politely.

"I thought you'd be taken with our menu. Oh, here comes the deputy chairman. Got to go."

He hurried in the direction of the parking lot while Abigail started across the patio. Almost everyone present was a member of one of two groups, each with its own agenda. One group was made up of very rich white men who were determined to keep what they had by enriching a small band of influential black men beyond any possible imaginings. The other group was made up of influential black men: politicians, senior bureaucrats, one former cabinet minister who had recently resigned to pursue richer pickings, all determined to be part of the group that was being enriched by the very rich white men.

Robert saw her long before she reached him and met her in the center of the patio. "You look great," he said.

A waiter swept up to them with a tray of crisply fried insects. Abigail waved him away. With her right hand she tried to reposition the offending label. "Have you seen the menu?" she asked. "Real African stuff, to make us darkies feel at home, no doubt."

"They're just trying to be accepting," Robert said. Abigail recognized his patient tone of voice.

"Mopani worms, locusts, fermented Amarula with sour cream? Palm wine, made by Zulu peasants? For God's sake. I grew up in Hampstead, just down the road from Buckingham Palace."

"Shhh . . ." He had a finger to his lips.

"Robert, you've got to get me out of here. I won't eat that to please anyone."

Robert took her by the arm and led her a few steps away from the nearest cluster of partygoers. "Listen, I need you to be on your best behavior tonight. Let me tell you what this is all about."

She hated it when Robert preached to her about being on her best behavior. Before he married her he knew that she was rarely well behaved. He should have made peace with it by now. Trying to avoid him, she looked into the depths of a garden, where flowering orchids had been arranged in the nearer trees for the evening. They would be returned to the nursery in the morning.

He leaned forward to bring his face close to hers. "Tonight the old man is announcing his empowerment deal. I'm getting ten percent of the company."

Abigail turned to face him, her head spinning in his direction like a toy operated by a windup rubber band. Her neck was still itching. "Ten percent of Vuna Corp?" The name of the company meant "harvest." It had been changed from National Media in the first year after the democratic elections.

"That's right. What's wrong with your collar?"

"Nothing's wrong."

"You keep fiddling with it."

"It's fine."

"If you keep fiddling, it looks as if something's wrong."

"Ten percent?" Abigail asked.

Robert grinned at her. "Sweetheart, we're rich."

Abigail realized that his pleasure was simply in anticipation of pleasing her. She heard herself say, "I can hardly believe it. What's it worth?"

"Half a billion."

"Half a million?"

"Half a billion."

"Half a billion rand?" It seemed impossible.

"Half a billion rand," Robert said emphatically.

"Good God, Robert, are you worth that to them?" She paused for only a moment, before hurrying on. "I know how good you are at your work. It's obvious to me, and everyone who knows you says so, but half a billion . . ."

He was leaning toward her again, so that he would not have

to raise his voice. "Look, they have to do it with someone. They can hardly do business in this country and interact with government without an empowerment partner. I'm the most suitable."

"And you pay nothing?"

Now Robert looked uncomfortable. Abigail's reaction was nothing like he had imagined it would be. "Nothing we have to worry about. There's some fancy footwork in the accounting. It will take five years before the investment is fully ours."

"Good God, Robert."

"What is it?" He was almost begging.

"Half a billion?"

"You act as if you're not pleased."

"I'm practically paralyzed."

A cluster of young black executives, drinks in hand, had moved closer to them. A broad-shouldered man, carrying too much weight and at thirty-five a leading office-bearer of the country's most influential youth organization, was the center of attention. The entire group was laughing loudly at something he had said. He was hanging on to an embarrassed-looking young woman. "Everybody with influence has got his Indian," he was saying. "It's the way the world works." He was referring to the local myth that all Indian South Africans were rich. His eyes fixed on Robert and he wagged a knowing finger. "What about you, Mokoapi? What do you say?" He waved a finger at Robert. "I can see you've got your Indian, my man."

Abigail was already moving away with Robert following. "Is that what Vuna Corp is—your Indian?"

"Don't be absurd," Robert said. "Big Vusi is a fool. Everyone knows that. I don't understand you, Abby. I swear I don't understand you. Don't you want me to get ahead?"

The chairman and his wife had been moving among the guests like royalty at a command performance, waving here, nodding there, a few words spoken somewhere else, all grace and graciousness. She was wearing a Ghanaian robe, complete with turban, no doubt part of the all-African ambience that

Martin had been talking about. She spotted Abigail with Robert and moved her husband in their direction. "Abigail, my dear," she said, as they approached. "You look lovely tonight."

"You too, Marcia. Your outfit is a perfect example of . . ." She caught Robert's warning eye. ". . . of genuine African chic," she finished. Out of the corner of her eye she thought she saw him relax.

"Thank you, my dear," Marcia said.

"This is an important night for your husband," the chairman said. "I searched for years to find a black editor of genuine ability. I was delighted when I found Robert."

"A personal triumph," Abigail said. She felt more than saw Robert move uncomfortably next to her.

"I like to think of it that way."

"Marcia, I was wondering . . ." Abigail began.

Marcia had been looking admiringly at the chairman, who was smiling modestly.

"Yes, dear?" Her eyebrows had risen involuntarily. Robert's eyes had also widened, no doubt wondering what his nonconforming wife might be up to now.

"Do you have some scissors I could borrow for a moment?"

Marcia glanced at her husband in a way that seemed to indicate that this was not in the script. "I suppose I can find something, my dear. Come along." She led the way through the sliding doors and up a staircase that reminded Abigail of *Gone with the Wind*. Her bedroom was decorated in lavender and was furnished with only a single bed and a hand-carved yellowwood dressing table. In the adjoining walk-in wardrobe that was almost as big as the bedroom itself she found a pair of nail scissors. "Will this do?" she asked. "I don't know what the problem is."

Abigail had already rid herself of her jacket. "This label is driving me crazy. It feels like it's made of sandpaper."

After the label had been dealt with and Abigail was ready to return to the party, Marcia held her by one arm. "Most young women would simply have suffered the label on an occasion like this."

"Maybe I'm not most young women."

"You certainly are not, my dear. You're altogether refreshing. Something else I should mention . . ." She waited for Abigail's full attention. "My husband gets a little overdone sometimes. When he called Robert a black editor of genuine ability, he simply meant that he was an editor of genuine ability."

Abigail nodded. "Thank you. That needed to be said."

When she got back to Robert, he studied her face for a moment before releasing a lungful of air. "You look happier."

"I no longer feel quite as patronized," she said, "and the label's gone. I'm sorry, Robert. Here I am, behaving like a bitch on your big night. Please forgive me."

"Let's just try to be a little tolerant. And I'm glad the label's gone."

"It was scratching the hell out of my neck."

Suddenly Robert was laughing. He hugged her briefly, not the sort of thing husbands did to their wives on such occasions. "We'll be able to afford clothing with gentler labels from now on," he whispered.

Robert was drawn into conversation with a business acquaintance, and Abigail moved to the edge of the patio. She watched her husband, smiling and shaking hands, as he was introduced to someone. He was so effortlessly gracious and as effortlessly honest. Watching him, she realized again how much she loved him. Dear Robert, she thought, you deserve an easier woman than me.

In due course the chairman made his unavoidable speech. Abigail saw similarities with that made by the minister earlier in the day. Both, according to their authors, had been about liberation. The minister had spoken about Michael Bishop's selfless devotion to the cause of political liberation. The chairman revealed his corporation's commitment to the cause of economic liberation. Each speech was full of praise, first for Michael Bishop and then for Abigail's own Robert.

In time it was over, the food consumed and the requisite interval had been spent smiling, sipping drinks and shaking hands. And, at last, Abigail could go home. With the afternoon and evening behind her and the label in an ashtray in Marcia's bedroom, life felt much better. She drove quickly along the highway between the two cities with the headlights of Robert's car in the rearview mirror, never more than a hundred meters behind.

4

The distance between their cars narrowed as they entered Pretoria, Robert stopping close behind her at the first traffic light. Abigail was glad that the drive home had been uneventful. She admired the safeness of his driving after the amount of liquor he had consumed during the evening, but she did not imagine that he would have passed a blood test.

A wind had been blowing across Pretoria all evening, and once they turned out of the main suburban artery the streets were sprinkled with lilac jacaranda blossoms. As far as the headlights reached, the little flowers formed a soft and colorful carpet.

Tonight Abigail waited till Robert had finished showering before entering the bathroom. "Come to bed, baby," he murmured in her direction as he sat on the edge of the bed. "I want to celebrate the occasion."

From the bathroom she saw him roll over slowly, quite naked, ending horizontally, his smooth, almost hairless body a deep brown splash on the crisp white of the sheets. Not tonight, she thought. She would stay a few minutes longer than usual in the shower and by the time she came out the liquor would have done its work, even on Robert's cast-iron constitution. And he would sleep through till morning.

Robert's approach to sex was essentially uncomplicated.

"Three generations ago Zulu men were still warriors," he had told her more than once. "And I was a warrior against the old regime. I need sex and I need it regularly."

She was not sure what the connection between warriorhood, if that was the right word, and sex was. Not that this was normally a problem to Abigail. They were both in their thirties, in excellent physical condition and their love-making had never been anything but enjoyable. On occasion it was ecstatic.

But tonight was different. She was trying not to think, but the memory that this afternoon threatened to reawaken was with her in a way that went deeper than thought. Despite the years between, it was never far from her and today's meeting, not the silly evening one with the men on both sides all jockeying for financial position, but the pompous afternoon one with a cabinet minister singing the praises of a man whom the minister did not understand and who had not bothered to attend.

Had not bothered to attend? she asked herself. Perhaps it was not like that. Perhaps attending was impossible. You had to know him to even guess at the reasons. And no one knew him.

On any other night the warm water cascading the length of her body and splashing around her feet would have been relaxing. On this night it was a shield, a protection against the advances of a loving and virile husband. God knows, she thought, he deserves a less complicated woman.

Leaving the water running, she took the few steps across the bathroom that would, through the crack of the door, give her a view of Robert on the bed. His arms and legs spread-eagled, he gave every impression of being unconscious.

She lingered another ten minutes in the shower, eventually emerging from the bathroom in a Chinese gown he had brought back from a fact-finding trip to the East during his days as a civil servant. By this time he was as she thought he would be. Robert would not be conscious again until morning.

Instead of lying down on the bed next to him, Abigail left the bedroom and made her way through the apartment to the French windows and onto the balcony. She stood for some time looking down into the street where splashes of blossoms could be seen wherever a street lamp lit one of the city's omnipresent jacarandas. Tonight Abigail saw neither the blossoms nor the city lights stretching away to the west.

She did become aware of something moving in the deep darkness of the shadow of a large house that bordered the secure complex where she and Robert lived. Whatever it was would be able to see her clearly, she thought. It was probably just a cat, but the thought was not convincing enough to keep her outside. She was retreating toward the French windows when she saw the pale form of the bull terrier emerge from the deeper shadow. The dog had a reputation earned by attacking messengers and deliverymen with a ferocity not expected in a domestic animal. According to rumors spread by the neighborhood's domestic workers, the house owners routinely paid hospital bills and small bribes to keep the incidents from the police. Abigail shuddered at the sight of the creature padding along a pathway, its narrow eye slits giving the appearance of being closed. The animal rounded a corner and again disappeared into the darkness. She stepped inside, locked the French windows and closed the steel security screen. By the faint light from outside she sat down in one of the easy chairs.

You are a fool, she told herself. There is no connection between the dog and the man. Even so, it was three o'clock before she came to bed and, even then, sleep was not possible.

5

The four female executives from the national rail carrier were seated in government-issue chairs around Abigail's desk. They all looked indignant, righteously indignant.

Her responsibility in the Department of Justice was the gender desk. This meant ensuring that new legislation did not keep women at a disadvantage, it being assumed that all women, especially African women, were already disadvantaged. It also meant that she could not avoid delegations like this one.

She had asked for a job that would allow her closer to major litigation, but the deputy director-general had answered through bored, half-closed eyes that the gender desk was an important part of the department. The department thought so, the party thought so, the president himself thought so and therefore she should think so too and do her best to make her section effective. It was clear to her that the deputy director-general himself did not think so.

She had cornered the minister at a conference once to tell him about her ambitions. He had nodded and smiled while he listened to her, then placed a large hand on one of her shoulders and said, "All in good time, my dear. I will not forget you." That had been that.

"Let me understand this," Abigail asked the four women.

"You cannot take this matter to your boss herself, because she is the problem."

"She has reduced us to the level of mere clerks," the one, who seemed to have been chosen as spokesperson, said. "We are not allowed to undertake overseas trips unless she has cleared them."

Abigail clicked her tongue in apparent sympathy.

"And we no longer have advertising budgets. Our company cars have to be in the company garage overnight—we may not even go home in them. And there is a total moratorium on new staff."

"I understand why you came to me," Abigail said.

The spokesperson looked at the others. "I told you we should come to Abby."

Abigail smiled her best public relations smile. "But, unfortunately I have been specifically forbidden to get involved with issues regarding parastatals."

"What point is there in a gender desk then?" one of the others burst out. "I thought it was to look after the interests of women."

Well, perhaps the intention may have been to look after the interests of impoverished rural single mothers, Abigail thought. Or perhaps to see to the interests of those women whose rights are being trampled by outdated tribal laws that should long ago have passed into history. Or to start eliminating the remaining statutes that treat women as minors. Perhaps the idea was not to fight for your right to fly overseas at taxpayers' expense. "I do sympathize," she said. "I really do."

It took her another fifteen minutes of sympathizing before she could turn her attention to the conference she had to run— the conference the minister had told her could very well define policy into the future. Its subject was the role of gender diversity in the administration of developing national economies in Africa. A list of speakers had been passed down to her by the deputy DG, who had made it clear that these names had come from higher than himself, hinting that the presidency had a hand in the matter. She had objected to some of the names on the list, especially that of the dictator running Zimbabwe who was no advocate of female advancement, but was told that there could be no discussion about the matter. She could suggest further names to fill out the list, but those on the original list were to be the keynote speakers.

She had completed the list of speakers, it had been approved by the minister without comment, Johanna had contacted them all and now the synopses of all the speeches lay before her on her desk. The speakers fell into two distinct categories: those she had added to the list would all be discussing things that the African countries themselves could do to promote economic growth. Those on the original list would all be talking about how much the West owed Africa and that it was time that reparations were made.

She had barely finished going through them when Johanna came in. She looked anxious, an unusual state for her, and puzzled, an equally unusual state. "There's a strange white man downstairs," she said. "He came without an appointment and he's asking to see you. He's wearing a suit that's too small for him. His hands are so big . . . you should see them . . ." Johanna was clearly proud of her powers of observation. "Also, his suit is old and a bit creased . . ."

"Tell me, Sherlock," Abigail asked, "did he mention a purpose for this visit?"

"He said it's personal. I told him that you were very busy and only saw members of the public by appointment. I said you were preparing for a major conference and could not be interrupted. I told him that he can't just walk in and expect to see senior justice department executives. But he's still there."

A white working man with dirt under his fingernails? "Might he have a name?" Abigail wanted to know.

"Leo Lawrence," Johanna said.

Abigail paused a long moment before she was sure that she would be able to speak. "Leon Lourens?" she asked, correcting Johanna. She had only heard that name once before and had never expected to hear it again.

"That sounds like it."

Abigail seemed to be looking straight at Johanna as if studying her face, but she was not seeing her. The younger woman moved uncomfortably from one foot to the other, sure that she had done something to displease her boss. "I'll send him away."

"No," Abigail said at last. "I'll see him."

"He looks quite rough."

"Take these." She handed Johanna the synopses. "And bring him up immediately."

"Right now?"

"This moment."

After Johanna had hurried away, Abigail rose slowly and came out from behind her desk. It would not seem right to be waiting, seated at the desk, when he came in. She went over to the office's only window which, had she looked in that direction, would have given her a view of the Schoeman Street traffic. Instead she turned to face the door. She had waited perhaps two minutes when the door opened and Johanna came in, her head swiveling anxiously back and forth between Abigail and the man following her.

Leon Lourens had changed in the twenty years since the night when she had first met him. He had been a boy of perhaps nineteen then, sturdy, but with the lightness of youth. Now he was broader, his shoulders heavier, thick-fingered hands protruding from the sleeves of a suit that no longer fitted well on his widening frame. His face, too, looked darker in the way of Caucasian faces that are exposed to the sun every day.

He took just one step into her office and stopped. Standing before the window, she was no more than a silhouette. He waited for her to advance across the room. "You've changed a lot, but I can see it's you," he said.

For the moment Abigail was unable to speak. She too could see that this man was the boy of all those years before. She reached out and took his outstretched hand in both of hers. Johanna, realizing that she was in the presence of something that she did not understand and where she was not welcome, retreated quickly, closing the door behind her. "I've followed your career," he was saying. "A few times there were things in the papers. When I read it I knew it was you." He spoke with a heavy Afrikaans accent.

At last Abigail found her voice. "I'm glad to see you," she said. "I've often thought about you." How could she do otherwise? On a night when she had been sure that she was going to die, he had appeared unexpectedly and she had lived. She had known him for just seven hours, but they had been hours that had left their mark indelibly on her soul. To say that she would not forget him did not describe it. She had been changed by those hours. Remembering or forgetting was not the issue. "You're not in the army anymore?" she asked.

He spread both arms in a gesture of helplessness. "They retrenched me after the 1994 elections."

"What do you do now?"

Again the helpless, almost embarrassed gesture. "I fix cars, I do odd jobs."

She led him across the room to the window where there were chairs and a coffee table. "Won't you sit down?"

Lourens accepted with the awkwardness of someone who was not often invited to sit down in the offices of senior people. He sat upright with his hands on his knees on a seat that invited relaxing. Abigail waited until he spoke. "You're big now, but you still look the same."

"I was big then." She found herself smiling. Something about the manner of this ungainly man was putting her at ease.

"But you were just young, still at school, I think."

"That's right. I was still at school."

"I heard that you and the others escaped the next night. I was glad that you escaped."

So you know very little about the next night, she thought. "You were not glad that my friends also escaped?"

He shrugged. "I don't know. I couldn't let you go myself."

"I know."

Again there was silence as Abigail waited and her guest looked for the words to begin. "Miss Bukula . . ." he began, looking down at his hands.

"Leon," she interrupted him, "had it not been for what you did that night I would not be here now. I would not be alive. You called me Abigail then. Please call me Abigail now."

He tried again. Her name came out uncertainly, almost experimentally. "Abigail, I think I need your help."

She could not help being aware of his hands and the poorly fitting clothes. "You need employment?"

"No, I don't need a job. I get enough work. I actually do better now than when I was in the army." Again the silence as he tried to begin, then finally, "You remember the Maseru raid?"

To Abigail it was a question almost without meaning. Every part of their conversation of the last five minutes related to it. "Of course," she said.

"We were quite a small team that actually entered the house."

"Yes?"

"I think there were only twenty or so. The main force blocked all the roads leading to the area." He was looking closely at her face now. "Do you think . . . ?" It was not easy to ask the question. "Do you think the government might be having us killed, the men who entered the house?"

"Come again?" Abigail was on her feet. "What did you say?" Lourens too, rose—but his movement was slow and tentative while hers had been sudden and decisive. Her tone was demanding. "What do you mean?"

"I'm sorry, but do you think it's possible . . . could the government be having us killed?"

"No. Absolutely not."

"You see, some of the men who were there have died."

"Sit down, Leon." Abigail herself sat down. Her hands were now moving restlessly in her lap. "There can be many reasons that people die. The government is certainly not having people killed."

But Lourens had not finished. It had taken considerable courage for him to come this far and now he needed satisfaction. "After the raid I kept no contact with the others, I don't even remember the names of most of them, but I have heard of three of them dying."

"That means nothing."

"I've been told that they were all murdered."

"I don't believe it."

"That's what I hear."

"This is an urban legend, Leon, a story concocted by those who feel they have no place in the new South Africa."

Despite his awkwardness, Lourens looked determined now. "I thought so too, but there is another thing." Abigail waited silently. "Do you remember what day the raid took place?"

"October twenty-first," she said. Remembering took no effort.

"Those men all died on October twenty-second, the night you and the others escaped."

"I don't believe it." But her eyes were searching the face of a wall calendar.

"Today is the sixteenth," Lourens said. "The twenty-second is in six days."

"This is impossible." Abigail made as if to rise, but restrained herself. "This is not right. I don't know why you come here with this story." It was said accusingly. She could give no credence to what he was saying. She felt as if he was tampering with the very foundation of her existence.

"What I heard is that they were murdered. But I do know that two of them died on that same day. One was reported in the newspaper and one was the only man I still had contact with. Then last week I met a policeman in a bar who told me that there were others killed on that day, but I don't know who."

To say again, in the face of his information, that this was impossible seemed crass. And she knew this man. It had only been for a few hours, but she knew what he had risked. More deeply than she knew anyone, even Robert, she knew this man.

He was speaking again. "You see, the thing is I am the only support my wife and children have. I don't even have brothers or sisters. She has a half brother, but that's all."

"Wait, wait." Abigail's anger had been replaced by concern

for this man whose concern was not for himself, but only for his wife and children. She realized that, had she anticipated such a situation, she would have imagined his reaction just as it was now. Abigail had not smoked for a year. Now she went in search of a cigarette. In the back of one of her desk drawers she found a pack that still held a few. "Will you have one?" she asked Lourens.

"Not for me. I don't."

"I don't suppose you have a light?"

"No, no." He patted his pockets ineffectually.

She opened the door into Johanna's office. "Have you got a light?"

"Are you smoking again?" Seeing the look on Abigail's face she continued almost without pausing. "I'll find one."

Abigail sat down again, the unlit cigarette twitching back and forth between two fingers. Lourens was a man who, if what he said was true, needed her help badly, more than anyone else ever had. "Where are you hiding? Are you hiding?"

"No, I work from home. Where would I hide?"

Johanna came in, waving a cheap plastic cigarette lighter in one hand. "Mr. Lesoro lent it to me. I told him . . ."

"Never mind what you told him." Abigail snatched the lighter. Her hands were shaking as she lit the cigarette.

"Are you all right?" Johanna tried inanely to whisper it so that only Abigail would hear.

Abigail handed back the lighter and waved her away. After the door had closed, she spoke to Lourens again. "Do you have the names of those who died?"

"The three I found out about, I know who they are."

"Do you know any of the others?"

"Just one, but he's in C-Max."

"Do you mean van Jaarsveld?"

"Yes."

Like everyone else who had been involved in the liberation struggle in the 1980s, Abigail knew all about van Jaarsveld. She knew that he had been the senior policeman that night in Maseru when Lourens had stood between her and van Jaarsveld himself. His reputation as a killer had been built during a career that had started in the sixties and ended only weeks before the 1994 elections. He had personally killed more activists than any other member of the apartheid security forces. But unlike his colleagues, when the opportunity came for him to confess to the Truth and Reconciliation Commission and go free, he had not taken it. Abigail had been in court on one of the days of his hearing. "I was fighting for my country," he had testified. "I won't, like so many others, say today that what I did yesterday was wrong. I knew it was right then and I know now that it was right. Look at this country. My people have lost their homeland, but no one cares." He had been sentenced to life in the country's maximum security prison. Parole would never be a possibility.

There was a new portent rising in Abigail's mind. "The ones who died, do you know how?"

"No," Lourens said. "I never found that out."

There was little left to say. She had nothing with which to reassure him. "I will try to find out about the other deaths. Leave me your number. I'll call you."

6

Johanna sat down carefully on the chair to which Abigail had pointed. She was armed with notebook and pen. One of the younger woman's strengths was a well-developed ability to read situations. While she did not understand what was happening, she knew that it was serious and that this was no time for joking or even small talk. She waited for Abigail to begin.

"Write down this date: October 21, 1985. Have you got that?" Johanna was nodding, but Abigail repeated the date to make sure. "On that night a team of South African Defense Force soldiers entered Lesotho and raided an African National Congress house just outside Maseru. The soldiers killed twelve of the people in the house and brought the rest—six, I believe— back to South Africa. On the next night, October 22, we escaped from the police cells in Ficksburg."

Johanna's eyes were open so wide that the whites were visible all round the irises. "You were there?"

"Yes, I was there. Now listen carefully. Someone at the army's headquarters must have some information about the old government's cross-border raids. I want the names of all the soldiers who entered the house that night."

"They've probably all confessed and received amnesty." The words came tumbling out of Johanna. "We can't touch them."

"I said, listen carefully. I do not want to prosecute them, but

I must have their names and I must have them today. You find them for me and you find them by lunchtime. Tell them the minister wants that list now."

"The minister?" Johanna had been impressed, now she was stunned.

"The minister wants that list by lunchtime," Abigail lied.

Johanna scurried back to her office and Abigail took the passage to the lifts. There she pressed the button for the top floor. She knew that if she was going to get the facts on whatever it was that had been happening and deal with it, she was going to need help.

The four corners of the top floor were occupied by the offices of the minister, the deputy minister, the director-general and the deputy director-general responsible for liaising with Special Operations. She walked purposefully down the passage to the last of these and entered his personal assistant's office without knocking.

The assistant was packing files into a broad black briefcase. "I need to see Mandla," Abigail told her.

"I'll make you an appointment," the assistant said.

"I need to see him now."

"He's not here. He's already on his way to the airport."

"Where's he going?"

"Parliament. Cape Town." She was one of the few personal assistants in the department, Johanna included, who did not act as if they were the keepers of the keys. In a whisper she added, "Something big has come up. I don't know what it is. PAs don't get told the big things."

Abigail had tried the offices of three other senior men and one deputy DG. Two of them had been out, the third was in a meeting with his staff and would not be free before lunch. The deputy DG listened politely, but had more important things to do than institute investigations into probably unfounded theories about apartheid soldiers being murdered.

It was almost three quarters of an hour before Abigail got

back to her office. Johanna followed her in. She could barely contain herself. "They didn't want to give it to me," she said. "They even said they didn't have it, but when I told them the minister was going to come over there himself if they didn't give it to me . . ."

"You told them that?"

"Yes. And I told them their jobs were on the line. I told them you said . . ."

"All right, Johanna. I'd better not hear any more of what you told them."

"But they still refused me."

By this time it was clear to Abigail that Johanna had the list, but she also knew that to keep Johanna in a state that was departmentally described as "motivated," she would have to listen to the rest of her story. "Can we get to the point?"

"I spoke to a Major Msibi and he said he would not release it without the permission of his minister."

Abigail looked at Johanna's sparkling eyes and sighed.

"But I found a Lieutenant Johnson in the same section and told him that the Minister of Justice was going to be very unhappy if he did not hand it over this morning. And you know what these civil service whites are like."

"So you got it?"

"Ta-raa." Johanna's fanfare was accompanied by her thrusting two faxed pages, taken from an obviously old document, at Abigail.

"Good girl," Abigail said from the heart. "That's wonderful." It really was wonderful, she thought. At the top of page one was the name of the operation and the date, October 21, 1985. Operation Good Neighbor, it had been called. This was followed by the actual address outside Maseru, Lesotho's little capital, that was going to be raided. They must have been very confident of their security, Abigail thought.

Below the address were two lists of names. The first one carried the word "Strategic" at the head of the column. It contained thirty-five names and their ranks and spilled over onto another page. The second list was headed "Strike" and was made up of just seven names. The name Lourens, L: Corporal, was among them. So was one of the other three that Leon had given her. This, then, was the list of those who had entered the house. But it was far fewer than the twenty or so of Leon's memory. At the bottom of the list there seemed to be an eighth name of which only the tops of the letters were visible. It seemed to Abigail that either the bottom of the original document had been torn off or some electronic spasm had erased the rest of the names. Still, there were enough for a start.

"I did well, didn't I?" Johanna was hopping up and down on the balls of her feet.

"You did brilliantly. But there's more I want from you."

Abigail explained carefully what it was that she wanted and how the information could be obtained. Then she told Johanna that she would talk to the supervisor of the library to get their new girl to help. She would also try to get a typist from the pool to assist further.

"You want to know if they have died and what year?" Johanna looked puzzled.

"And the date each one died . . . most of all the date. That's the most important part."

"This is so exciting . . ."

"Listen carefully," Abigail said. She found that she was often using those words when talking to Johanna. "This happened twenty years ago, and these men would all have been between eighteen and forty-five or thereabouts. They will be between forty and sixty-five by now. Obviously the higher ranks will be older."

"This is thrilling."

"Just do it," Abigail said. "Do it now, do it fast, and do it right."

"Yes, sir," Johanna said, clicking her heels together and fashioning a mock salute. "The twenty-second of October— that's the day of our conference."

"I know."

"Is that significant?" Johanna's voice was eager. She wanted it to be so.

"I don't think so. And, oh . . . go down to Human Resources—
I think they arranged the presentation for Michael Bishop, and
get his address and phone number."

It was mid-afternoon before the deputy director-general discovered that Abigail was conscripting typists from other departments. He entered her office five minutes later. The look
on his face suggested that now he had something on the minister's pretty favorite.

He was within five years of Abigail's age, but that had not
stopped him from addressing her as "girlie" the first time he
gave her an instruction. Abigail had replied that he was at lib-
erty to call her either Abigail or Ms. Bukula, but nothing else.
Since that day relations between them had been frosty at best.

The deputy director-general was physically a small man. He
had a lean, fleshless head that made him look top-heavy. His
tight African curls had been allowed to grow, spreading a few
more centimeters all around and so adding to the effect. He
stared at her with what was intended to be unsettling intensity.

"You have something to tell me, I believe." The words came
out in tight little syllables, a way of speaking that Abigail pri-
vately thought of as his pinched-arse mode.

Speaking to this man without permanently destroying her
career prospects was always a special challenge to Abigail. At
times like this it was still more difficult.

"Not that I'm aware of," she said, keeping her voice flat and
expressionless.

"I fail to see how you can be unaware that you are hi-
jacking girls from all over the building to undertake some
private project of which I know nothing."

"I have authorization," she said.

"From whom? It didn't come from me."

"It came from Mandla Nyati." Abigail lied well when she
felt the cause was a good one.

This piece of information gave the deputy director-general
reason to pause while considering the best course of action.

Nyati was technically of the same rank, but anyone associated with Special Operations or the Asset Forfeiture Unit automatically rose a step or two in rank. "He's not your line manager," he said carefully. "Instructions should come through your line manager."

It was time to give the fish a little line, before reeling him in. "That's quite true" she said innocently. But she stopped there. That was enough line. Let him thrash around on the end of it. If he did not have the courage to countermand what seemed to be a Special Operations instruction, that really was his problem.

"Well," he said. "I trust you have it in writing." It was a desperate attempt to regain a little dignity.

"Oh, yes."

He waited for Abigail to offer the written authorization, but she remained silent and motionless, looking back at him in the expressionless way that she hoped would have done justice to a good poker player.

"Well, where is it?" he asked.

"In my car." One of her hands was partially covering a sheet of paper that lay face down on desk.

The deputy DG's eyes flickered toward the piece of paper. There was nothing in Abigail's posture to suggest that she might be thinking of showing it to him or of fetching the document she had told him was in her car. He waited only a moment longer before starting to rise. "I would appreciate a copy," he said. The enemy was in full flight.

"Of course," Abigail said, still without moving.

"And let's not forget the conference. It's only days away."

"I won't."

Before he had left she lowered her eyes to the papers on her desk. She did not look up as he went through the door. Small victories, she told herself—small victories can lead to big defeats, if I give him the opportunity.

Abigail looked at the copy of the fax that Johanna had left her, reading the names of those who had entered the house on that night twenty years before. Apart from Leon's name and the three he had given her, there was only one that she recognized. It was van Jaarsveld, M: Captain.

Marinus van Jaarsveld, the only one of the raiders to make the pages of the newspapers because he had been the only one to refuse the promise of amnesty that the Truth and Reconciliation Commission had offered, was now in prison. She had been told that he occupied a cell on what had been death row in apartheid days. But he was not waiting for impending death.

She had only seen van Jaarsveld on that day near Maseru and again in court when a changing country had finally caught up with him. But, in his case, she had no desire to resume the acquaintanceship. While Leon had retreated from contact with any of his colleagues of that night, van Jaarsveld had stayed at the center of the security forces and may have kept in touch with some of the others.

He was in the care of the Department of Correctional Services and Abigail had a good contact there. She had met Fransina Wolmarans of their communications office a year before at a departmental management seminar. Abigail had a tendency toward unlikely friendships and Fransina, who had worked for the department under the apartheid government, was one such. Fransina's mixed race parentage had delayed her promotion under the old government, but she had been given more responsibility since then and her salary had since moved up a couple of notches. The absence of tertiary qualifications meant that her career had probably now reached its limit. The warm relationship between a well-educated black activist who was manifestly destined for big things and a lower-level bureaucrat who spoke Afrikaans at home had surprised many.

Abigail dialed her number. When Fransina answered Abigail told her what she wanted.

"It's easy to visit a prisoner, specially for someone like you," Fransina said. "What's the prisoner's name?"

"Marinus van Jaarsveld."

"The mad old supremacist?"

"I suppose that's him, yes."

"I'm sorry, Abby, but I don't think you'll be allowed. Visits to C-Max are tough. Visits to people in C-Max who have been found guilty of political murders are still tougher. And visits to van Jaarsveld are the toughest of all."

"Why so?"

"There seems to be some intelligence that his friends want to free him. And you know what he did. The government won't take any risks with him. I don't think they'll let you in."

After she had hung up, she tried one other possibility in correctional services, then a few more in her own department. Those who had no real influence in the prisons told her so and those who may have had influence lost interest when she mentioned the name Marinus van Jaarsveld.

"Why, Abigail? Why do you want to speak to this dinosaur?" one had asked.

"I can't really say," she had told him. The truth seemed so unlikely and was so difficult to explain.

"You want to see Marinus van Jaarsveld, but you won't say why. Forget it, Abigail."

It was mid-afternoon when Johanna returned, looking both stunned and triumphant. "We've only tracked three so far. And they all died on October 22. How did you know?"

7

When Robert Mokoapi got home around eight o'clock, his wife was sitting in one of the easy chairs in front of the French windows which she had left closed. The apartment had been in darkness until he switched on the light in the hall.

"And this," Robert said, "sitting alone in the dark? Something wrong?"

Abigail waved a hand in a gesture that, while avoiding the need to speak, was intended to tell him that all was fine.

The gesture did not work. Robert put down his briefcase, threw his jacket on a sofa and came over to her. He dropped to his knees in front of her and reached out gently to take her in his arms. Abigail held back for only a moment before allowing him to embrace her. "I think you'd better tell me," he said.

He was a good man. Abigail appreciated that fact almost every day of her life. She sometimes felt vaguely guilty that such a good husband should be saddled with someone as opinionated and ready for a fight as she was. On the other hand, she sometimes thought that, in her, Robert had a pretty good deal too. She was not all arguments and volatility.

To her intense irritation she found herself sobbing in Robert's arms. "Hey?" he said. "What's this?"

"It's nothing. I had a hard day." Her voice came out in little snatches between the sobs. The little-girl sound of her voice irritated her intensely.

She tried to free herself from Robert's arms, but he was holding her too firmly. "Tell me about it," he said. "I'm your friend, remember. We're the ones who listen to each other's problems."

When she stopped sobbing Abigail made an attempt to speak. "I like you," she said.

"I should hope so," he told her, and they both laughed, he with real restraint and she with tears in her eyes.

When the sobbing eased, Robert released her and started across the room. "I'm going to pour us both a drink, a stiff one." Abigail did not protest when he poured whiskey into two glasses. He placed the glasses on either side of the sofa, then led her to it so that they could sit next to each other. "So what happened today? Did that little weed of a deputy DG do something?"

By now Abigail had composed herself. "Today I met someone I knew long ago. He was good to me then, but now he's in trouble."

"An old boyfriend?"

Abigail knew that Robert was aware of the Maseru raid and that she had been present, but she had never told him anything about that night and she had never told another soul about Ficksburg. Abigail was determined that she would never in her life tell anyone about either. She could share every other aspect of her being with Robert, but not this. There were some things that Abigail had buried deep and that she preferred to leave that way. She shook her head in answer to his question. "He's a white man who was a policeman of the apartheid regime." Robert was a newspaperman and not easy to surprise, but it was clear by his face that this surprised him. "He saved my life."

"In Maseru?"

"He shielded me from one of the others who would have killed me."

"Where did you run into him?"

"He came to see me today."

"So what's he need—money?"

"No." She looked intently at Robert's face. "He thinks there are government agents trying to kill him."

"Ah, bullshit." Robert's disgust for the old regime and all those involved in it was showing. He shook his head. "These guys, they'll believe anything bad . . ."

"Some of the soldiers who were in Maseru seem to have been murdered." Abigail had already decided not to tell Robert about the matter of October 22. She loved him, but he was newspaperman and you did not tempt newspapermen with some things, even if you loved them.

"You believe this?"

"Some of them have been murdered. That much is true."

Robert needed more than that. "Do you believe a government agency is responsible?"

"No."

"Good. I'll drink to that." He held his glass toward her and they clinked them. "Let's take your friend to lunch and reassure him."

"I don't believe a government agency is involved." She was watching his face as she spoke. "I believe Michael Bishop could be." Abigail closed her eyes and rocked back as if she had been struck. Until that moment she had not even admitted that belief to herself. It had been lurking somewhere deep within her in the place that conscious thoughts avoid. If she truly believed that Bishop could be involved, it was only now that she knew that she did.

"Michael Bishop." Robert was searching his memory for an identity to match the name. "He's the one they called the Ghost. Are you sure he's real? I always wondered if he wasn't a myth."

"He's real all right. Yesterday they held a meeting at work to honor him." That was not all. There was much else, but that would be enough for Robert. Or enough for her. At least, enough for now.

"Really?" Already his curiosity was becoming a problem.

"Listen, Robert, this is not a story. This man may be in danger. I need to help him. I owe it to him."

"Tell me why you suspect this Michael Bishop."

"I can't."

"You can't or you won't?"

"I can't."

Robert had both of her hands in his. "Listen, pal. I'm on your side, remember?"

"I can't. I can't now."

"Will you be able to later?"

"No. Maybe. Perhaps . . ."

Robert smiled faintly. "A good maybe is almost as useful as a sturdy perhaps."

"I had dealings with him in the old days, during the struggle. I don't believe anyone else could have done it. Most of all, I don't believe anyone else would have wanted to do it."

"And you won't tell me more?"

"I just can't."

"You're a bit tough on your allies, pal. But all right, you tell me what to do for this Lourens. If he saved your life, I'll do whatever I can to lend a hand."

But for the moment there was nothing Robert could do. She had no option but to leave him with the idea that what she had told him was based on nothing more than the meandering thoughts of an old apartheid-era soldier and her own hunches.

Then there was the bedroom and this time there was no chance of Robert falling asleep in time to save her. But there was his puzzlement, almost hurt, and soon his asking, demanding even, to know, "What is it? Has it got something to do with the money?"

And a long moment in which she wondered what he was talking about, before she realized. "No, it's not the billion."

"Half billion," he told her.

"No, of course it's not that. It's just that it's upset me and . . ."

Then he was striding around the room, wearing only his sleeping trunks. "I'm a Zulu man. I need sex the way other men need food."

It was not possible though, especially not now, not since she had admitted her fears to herself. Eventually he did sleep and she went back to the French windows. By the lights in the neighboring garden she could again see the bull terrier ferreting among the shrubs. A female figure walked by in the street, carrying a shopping bag. Probably a domestic worker going home to one of the townships, she thought. Immediately the bull terrier surged toward the garden gate, snapping and biting at the steel bars to get to the woman outside.

Jesus, she thought, do we have to put up with these reminders of apartheid days? In those days many a domestic servant had been savaged by a dog belonging to the employer or the employer's neighbor. Very few had ever been compensated in any way.

As the domestic worker moved away, the dog's growling slowly died down, then stopped altogether. She sank slowly into the chair she had used the previous night. From the position where she was sitting she looked out into a night in which the black of the sky glowed vaguely gold with the reflected lights of the city.

She tried not to think. She also tried not to remember. Maseru had returned to her more strongly than at any time in the intervening years. It was too late to do anything about it, but perhaps she could keep the door closed on Ficksburg. She could leave it as a dark cave in the vault of her memory. But it was a cave that was haunted by the insubstantial figure of Michael Bishop . . . the Ghost, as Robert had called him.

8

Monday, October 17

Yudel Gordon, former senior psychologist in the Department
of Correctional Services, drove through the Pretoria Central
Prison complex. Over the last thirty years he had traveled the
road many times.

He passed the main section where most of the prisoners were
kept, the administration block where the year before a bored
bureaucrat had mislaid the files of four prisoners and as a result
had kept them inside for an extra two months, the houses of the
warders where uncomplicated men and their families lived in
a world that was becoming increasingly complex, the sports
field where the prison officers' soccer team competed with more
enthusiasm than finesse, and the recreation club where off-duty
warders spent time when the need to escape female disapproval
was upon them—all of it as immaculately maintained as the
prison itself.

Yudel considered how faulty the impression of order was.
Prisons throughout the country were filled beyond capacity.
Having five prisoners crowded into a cell intended for three
was normal. It was a situation inherited from the apartheid
government eleven years before, and had not improved since
then.

In some years, the department's budget ran out before the year
did. Room was sometimes made for new prisoners convicted of

relatively minor offenses by releasing others whose crimes were far worse. This too was a method inherited from the old regime. In recent months two convicted murderers, serving twenty-five-year sentences, had been released before the end of their fifth year and within months had been rearrested for further killings. A third prematurely released murderer had been arrested for multiple rapes.

There had been a time immediately after the first democratic elections when the new authorities had seemed to think that the guilt of anyone convicted of anything during the apartheid years had to be in doubt. Tens of thousands of prisoners were released early in those days, temporarily easing the overcrowding in the prisons. Most were back inside within six months, and the situation returned to normal.

These releases were in addition to the politicals, who had all been freed regardless of their crimes, the official position being that none of them would have committed their crimes in a normal society. While apartheid had certainly produced an abnormal society, Yudel was not sure what a normal one looked like. And he would not have released all the politicals who had been freed. They had been imprisoned by the old regime for setting off bombs in public places, shooting at and occasionally killing policemen and civilians, planting bombs on country roads and of being enthusiastic members of the necklace mobs which burned to death informers, witches, spies, boycott breakers, scabs and other traitors to the revolution.

Many years had accustomed Yudel to dealing with criminals, but he doubted that he would ever grow accustomed to the sanctimony and self-satisfaction of the politically motivated killer. You don't understand, he had been told many times. You have to see it in context. We did it for freedom. It's easy for you. You've always been privileged.

Among the politicals who had fallen under his care and been released was Simon Mkhari, who had burned to death a woman of sixty. Her crime, in Mkhari's eyes, had been that, during a boycott of white shops, she had bought a small packet of groceries from a shop owned by a white man. Yudel had felt that Mkhari was an opportunist who had found, in the country's political situation, a morally acceptable reason to kill. Yudel remembered eyes that held a wild unruliness and an inner tension that distorted the area on either side of his mouth, an uncontrollable restlessness that went beyond the reach of discipline. Yudel had seen those eyes as the product of a life that had taught him that there were no friends to be found anywhere and only temporary allies. Men had to be subdued by force and women taken in the same way. He had opposed Mkhari's release, believing that he was more than likely to kill again. As he had expected, he had been overruled without discussion. Recently, Mkhari's name and photograph had appeared on police "wanted" posters. He had not possessed the skill or education to make use of the opportunities offered by the new South Africa, and the wild unruliness was still a part of him.

There had been other releases with which Yudel had agreed. The Grysbank Six, as the media had called them, had been part of a mob that had beaten, kicked and finally burned to death a female schoolteacher by the name of Maggie Twala, who was rumored to have been the lover of a policeman. Those had been extraordinary times . . . none of them had ever before been found guilty of any crime, but had been swept along by mob passions in the heat of a political upheaval such as the country had never seen before. They were not likely to kill again.

Yudel was aware that many people, perhaps most people, would sneer at his opinion of political killers. After all, he had stayed in the employ of the prisons department throughout the apartheid years. It was true that his actions and his sympathies in those years had removed any possibility of promotion, but still he had never resigned. He had been aware of the beatings and the torture dealt out by the security police, sometimes in the prisons, and he had objected officially. He had once tried unsuccessfully to have a senior security policeman arrested for rape and murder. But when nothing came of his protests, he had stayed in the department's employ, telling himself that he was doing good. Not everyone had agreed.

This was the first time Yudel was to meet with the commissioner since he had been retrenched three years before. Their last meeting had not been easy for either of them. In previous meetings the commissioner had always tried to show special friendliness to Yudel. "I'll be sorry to lose you as a staff member," he had said. "This retrenchment is no reflection on your ability. You know the reason as well as I do. The transformation of the department demands it. I have received employment equity targets from the minister and I don't have any choice. When I took over, ninety-six percent of my professional officers were white. I brought it down to twenty-seven percent before I even considered retrenching you."

"Thanks for telling me yourself," Yudel had said.

"You have my respect," the commissioner had said.

"Thank you."

"And I liked your approach to rehabilitation."

"I've worked on it for a long time."

"I know. I can see that. Maybe private practice will work out for you."

"Maybe."

Yudel had not told the commissioner that he considered this just as racist as the actions taken by the old government that excluded black South Africans from the mainstream of the country's life. In his farewell speech to the staff, he had said that you cannot sail a ship without its crew. The commissioner had not answered him.

The road wound round the last of the warders' houses and ended in the parking area beneath the walls of C-Max, the country's top high-security prison. The outer gate was a black, heavily studded vehicle entrance, set into a recess in the wall. A narrow pedestrian door in the gate opened for Yudel, where he was subjected to a quick electronic search for weapons. The search showed up something suspiciously large and metallic in his brief case. On examination the guards found the suspicious object to be a modest roll of banknotes. Each note contained a thin metal thread that set off the alarm. After they were satisfied that Yudel posed no threat to the prison's security, he was allowed in to wait for the warder who would accompany him to the inner wall. Only one prisoner had ever escaped from C-Max, and he had achieved that distinction by bribing a warder with more money that he would have earned in five years. Both escapee and warder were now prisoners in this same institution.

A narrow strip of lawn filled the space between the two walls. Guinea fowl and rabbits grazed on the grass, apparently at ease in these forbidding surroundings.

At the second wall a warder unlocked a barred gate with a key so big that he could manipulate it only by holding it in both hands. Yudel was passed to a new warder who took him deeper into the prison. Ten paces farther, at the foot of a broad flight of stairs, the process was repeated.

As gate after gate opened and wall after wall enclosed Yudel, all outer sounds faded and the sounds of the prison rose around him. The continual opening and closing of gates, steel sliding and jarring heavily against steel, shouted voices issuing the endless streams of orders by which prisons function, the clatter of buckets from a passage and steel plates from the kitchen and, as he passed the entrance to a cell block, the hum of the prisoners' voices: all seemed to reinforce the walls and bars, drowning the evidence of a world outside.

The cell block where the commissioner had chosen to meet Yudel was in the innermost keep. Here the only eating utensils allowed were plastic spoons with the shortest handles. Materials like wood and porcelain, let alone steel, lent themselves too well to making weapons. For the same reason no belts and buckles were worn in these cells. This was also the only place in the country where toothbrushes without handles were provided to prisoners.

C-Max held a motley collection of murderers, rapists, the most ambitious white-collar criminals and those prisoners whose possible future testimony made them targets, but this particular block was home to those who would probably never be freed. Its population was made up of serial killers, the senior members of organized crime gangs, dangerous sex offenders and the last solitary political killer of the apartheid government who had refused to confess and so earn his freedom.

Deep interest surrounded each new addition to the cell block, news passing fluidly along the cells between prisoners who could hear one another, but only see the man directly opposite, and then only when he was looking through the inspection hole in the solid steel door of his cell. They knew one another's crimes, their victims, their sentences, appeals and petitions.

In the old days this had been death row. In those days tragedy was present here in an even starker form. Reality had been reduced to its simplest elements. In those days and in this place tragedy had not been a market collapse, a run on the nation's currency or a doubling of interest rates. Matters of this sort had stood exposed as trivia. Reality came at seven in the morning with the visit of the sheriff and his list of those who had a date with the gallows in seven days' time.

Today, the men in this block were virtually all permanent. There were few new arrivals and few releases. It was the most stable prison population in the country. Occasionally a new serial killer or senior member of an organized crime ring was added to the tally. Those who were in C-Max were not going anywhere soon.

Like any other prison, C-Max had seen its share of breakout attempts. Just a year before Yudel's visit, the head warder himself, a second warder and two prisoners had died during an unsuccessful break-out. The only successful one had taken a bribe of 80,000 rand to get the escapee past the prison walls.

In apartheid days, no one in this section had been permanent. New men had been brought in. Old ones left, either downstairs to the main prison after their sentences had been commuted, or across the yard to the chapel to make their final preparations, or simply to await the moment.

Apart from the prison's sights and sounds—the gleaming tiled passages, the gray steel gates with bars polished to a bright glow at shoulder height by the handling of many years, the shuffling prisoners and striding warders—there were also smells. Disinfectant, floor polish, food and the pungency of cheap soap: the smells formed powerful associations in the minds of those who spent time in prisons.

The smell that had always been the most powerful and most troubling to Yudel was gone now. In years past, when the cell block had been used as death row, a ripe body odor that Yudel had never experienced anywhere else had always been present. Many years before, a new head warder who had never before served on death row had tried to remove it. For a week prisoners from other sections had scrubbed the passages and cells with every soap and disinfectant available to the department, but the moment the scent of the cleaning agents began to fade, the other returned. A young white sociologist from the University of the Witwatersrand who had visited a prisoner there had written in an academic paper that this was the smell of fear. An old black woman whose son was awaiting execution had told Yudel that it was the smell of approaching death.

Whatever it had been in those days, the prison authorities had never been able to eradicate it. It had simply been the smell of death row. Within days of the repeal of the death penalty it had disappeared.

Few of the former inmates of death row were still in prison. By the time the death penalty was repealed there had been just over two hundred and fifty souls on death row. Only a few of them were not political prisoners and those were the only ones who had not been set free. Most of the freed politicals, members of necklace mobs, had returned to the obscure lives they had led before that moment of insanity had swept them away. Others had been rewarded for the roles they had played in the revolution. One, who had planted a bomb in a bar, killing a few late-night revellers, was now a manager in a department of one of the cities. Another had returned to his old position in a trade union. Some others filled fairly senior government posts.

Yudel reached yet another gate. Commissioner Joshua Set-laba and two other officers that Yudel recognized, without knowing their names, were waiting for him in the block's shift office. They rose as Yudel entered.

9

"So, Yudel." The commissioner held out a large hand, enveloping Yudel's smaller one and holding on tightly. It was an altogether friendly gesture. "How are you?" This too was not just a formality. He waited with real interest for Yudel's reply.

"I'm well, Mr. Commissioner," Yudel said. "I hope you are too."

"I'm very well." The other officers both offered the firm handshakes that are part of the makeup of uniformed officers everywhere.

Yudel shook their hands, nodded at them, then waited. He was the one who had been invited.

"How are things going with you?" the commissioner asked.

"All right." Yudel wondered where this was going.

"I suppose you're wondering why I wanted to meet you here."

"No," Yudel said truthfully. "I'm wondering why you want to see me at all."

"Ah," the commissioner nodded. "I wanted to meet you here because I want to talk about this place."

"All right."

"Are you making a living?"

"I'm getting by."

"Some private practice? Old white ladies who feel unsafe in the new South Africa?"

"Sure. And some white businessmen who have given chunks of their businesses to black partners and are now regretting it." The last part was not entirely true. There were many such cases, some of them known to Yudel personally, but he had no patients in that category. They went to see their attorneys, not their psychologists, the objective being to draw up contracts that would give away as little as possible to their new empowerment partners.

The commissioner grimaced slightly. Yudel had a way of raising awkward subjects. "How did you spend your retrenchment package?"

"Ah, Mr. Commissioner," Yudel waved an admonishing finger at him. "You're going into the financial advisory business."

"No, Yudel, certainly not. I only . . ." Then he read the look in Yudel's eyes and returned the admonishing finger with a throaty chuckle. "Ah, Yudel, you got me there."

"I paid off my house bond and bought a car."

The commissioner nodded. "Tell me, are you getting any criminology work?"

"Not much."

"Want to get back into it?"

"Mr. Commissioner, what is this about?"

The commissioner turned to the two officers who had come with him. "You two wait for me outside." To Yudel he said, "Can you call me Joshua? You're not on my staff anymore. Otherwise I'll have to call you Mr. Gordon. It seems a bit silly."

"All right," Yudel said. "I'll call you Joshua."

The two officers had left. "Good," their boss said. "Now, do you want to get back into prison work?"

"Are you offering me my job back?"

The commissioner opened his mouth wide, as if taking a deep breath, before answering.

"If so, will I have an equal chance of promotion in future?"

The commissioner waved a hand impatiently. "You know the

answer to these questions Yudel. No, I want to offer you something different." He waved a hand at the cells that occupied both sides of the passage beyond. "You've been here before . . ."

"Once or twice," Yudel said.

The commissioner threw back his head and his laughter came roaring out. Before it had eased altogether, he began again. "That's what I like about you, Yudel. Understatement. That's right, isn't it? Understatement. Once or twice? One or two thousand times, I think." The laughter stopped as suddenly as it had started. He pointed a finger at Yudel in what almost seemed to be an accusation. "Do you know how many prisoners I have?"

"In all our prisons? One hundred and fifteen thousand, six hundred and forty-five, last time I saw the figures."

"What a memory. But that figure's not right anymore. It's now one hundred and sixteen thousand, two hundred and twenty."

"I'm out of date," Yudel said.

"And how many psychologists?"

"Twenty-eight before you retrenched me. Twenty-seven, I suppose. But that figure's probably out of date too."

The commissioner shook his head briefly, ridding it perhaps of Yudel's repeated references to his retrenchment. "The remaining two white psychology officers, two colored officers and the last Indian have resigned. And I've hired two new youngsters and an academic from UPE. You'll get on well with him, a highly educated man. He'll be invaluable to you. So I've got twenty-four now." He paused for dramatic effect that was not needed on Yudel. "Twenty-four psychologists and one hundred and sixteen thousand . . ."

". . . two hundred and twenty prisoners," Yudel completed the number for him. "So what do you want from me . . ." He paused for a moment before experimentally using the commissioner's first name. ". . . Joshua?" he finished.

"I want you to train selected, ordinary warders to use your system. I want you to coordinate the program nationally and Lesela to be in charge in this province."

"Lesela?"

"The academic. We can call the warders you choose parapsychologists, like paramedics."

"I understand, but we'll need a different name. Parapsychology is something else. We could call them psychology interns."

The impatient hand was waving again, but the beginnings of a smile were in the commissioner's eyes. "Any name, I don't care. But I think you are not against the idea."

"It can be done," Yudel said. "We'd need to select the men carefully, both interns and prisoners. It doesn't work with all prisoners."

"I know. You'll have to do it all."

"There's one other thing," Yudel said. Despite always having done some private work in his own time during his years in the department, he had always been embarrassed about discussing money. Three years without his monthly paycheck had cured him of that. "I need to make a living," he said.

The commissioner had thought of that. "I'll give you a year's contract and I'll pay you three times what you earned when you were with us. I will also not expect you to come in for the usual forty hours a week. I know I'll get my money's worth from you."

Yudel considered the matter briefly, very briefly. He tried unsuccessfully to restrain his right hand from shooting out in the direction of the commissioner. He was still trying to avoid looking too enthusiastic when the commissioner started shaking his hand, a lot more vigorously than their earlier handshake.

"I need to do something about my psychology section, Yudel. Right now it's a joke. And the country is suffering because of it." Yudel had always seen him as a man who was determined to do his job well. Holding that view of him had made Yudel more surprised and disappointed at his retrenchment than he would otherwise have been. "And I like your methods. I believe in them."

In several long meetings in the past Yudel had told the commissioner that teaching a criminal to lay bricks did not turn him into a bricklayer. It made of him a criminal who knew how to lay bricks. Yudel's thinking was that, while teaching crafts to criminals was not a bad thing, it did nothing toward rehabilitating them. To Yudel, criminals were a subculture in rebellion against mainstream society. Their code of morals was different from that of other people. For them, to give evidence against other criminals was immoral. One of them who ratted on another was an outsider to be shunned. In extreme cases they were lowlifes to be killed. Anyone who had dealings with criminals knew that they did possess a moral code; it was just that it was an inverted form of the one that applied to regular society. Straight society was out to get them and they had to fight back.

It was this basis of the criminal culture that had to be confronted before rehabilitation could take place. In Yudel's view, until the criminal had come to the realization that the rest of humanity was not the enemy, there could be no reconciliation between them. And rehabilitation, ultimately, was a matter of reconciliation. He agreed with the commissioner that the department did not need trained psychologists to apply his principles. Interns, taken from among the brightest and most empathetic warders, would be able to do the job.

Looking at the commissioner, Yudel was so excited by the prospect of getting this opportunity to apply his ideas that he did not trust himself to speak. The commissioner was offering him something he had never had while employed by the department. And he was getting paid for it—three times his old salary. Suddenly it seemed to him that the new South Africa was not all bad.

"So you accept?" the commissioner asked.

"Damn right," Yudel stammered.

"Oh, one other thing. You don't have a black partner yet?"

"No," Yudel said. "I don't have a partner at all."

The commissioner seemed to reflect a moment. "I'm sure we can manage it anyway. You may need one for future contracts. I'll tell them you've entered negotiations with various black psychologists."

———

The thought of facing Marinus van Jaarsveld again, twenty years after the night in Maseru, was more than repulsive to Abigail. But he had been there. He had been one of the inner circle of the apartheid regime in a way that an innocent like Leon Lourens could never have understood, more even than most apartheid politicians could have understood. They had done the regime's talking. Van Jaarsveld was one of those who had done its killing.

It was likely that he would have kept contact with some of the others who had entered the house in Maseru that night. Abigail believed that there were things he would be able to tell her about the way the other members of the squad had died in the years since then, and how they had died.

She had spent much of the previous afternoon and more than an hour this morning calling senior people she knew, trying without success to arrange a meeting with van Jaarsveld. Fransina had advised her against even trying to see him. But Fransina at least had some of the right connections. Abigail phoned her again. "You must know somebody who can help me," she said when Fransina came on the line. "Anyone with some old-fashioned guts."

"Please, Abby." Fransina sounded distressed. "You're going to get us both into trouble."

"Listen to me," Abigail said. "Listen."

Something in the tone of Abigail's voice got through to Fransina. "Speak then. I'm listening."

"I believe a man I know well and whom I value is in danger."

"And mad old van Jaarsveld can help you?" She sounded skeptical. To Fransina, this was clearly a ridiculous idea.

"It's just possible." Fransina was silent for so long that Abigail thought she may have hung up. "Are you still there?"

"I can think of only one. He's a strange one, Abby. He's been in the department all his life, under both governments, like me. In the old days he was often in trouble, apparently because he did not agree with the way the old government treated prisoners. It seems he lost out on promotions because they were unsure about his loyalty."

"He sounds all right," Abigail said.

"Maybe. He's also been in trouble in recent years for the same reason."

"Surely we treat our prisoners better than the apartheid regime did?"

"Not according to Mr. Gordon."

"Gordon?"

"Yudel Gordon."

"Who Gordon?"

"Yudel. Y–U–D–E–L. A lot of people say good things about him. Although he was apparently sympathetic to the liberation struggle, he worked for the old government throughout those years. I suppose he needed a job, like I did."

"Okay, thanks," Abigail said. She was getting ready to hang up.

"Abigail?" Her friend's voice was suddenly urgent.

"Yes."

"He was retrenched some time ago and is being brought back as a contractor."

"I see."

"I don't know if he will want to help and I don't know if he can."

"All right."

"He's a funny-looking little man—wild hair going gray, stoops a little when he walks. And you can never predict what he might do."

After she had hung up, she looked up Gordon, Y. in the telephone directory. It listed only one. She dialed the number. A woman answered and told her that Yudel was at the prison.

"The regular prison or C-Max?" Abigail wanted to know.

"C-Max, I think," the woman said.

Abigail Bukula sat in her car in the parking lot outside C-Max. Half an hour earlier she had used her Department of Justice ID and her status in the department to bluff her way past the gate in the outer perimeter, but had got no farther. She had been refused entrance by a pair of stony-faced guards who would not listen to any arguments that were not backed up by permission from their own department.

As she watched warders came in and out through the narrow door set into the vehicle gate to fetch individual visitors to prisoners. Each visitor went through a name check, then entered the prison accompanied only by a warder. Most of the visitors were working-class people, both black and white. Many were wearing clothes that had not been bought in the last twelve or even twenty-four months, but that seemed to have been washed and ironed specially for the occasion.

One woman of perhaps fifty looked like a caricature of a white, working-class grandmother. She was a little overweight and walked slowly, as if her feet hurt. On her left ankle there was a bright pink scar or birthmark. Maybe it's a scar and whatever caused it is why her feet hurt, Abigail thought. The woman's gray hair was pulled back into a bun. She was carrying a basket over one arm that was searched at the gate before she was allowed inside.

Abigail had no way of knowing that this woman was Annette van Jaarsveld, Marinus van Jaarsveld's altogether loyal and devoted wife. What is such a woman doing here? she asked herself. A mother visiting her son in this place? Or her grandson?

And what about me, why am I sitting here? she wondered. Van Jaarsveld was deep inside this seemingly impregnable fortress, and she was outside. It was clear that they were not going to let her in unless she could get some real influence on her side. And sitting here in the parking lot was not going to do it. But still she waited.

There are better things I could be doing, she thought.

All her life, unplanned and seemingly inexplicable incidents had come to Abigail's aid. Sometimes, as on this occasion, she had found herself waiting for something that she had no reason to expect. In fact, she had no idea what it was that she was waiting for.

She was still asking herself why she was waiting when the reason became apparent. The narrow door into the prison opened and a white man, Jewish in appearance, slight in every dimension and wearing a rumpled gray suit, stepped through it. His unruly bush of graying hair did not seem to have been combed recently, certainly not today.

He looked exactly as Fransina had described him. While Abigail watched, he stopped and looked around. He had obviously forgotten where his car was parked. He was still scanning the parking lot when a warder who had taken up a position outside the gate pointed him in the right direction. He nodded to the warder, seemed to say something and set off in that direction.

Abigail was already standing next to her car. The small white man was following a path that would bring him close to her, but looking down at the ground in front of him as he walked. His lips were moving slightly, as if he were talking to himself. She took a step forward as if to intercept him. He glanced up and their eyes met for a moment. Abigail smiled, but he looked down immediately and hurried past. She watched him get into a new sedan. She did not know it, but it was the car he had bought with his retrenchment package from the Department of Correctional Services. Abigail watched him drive away.

By the time she turned back to the gate, the warder had opened the narrow door and was about to go back inside. Abigail called and waved to him to stop. He looked curiously at her, but he stopped. From close by she recognized him as having been present when she had been refused entry earlier that afternoon.

"Hello, sister," he said. There was something exasperated in the tone of his voice. "What can I do for you now?"

"That man who just left, who is he?"

He looked quizzically at her, as if wondering whether he should be giving her this information. He was just an ordinary warder, but she was someone who had been refused permission to see a prisoner. To him, this meant that she was not a very important person. In the civil service, as he understood it, important people were not refused much. "Why you want to know?"

"Oh for God's sake. I just want to know his name."

He was not well educated but, from her way of speaking, he knew that she was. She therefore had money, but he was in charge here. "Why?" he demanded.

Abigail, who had never in her life paid a bribe for anything, found herself scratching in her bag for money. She found a fifty-rand note and handed it to the warder. Robert would kill me if he could see this, she thought. She had often heard him intone, "If we give in to bribes we will end up like the worst African countries."

The warder had no such reservations. He took the money. "That's Mr. Gordon," he said. "Mr. Yudel Gordon. He used to work here."

Damn, Abigail thought. He was right here. I had the chance to speak to him. Why didn't I speak to him?

Back in her office, it proved to be only a little easier to get information about Yudel than it was to see Marinus van Jaarsveld. She called Robert, but he had never heard of Yudel. He had his librarian look for references to Yudel in past editions of the newspaper though, and had found only one obscure report relating to disciplinary action being taken against Yudel by the department in the old days. The reporter had not been too clear on the matter, but it seemingly had to do with a complaint laid by the security police. Apparently they felt Yudel had interfered in one of their investigations.

On the Department of Correctional Services Web site she had read a ten-page description of their new methods of rehabilitation, the author of which was listed as Y. Gordon. It was dated 1993, twelve years earlier. So he was a psychologist. She wondered if his methods of rehabilitation had ever been implemented. Knowing government departments as well as she did, she doubted it.

Abigail had to see this man. She had his home address, so if he was now operating from home, there was a fair chance he would be there. She reached for the phone, but withdrew her hand. In her experience, people refused her more easily over the phone than face-to-face. She was at the door of her office before Johanna, spotting her escape attempt, caught up and took her by the arm. "I found out about two of the others. They also died on the same day. And I found out about how one of them died. He was strangled, with a wire, the police think."

Abigail made her way to the lift. She was having some difficulty with her balance. Twice she stopped to steady herself against the passage wall. If she had not been altogether sure before, now she was certain about the identity of the killer. And about what Leon Lourens believed was true. There was no doubting any of it.

10

Yudel Gordon circled his wife's kitchen stove. After a considerable struggle he had managed to drag it far enough from the wall to go right round it. He was looking for the fuses.

Rosa, his wife, was sitting at the kitchen table, observing this singular scene. Yudel rarely attempted to repair anything and, on those few occasions, he was even more rarely successful. "We could get a repair man," she suggested. "I know they're expensive, but at least they have experience."

Yudel did not answer. This was a matter of pride. He had asked about stoves at the local hardware store and was trying to remember what the assistant had said. He recalled being advised that the fuses were probably behind a little lid or a flap.

"Perhaps it's time to get a new one," Rosa suggested, "the kind where the plates are sort of part of the surface. Everyone says they're so good."

"I spoke to a man who knows about these things," Yudel said. "I got the very best advice and he says it's probably just a fuse."

"A fuse? What does a fuse do to it?"

"It blows. And once it has blown the stove stops working."

"How can you tell whether a fuse is blown? Once you have it in your hand, I mean, how can you tell?" Rosa was trying to discuss the matter intelligently, exploring ways to be helpful. "You may not realize that the fuse is blown, or in the act of blowing. And what if the fuse has blown or blows while you are handling it? What action do you take to un-blow it?"

"I don't know," Yudel answered patiently. "Perhaps once I find the fuses all will become clear." He had completed two full circuits of the stove, but had seen nothing that looked like a suitable place for hiding away fuses.

"Do you need a screwdriver?" Rosa asked.

"I don't think so."

"There's one in the kit of my sewing machine, if you need it. It's a nice little one. I've used it myself, around the house. I'll get it if you like."

"It's quite all right," Yudel told her. "I don't think that screw-drivers are useful in dealing with fuses." As an afterthought and a little vindictively, he added, "I think they're used for screws."

"Of course they're used for screws, but they may work equally well for fuses." She watched Yudel skeptically in si-lence for a moment, then she tried again. "You look as if you're afraid to touch it. You can't fix it if you're afraid to touch it."

"I'm not afraid to touch it. I don't know where to touch it." To demonstrate his confidence Yudel tugged at a small, em-bossed fascia plate next to the control panel. It swung open on hinges, revealing a row of six round glass objects.

"Are those the fuses?" Yudel felt that the intensity of her interest was excusable. She was, after all, the one who did the cooking.

"I think so," he said.

"The little devils," she said, "causing so much trouble. They shouldn't put them in. Are you sure about the screwdriver?"

"Quite."

"How do you get them out to see if they're blown?"

"Like this." The two words had a heroic ring. Yudel grasped one of the fuses and twisted vigorously. It remained unmoved, as if set in concrete.

"The other way," Rosa said. "Turn it the other way."

Yudel twisted the fuse in the other direction and it came loose. In a few seconds he had it out and was examining its transparent sides for signs of blowing, whatever that was. "How did you know I was turning it the wrong way?"

"I reasoned that it turned the same way that screws do." Yudel looked quizzically at her, expecting a more detailed explanation, so she continued, "Someone has to do the occasional screw around here. You don't."

One at a time Yudel removed all six fuses and placed them in a row on the kitchen table. "Now," he said, trying to impart a businesslike tone to his voice, "let's have a look."

Rosa had already looked. "These two are blown," she said. "See. They're all blackened inside. That must happen when one blows. It sort of burns. The others are still perfect."

Yudel looked at the two Rosa had indicated, then at the others, then back at Rosa.

"When you're in town tomorrow, get us two." She held out the two faulty fuses to Yudel. "Take these with you so that you bring back the right thing." As a sop to his masculine pride, she added, "I thought you did quite well. You did find them."

The hallway chimes, an insistent connection to the world outside their home, intruded suddenly, driving away all pre-occupation with fuses and screws. Yudel tried to ignore the sound. He was pretending to be busy with important matters.

The voice that reached Abigail over the intercom from inside the house was female and demanding. From a main artery a few blocks away there was a fair amount of traffic noise, so Abigail had got out of the car to get an ear close to the loudspeaker. "Yes," the voice demanded. It was so strong and clear that it was unnecessary for Abigail to get out of the car.

"Is this the home of Doctor Yudel Gordon?" Abigail asked.

"It is," the voice said, offering nothing more.

"I wonder if I could speak to him. My name is . . ."

She could see the front door of the house from the gate. It had opened, cutting off her sentence before she could finish it. An imposing woman, perhaps in her late fifties, stood in the doorway. Her long, graying hair had obviously been left its natural color and hung down to her shoulders. Her skin was the olive color of many Mediterranean people. The skin around her eyes was darker, as if she had been too enthusiastic in the application of eye shadow. But it did not look to Abigail as if this woman ever used eye shadow. She stood still in the doorway, clearly studying both Abigail and her BMW. When she had satisfied whatever reservations she had, she started down the path toward the gate, at the same time pressing a button on a remote control that opened the gate and allowed Abigail to drive in.

The house was a typical Pretoria middle-class dwelling, which meant that there was no shortage of space either in the house or the half-acre garden that surrounded it. Like the mansion she had visited two nights before and all the neighboring houses, its garden walls were topped by electric fencing. The woman who had let her in held out a strong hand. "I'm Rosa Gordon," she said without smiling.

"Abigail Bukula," Abigail said.

"What can I do for you?" Rosa looked straight into her eyes without any indication of hostility, but also no sign of friendliness.

"I work for the Department of Justice. I hoped I might see Doctor Gordon."

Rosa seemed to take a deep breath. "What has he done to alert the Department of Justice?"

So it was the way Fransina had said. "He's done nothing. I was hoping he could help me with a problem I have."

"Yudel?" The disbelief in Rosa's voice was unmistakable. "He usually manages to complicate matters." But she stepped aside, gesturing to Abigail to come into the house.

Rosa led Abigail to a closed door and paused before it. "He also does some wonderful things." Having satisfied herself that she had not left a poor impression of her husband, she knocked once before opening it. "Yudel, there's a visitor for you," she said.

Abigail found herself stepping into a large untidy study. Instead of standing vertically on the bookshelves, the study's hundreds of books were stacked in horizontal piles on almost every surface, including some patches of the floor. An effort seemed to have been made to create a clearing at the center of the desk. The eccentric-looking man she had seen in the C-Max parking lot had his back to her. He was facing a mirror hanging from a nail in the wall. At that moment he was trying, with paper scissors, to cut away a strand of hair that was even wilder than the rest. It came away and he snipped at a second strand. The overall impression his hair made was that its trimming may normally have been accomplished in the same way.

Abigail was suddenly overcome by an unexpected wave of shyness. There was something so private about the man, what he was doing and even the room she had entered, that she looked for a way of escape. She turned to look for support behind her, but Rosa had already left. By the time she turned back again Yudel was looking at her. "You were at the prison," he said.

She told Yudel her name and where she worked. Then she held out a hand across the desk for him to shake, careful to avoid the piles of books. He put down the scissors and took her hand tentatively. The way he did it seemed to suggest that he was unsure of the wisdom of physical contact with this pushy black woman. Yudel dropped her hand and looked at her without speaking.

This is quite a pair, Abigail thought. Are they husband and

wife, or brother and sister? At least, from what others said, the weird little fellow was not overly respectful of authority. That trait could be helpful. "You seem to have access to C-Max. I need to get in to see one of the prisoners," she said.

"His name?"

"Marinus van Jaarsveld."

Yudel's eyes widened. He made no attempt to hide his surprise. "He is allowed very few visitors. If you're not on his visitor list, they are not going to let you see him. Van Jaarsveld himself has to give permission and he's not allowed many visitors."

"You were in C-Max this afternoon."

"I was invited."

"Doctor Gordon, I need to get in very badly." Her voice held a certain restrained determination that, for the first time, seized Yudel's attention.

"You had better tell me why."

"It's a complicated story," she said. And you will probably not believe me, she thought.

"Would you care to sit down?" Yudel asked.

At least I have his attention, Abigail thought. She had to remove a two-volume set called *Abnormal Psychology* from the offered chair. She dusted it with a tissue before sitting down. She had expected dust, but there was none.

"Do you always do that before sitting down?" he asked.

"No."

"You made an exception for me."

"Well . . ."

"Well, you thought that a study that looks like this must be dusty too."

"Look, Doctor Gordon, I just need some help. I apologize for dusting the chair."

"Mr. Gordon," he said, "but Yudel will do." He was still looking intently at her face.

"I beg your pardon?"

"Yudel. That's my name. You can call me that."

"Thank you. I knew that. I'm Abigail." She had decided that

telling her story was the only way she was going to get any-where with him. She placed the books on the floor next to the chair and reluctantly began.

As she told the story, Yudel at first studied her face, then closed his eyes and leaned back in his chair. It tilted over so far that there seemed a real danger that gravity might bring their meeting to an abrupt end. There was something about his obvious absorption in her story that put her at ease. She found herself again reliving incidents she would rather have forgotten. This strange man's presence gave her a courage she had not expected. She told the story only in the detail that she felt was necessary to persuade him. He needed to know about the raid and that Leon had come to her aid, and he needed to know about the dates when the killings took place. The rest he did not need to know, and she had no intention of telling him. When she finished, Yudel slowly righted himself and opened his eyes. "You were at the raid in Maseru?" he asked.

"Yes. I was fifteen."

"Marinus van Jaarsveld led the raiding party?"

"Yes."

"Your friend was under his command?"

"Yes."

"And these murders that have taken place since then were all on the same date?"

"Yes. It seems impossible, doesn't it?"

"Nothing is impossible in human behavior," Yudel said. "The only thing . . ." His voice trailed away as his thoughts impeded the words.

"Only what?"

"Only, these killings are the work of a man, not an organization."

Abigail already believed that, but hearing Yudel say it was as much a shock as if she had never guessed it. "Why?" Her voice was suddenly hoarse. "Why do you say that?"

"This is compulsive behavior. Only people behave compulsively. Organizations may behave in aberrant ways, but compulsion is the preserve of the individual." Yudel suddenly became aware of the change in Abigail. She seemed to be shrinking back in the chair. It was only a moment before he realized that it was what he had said that had caused the change in her. He rose slowly and started round the desk. "Why do you want to see van Jaarsveld?"

11

Abigail had told Yudel that only five days remained, that there may be something van Jaarsveld could tell her and so she had to see him, not just soon, but immediately. Clearly the next step would have to be Yudel's.

He picked up the phone and dialed a number without looking it up. "Hello, Susan," he said. "It's Yudel Gordon." Abigail watched the expression of his face soften as he listened to the voice on the other end. "Thank you," he said. "Yes, I'm well. Rosa's fine too. I hope you're well?"

It seemed to Abigail that Yudel would try to do what he had promised. She rose while he was not looking at her and went into the passage. If this was going to work, there was something else that needed to be done. The woman, whether wife or sister, needed to be won over. She found her in the garden. Rosa was wearing gardening gloves and, with a pair of pruning shears, was trimming back a row of ornamental peach trees.

"I'm late," Rosa said, as Abigail approached. "I should have done this months ago."

"I don't suppose Yudel likes gardening," Abigail said, anticipating the answer.

"As it's almost impossible to get him into the garden, it is equally difficult to know whether he would enjoy it." She smiled at Abigail for the first time. "A good man by the name of Alpheus helps me. He comes every Saturday." Abigail nodded. It was what she would have expected. The basic patterns of South African life had not changed much in the eleven years since the first democratic election. "You said that you work for the Department of Justice," Rosa continued. "What's your position there?"

"I head the gender desk."

"Really? You're so young."

It was clearly meant as a compliment, but Abigail was less enthusiastic about her position in the department. To her it was the sort of position senior men used to pretend that women were getting important jobs. "Why can there not be a man heading the gender desk?" she had once asked the minister. She had wanted to follow up with "then I can get into court," but thought better of it.

While Abigail was in the garden with Rosa, Yudel had not been able to speak to the commissioner, but had been put through to his deputy who, after Yudel had let him believe that what was wanted had been approved by the commissioner, had agreed to make the arrangements.

"Another thing," Yudel said. "I want to go into the cell. I don't want to do this through two sheets of bulletproof glass."

The commissioner's deputy had agreed to this too. A new psychologist, one of the department's relatively few current recruits, would be there to escort him and his guest to the prisoner he needed to see. There would also be two heavily armed warders with them.

He looked up with a self-satisfied smile in the direction in which he expected to find Abigail. A movement in the garden caught his attention. She was chatting to Rosa, as if they had known each other forever. As he watched, Rosa laid a hand on Abigail's shoulder and the two women seemed to pause in their discussion. Both were smiling warmly.

Women, Yudel thought. What did they talk about when there were no men present? It had always been a mystery to men and always would be. They never divulged the secrets of their gender to the other half of humanity. He had been doing her an important favor—according to her, a life-and-death one. But, instead of waiting to hear the outcome, she had gone outside to discuss recipes or knitting patterns or man trouble or something similar with Rosa. Understanding females was beyond the scope of the male intellect.

If Yudel could have overheard the conversation in the garden, he would have heard Abigail telling Rosa that her thesis had been on crimes against children and how the patterns had changed during and after apartheid. "I wish you could make the time to tell me about it some day," Rosa said.

"I'd love to," Abigail said.

"I'd like to read your thesis."

"I'll have a copy delivered."

Rosa waved a hand in the direction of the study window. "It looks as if Yudel has finished," she said. "He has that impatient look he gets when he's done something he thinks is pretty good, but there is no one present to applaud."

Yudel saw them start toward the house. They've probably exchanged e-mail addresses to expedite the exchange of dream vacation destinations, he thought.

12

For the second time that day, Yudel set out for C-Max. Abigail had left her car in the driveway of his home and was seated in the passenger seat next to him. "Thank you for this," she said.

Yudel nodded, but drove in silence until they entered the prison complex. "Are you sure you want to meet him again?" he asked eventually.

Abigail was sure that she never wanted to see this man again. She was glad that he was being held in the depths of C-Max with no practical hope of escape. Of all human beings on earth, there were just two Abigail prayed that she would never have to face again. Van Jaarsveld was one of them. She had seen him only briefly and knew what he had done. His actions that night were a continuing nightmare that had been dimmed only slightly by the passage of twenty years. Seeing him again was something that she would never have chosen. But now, since Leon Lourens had entered her office two days before, everything was different. "I'm sure," she said.

"When we're in front of him, you'd better let me start," Yudel said.

She nodded.

They had to wait outside the pedestrian gate for almost half an hour before they were let in. A bespectacled man, taller than Yudel and lean, was waiting just inside. He was one of a kind of African man whose age is almost impossible to judge. Even to Abigail he could have been anything between thirty and sixty. The guard who had opened for Yudel and Abigail waved them in his direction. He held out a limp hand to Yudel. "I'm Patrick Lesela," he said.

Yudel introduced himself and Abigail. The academic, he thought. "You're from UPE, I believe?"

"I've spent some time there, fine institution."

"And now you're the psychologist for C–Max?" Yudel asked.

"And for Modder B, Central and Zonderwater." His tone of voice revealed no enthusiasm. He had met Yudel's eyes only momentarily. He averted them as he spoke.

"Alone?"

"Yes. There aren't enough of us."

They had started toward the inner wall, Abigail walking next to Lesela with Yudel a few steps behind. There was a passivity about Lesela's manner that Yudel found disturbing. "Are you running any sort of rehabilitation program?" Yudel asked, wondering if Lesela knew what the commissioner was planning.

"No. I've been dealing with prisoner complaints." His head was tilted forward so that he seemed to be looking at a patch on the concrete path a pace or two in front of his feet. He had made no attempt to look back at Yudel as he answered.

"Complaints?"

"Conditions and so on."

They had practically no psychologists and one of the few spends his days listening to complaints? Yudel wondered about it. "Are you happy with that?" he asked.

Abigail glanced back at Yudel. There was a pleading in her eyes that seemed to ask, Did we come here for this?

"I understand we will soon be implementing the rehabilitation methods of an outside consultant. If I'm not mistaken, you are the consultant. I'm waiting for that."

So the commissioner had been talking about his new program before even getting Yudel's agreement. I suppose he knew his man, Yudel thought. "My methods are partly based on Zimbardo's prison studies. You're familiar with them, of course?"

Lesela answered in the same flat monotone in which enthusiasm would have been an alien intrusion. "I also agree with that study."

"Which study?"

"That Zimbalist study."

Zimbalist? Yudel thought. An academic? Which academy? And they retrenched me for you. And now you are going to be my trusty right hand. This time he was silent though. Abigail had again turned to look briefly at him. The reproach in her eyes was unavoidable.

Before they reached the inner wall they were joined by two armed warders. The group followed the same route Yudel had taken earlier in the day, gate after gate being opened to let them pass, then locked behind them. When they reached the section that had once been death row, Yudel led the way to the catwalk that ran over the top of the cells, with Abigail close behind and Lesela and the warders following. Below them the prisoners, one to a cell, sat on their bunks, paced, read or stood at the cell doors, talking to the man opposite. The walls between them were solid concrete and the ceilings open, but barred.

The man they had come to see was standing in the center of his cell, his feet spread wide and looking up as if expecting them. The light from the fluorescent fittings reflected off the white walls so that the thickset man below in his green prison uniform seemed to be standing in a sea of brightness. He looked older than his sixty-five years. "Marinus van Jaarsveld?" Yudel asked.

"Ja," he said and then softly, more to himself than to them, "fokken Jood." But he was not looking at Yudel. His eyes were fixed somewhere further back.

Yudel turned to find that he was almost alone. Considering how well insulated he was from the man in the cell, he felt surprisingly vulnerable. Abigail had stopped as soon as van Jaarsveld had come into view, but she was the focus of his attention.

The warders were behind her with Lesela still farther back and barely looking up, as if all of this had nothing to do with him.

"If you've no objection, we'll be coming down," Yudel told the prisoner.

"Come, then," he said, his eyes still fixed on Abigail. To Yudel it was the look of a predator studying its prey.

Van Jaarsveld was facing the door when one of the warders opened it. He was above medium height and had once been powerfully built, sloping shoulders ending at long arms with surprisingly delicate hands. A warder entered first, followed by Yudel and Abigail. Lesela and the second warder stayed in the corridor with the door open. Both warders had slipped the revolvers from their holsters.

No one made any movement toward shaking hands. "Thank you for seeing us," Yudel said.

Van Jaarsveld said nothing. He was again staring at Abigail. His head moved slightly from side to side as if he was clearing the way for some distant memory. He took half a step in her direction. The slow beginnings of a smile were forming around his mouth and eyes.

"Stay where you are," one of the warders said.

"We have a matter that we want to discuss. We think it may be of importance to you," Yudel said.

By now the smile was fully formed. It was an expression that suggested that he knew and there was no use denying his knowledge. Yudel glanced at Abigail over his right shoulder. She had stopped a pace behind him, but a little to the side to give herself a clear view of van Jaarsveld. The look on her face showed that whatever vulnerability Yudel had felt when they were up on the catwalk was nothing compared to what she felt now.

"I know you," the prisoner said to Abigail. His voice had the slightly jeering tone of one who had found them out. "You were in Maseru. You were smaller then, but I remember you. I let you go that time. You were lucky, very lucky that I let you go."

"You did nothing to let me live." To Yudel's surprise her voice was strong and even. It was also cold and she was moving forward. "Leon Lourens saved me. You wanted to kill me."

"You were lucky I was in a good mood." He was nodding his head for emphasis. "If I'd been a bad mood you and that little wind-arse Lourens would both have been dead. I let you live."

"Like hell you did. You saved your own life."

"I was good to you. Not everyone was so lucky."

Abigail's shoulders shook with a brief convulsion. It passed, leaving her shaken, but still closer to van Jaarsveld.

"Stand back, Miss," the warder's voice carried the note of command that came with years of authority over other human beings.

"Yes, stand back," van Jaarsveld jeered. "What did you think you were going to do anyway?"

"Stand back, Miss. Right now," the warder ordered.

Yudel had her by the arm and was drawing her back. "Lourens was a comrade of yours in those days. We believe he may be in danger."

The disgust in van Jaarsveld's face was visible. "Leon Lourens was never a comrade of mine. None of those bastards who kissed the ANC arse at that truth and reconciliation thing were comrades of mine. What I stood for then I still stand for now. I was protecting my people. I will not say, the way Lourens and all the rest did, that what I did then was wrong. Events have proven us right. Today the white man has been kicked out everywhere. We have lost our country."

"Listen," Yudel said to van Jaarsveld. "We've come here because we are trying to help some of your old comrades, not just Lourens. You may not realize it, but some of the other soldiers that were with you that night when you saw Miss Bukula in Maseru, have been murdered."

"I may not realize it." Now he was crowing with the pleasure that comes with superior knowledge. "My little Jew friend, I know as well as you that there are only two of us still alive. And I am in here." He turned his attention to Abigail. "In five days your little friend Lourens will be dead." He stopped and looked from Abigail to Yudel and back to Abigail, a look of genuine surprise appearing on his face. "You didn't know? You didn't know that we are all that are left? Do you also not know that they all died on the same day of the year? And that day is only five days away." He smiled at Abigail. "Lourens is as good as dead," he said with real satisfaction. "Your own people are doing it. I thought you came here to tell me something. But it looks like you came so that I can tell you something."

"Perhaps you do know more than we do," Yudel said. Abigail was looking at him, wondering where he was trying to lead van Jaarsveld. "Perhaps you do know more. Perhaps you can help us. We're not just talking about Lourens's safety. There's your own safety to consider."

"If you want to do something for me, my little friend, let them give me my freedom on the big day. Broadcast the fact in ANC party circles that I am out of prison. Give them my address too. Then let them come for me. Give me the chance to kill a few more of them to add to my score."

Abigail had to ask. She hated wanting to know, but she could not stop herself. "How many have you killed?"

"Not enough." His smile was again directed at her. "Some of them were very special ones." Now his eyebrows were raised, as if asking her a question.

Yudel was aware that there was something here that he did not understand. Abigail recoiled as if van Jaarsveld had struck her. He looked at van Jaarsveld's self-satisfied face and knew he had to do something to stop his gloating. "What makes you think you're safe? You exercise with the other prisoners. Even criminals have political feelings."

"I hope one of them tries. I can look after myself. It's a long time since I last killed one of them. In any event, I know who's doing the killing." He was again looking at Abigail. "And so do you, *meidjie*. And he's not in C-Max. He's not in any prison, even though he's killed far more than me."

Abigail was staring at him, an antelope trapped in the headlights of a car. It was not that he had used the Afrikaans word for a housemaid when addressing her. Yudel could see that something far deeper than van Jaarsveld's gratuitous insult had affected her. "He's not in any prison," the old extremist had said.

Out of the corner of her eye Abigail could see Yudel turn to look at her. She had given him only the broadest outline of the story. Without looking at him, she could feel the question: Who is he talking about? "What is this?" Yudel's question was directed at Abigail.

"It's Ficksburg all over again, but on an even bigger scale."

Yudel also did not understand the reference to one of the South African towns close to the Lesotho border. "You mean Maseru?" he said.

"Ficksburg." It was said heavily, as if from a deep sense of exasperation. "You know fuck-all, my little friend. Ask your black lady. She knows all about Ficksburg. She was there."

Abigail could feel Yudel looking at her. "Abigail?" His voice was a whisper.

"She's not telling you everything, my Jewish friend. I'm the one who is telling you what you want to know. I can give you the name of every man and what year he died and I can give you the name of the man who killed them." He laughed his humorless chuckle again. "But then, so can she."

13

Yudel drove quickly through Pretoria's late-afternoon streets, using side roads to avoid the commuter traffic. He was silent, pointedly avoiding even looking at Abigail. She looked at his face only once, saw the disapproval there and fell silent herself.

Only when they arrived at his home, where her car was still parked in the driveway, did he speak. "How do you expect me to help you, if you hide what you know from me?"

Abigail was expecting something of the sort and was waiting for it. "I only asked you to get me in to see van Jaarsveld. You've done that and I'm thankful. I'll be going now."

"Where are you going from here?"

"That's my business." She already had a hand on the door handle.

"What did happen in Maseru? Who were the very special people he says he killed? And what's Ficksburg got to do with anything? And he thinks you know who is committing these murders. Do you?"

Abigail looked briefly at Yudel's angry face. Every impulse within her was urging her to go and go now. The meeting with van Jaarsveld had been almost beyond her ability to endure. Now she wanted only to flee it all. It was past and should have remained buried, but Leon Lourens had brought her back to

Maseru and to van Jaarsveld and even Ficksburg. And this unusual man, what was he? Abigail looked again into his eyes and
she knew what he was. He was an ally.

But he had served his purpose. "Thank you, Yudel," she said.
She pushed open the door and was out before he could object
further. With the driveway gate closed, she had to wait in her
car until he got out and stood looking at her, a strange man in
a rumpled suit with a wild fuzz of poorly trimmed hair. For a
long moment she thought he was going to come closer to try
again to speak to her, but eventually he took a remote-control
switch from one of his jacket pockets and, with an almost
imperceptible movement, pressed the button that opened the
gate.

It took Abigail just a few minutes to reach her office in the
late-afternoon traffic. It was half past five, and only the twenty-
four-hour security officers on the ground floor were still in the
building. The staff had already left in the usual late-afternoon
stampede to get out of government offices. Abigail waved her
security card at them and entered the elevator.

When she entered her suite of offices, she was met by the one
employee of the department who was still in the building.
Johanna leaped to her feet as Abigail came into the room. The
expression on her face was close to panic. "Oh, I'm so glad you're
here. Those other men, we traced them all. They all died on the
same day."

"I know," Abigail said.

"How?"

"I spoke to their leader this afternoon."

"Van Jaarsveld?"

"Yes."

"Oh God, Abby. What's been happening? I'm so afraid."

"So am I."

"And they all got strangled."

"I know. And I've got the list of the others who were there."

"Shall I try to check them tomorrow?"

Abigail considered the suggestion for only a moment. "No. I don't think so. I think we already know the answer."

Johanna was looking down. "Your hands are shaking," she said.

"No, they're not." The response had been automatic, but now she also looked at her hands. "It doesn't matter," she said.

"Mine too," Johanna said.

"You go home now. Nobody's trying to kill you. Go home."

"And you? Do they want to kill you?"

"No, of course not. Go home now."

"Can I?"

"Take a sleeping pill tonight."

"Do you think so?"

"Yes, do it. Go home now." As Johanna turned to leave, Abigail remembered the other matter. "Have you found Michael Bishop's contact details?"

"I found that we never had them. We sent the invitation to Luthuli House. They said they would try to forward it. Maybe he never got it."

"Maybe not. All right, you go home."

"Right now?"

"Immediately, and tomorrow get back onto the conference. One of us has to work on it."

Seated at her desk, Abigail studied the list of names, and the dates and places each man had died. She ticked off the ones that Johanna had already tracked down. Of those that remained, one stood out among all the others. While the rest had all died inside South African borders, this one had been killed in London. And it had happened while she was there, during her university years. There had been a lot of talk in the exile community about the murder of a South African businessman. She remembered the talk and she remembered her father showing her the place where he died. That he had been part of the raiding party in Maseru was a complete surprise. No one had said anything like that at the time. Perhaps they had never known.

Or perhaps only a few had known. She filed away his name in her memory. It was possible that someone from the movement might remember something about the manner of Michael Whitehead's death.

Johanna had written a pile of notes to Abigail. It appeared that during the day every new discovery had excited Johanna so much that she had to write it down. A new note was written for every new confirmation that one of the men on the list had died, every discovery of a date of death and every time the means of death was revealed. At the bottom of the pile were a number of death certificates which, at a glance, seemed to confirm everything Johanna said. There was also a note in which Johanna anticipated her instruction, reminding her that the conference was drawing closer and that she, Johanna, would devote the next day to it.

Abigail stuffed the pile of paper into her briefcase, along with her purse, her mobile phone and other assorted documents. On the way to the lift, the passages were as empty as before. The security guards were still maintaining their bored vigil in the lobby. Down in the parking garage, the bays were deserted except for the fleet of vehicles that belonged to the department. From the road, the traffic was still audible as Pretoria's workforce struggled to get home for the evening.

Even afterward, Abigail did not remember hearing any sound that might have warned her. The man's left arm had wrapped itself around her neck before she had the chance to react. At almost the same instant his right hand rose to her neck, pressing a knife against her jugular. An African voice whispered something in her ear in a language she did not understand.

Suddenly the cluster of crumpled papers in her bag seemed absurdly important to Abigail and she answered in English. "Listen, I'll give you money, but . . ."

Before she could finish she was pushed heavily from behind, stumbling then going down on hands and knees. Her head struck a concrete pillar just behind her right ear. It seemed to her that almost immediately she was scrambling to her feet.

She tried to take a step forward, but had to reach for the pillar to steady herself. She went down on her hands and knees a second time. Her briefcase was gone and there was no sign of her assailant.

Abigail waited five minutes before starting the car engine. The day had been dense with enough incidents, without her causing an accident on the way home. Oh God, she asked herself, did they really want the contents of her briefcase that badly? And if they did, who were they? And the damned security guards, sitting in a cozy knot in the lobby, they seemed more interested in their own security than that of the building or their clients.

When she finally got home Robert was not yet there. There was a message from him on the apartment's phone, saying that he may be late, but he would pick up TV dinners on the way home, if she would wait for him.

She sat down in the chair in front of the French windows with the curtains open. The chair seemed to have become her favorite. Robert arrived an hour later with a plastic bag that contained the promised TV dinners and some cans of beer. His expression turned from good humor to alarm the moment he saw her. "Your clothes," he said. "What happened?"

Abigail had not noticed the smear of old grease across her jacket and blouse that she had picked up from the floor of the parking garage. Her hands, too, were covered in dust. For the first time she touched the place where she had struck her head. When she withdrew them, the tips of her fingers were covered by partly congealed blood.

"What the hell happened?" Robert was saying.

"They took my briefcase."

"Who did?"

"I don't know. This matter . . . the Leon Lourens matter. There were documents in it. I can replace them all, but . . . I don't know what they'll do next."

"You sit down," Robert said. "I'll pour you a drink." It was Robert's cure for most crises.

Once she had her drink, he cleaned the graze on her head.

Having him moving around her, tending her wound, plying her with drink, gave Abigail a feeling of real security for the first time since Leon Lourens had entered her office some eighty hours before.

When Robert was done he went to the telephone and lifted the receiver. "Are you calling the police?" Abigail asked.

"First I'm going to call your mobile. I presume it was in your briefcase?"

"Wait, Robert. I don't know who might be on the other end of the line."

Robert was a man angered by the attack on his wife. "Let's hear what they have to say for themselves."

"Shouldn't we wait?"

"For what?" Robert called the number.

From where she was sitting Abigail heard a male voice answer.

"Good evening." Robert always sounded impeccably polite when his anger was raised. "My name is Robert Mokoape. You or someone you know attacked my wife this evening. I'd like to know who you are and why you acted in this way."

Abigail heard the answering voice. She could not make out what was being said, but Robert's eyes widened in surprise, then the faintest trace of a smile formed round his mouth. "Hold on," he told the voice on the other end of the line. "You'd better tell her." He gestured to Abigail to come to the phone. "It's for you," he said. Then he smiled. "It's all right."

Abigail could barely believe what Robert was doing, but she came to the phone and took the receiver from him. "Yes?" To her own ears her voice was quivering.

The voice on the other end of the line was clearly the one that had whispered into her ear in the parking garage, but now it was an octave higher and had taken on a pleading tone. "Hi, comrade. I'm so sorry about tonight, but times are tough and a man's family has to eat."

"What are you talking about?"

"Comrade, I found your ANC membership card in your

bag. I'm so sorry. I didn't know you are a member of the party. I've taken your cellphone and the cash in your purse, but I left your briefcase with your credit cards and your documents with your building's security. I can see they might be important and I don't want to hurt the party. I'm so sorry I pushed you, sister. I hope you're not hurt badly."

"No. I'm not hurt."

"I'm happy. I'm very happy."

And I'm happy, Abigail thought, that you are just an honest mugger and not some political crazy. After she hung up, she turned to Robert. Suddenly they were holding on to each other and laughing, tears running from their eyes, as if nothing had ever been funnier.

Abigail finished her drink, showered and ate Robert's TV dinner. He tucked her into bed. Inside a minute she was asleep. Robert poured himself another drink and drank it slowly before coming to bed himself. The matter of the mugger had been funny, but there was still the other matter. He was concerned about where it could be leading Abigail and what he could do—if anything—to protect her.

While Abigail slept, Yudel Gordon was awake. For a long time he lay still next to Rosa, not wanting to disturb her by getting up. He waited for her breathing to become deep and regular before slipping out of bed, scooping up his dressing gown and going to his study, where a notebook with a few jotted thoughts on the Abigail matter lay open among the clutter of his desk.

Yudel forbade all tidying in his study, and he rarely undertook it himself. As a result, papers, note scraps, unpaid accounts, even books disappeared under the growing, shifting sea of paper on his desk. Rosa referred to his desk as a pocket of immaturity in his makeup. It was a phrase that he had often used until she started applying it to him.

Like Abigail, he had not enjoyed the latter part of the day. During the liberation struggle he had on a number of occasions been exposed to the insufferable self-righteousness of those who had placed bombs in public places to kill randomly, or had burned to death people who may or may not have been informers for the system. And, on the other hand, he had also occasionally been exposed to those who told themselves that they were killing to protect their people from the murderous black hordes. Today's meeting with van Jaarsveld was a reminder of those days. As far as Yudel knew, this man was the last of the apartheid killers still to be telling anyone who would listen that they had been right all along. No doubt many were still telling themselves the same in private.

Yudel's inability to sleep resided in a single phrase, used by van Jaarsveld, and by Abigail's reaction to it. It had been lost in everything else that was said at this afternoon's meeting in C-Max, but now it came back and drove away every hope of restful unconsciousness.

It was not even the thought that possibly Abigail knew who was killing the policemen who had been in the raiding party twenty years before. It was a little phrase of five words that kept Yudel awake. They hung in his mind, a clear, sharply delineated indication of the horror of those days. "Not everyone was so lucky," van Jaarsveld had said. Abigail had shrunk from those words, as if facing a death sentence. Perhaps there resided a death sentence within those words. Who did Abigail know who was part of the "everyone" who had not been so lucky?

Then suddenly he knew. He got up and walked to the window. Before opening the curtains he switched off the only light in the room, the reading lamp on his desk. It was a clear night and the nearer flowers in Rosa's garden looked pale silver in the relative darkness of the Pretoria night.

Abigail had been fifteen at the time. Van Jaarsveld had killed her parents. Yudel had no provable way of knowing it, but he was as sure as if he had been present that night. He stood at the window for a long time. He saw neither the garden, nor the floodlit form of the Union Buildings against the hill on the far side of Arcadia. He thought about Abigail, the things she would not tell him, the raid on a house in Maseru so long ago and the price the perpetrators were now paying.

When Rosa found him at three o'clock, Yudel was still at the window. "Come to bed," she said. "This will solve nothing."

14

Tuesday, October 18

Chief Albert Luthuli House, the ANC headquarters in down-town Johannesburg, did not seem to have woken when Abigail arrived at nine in the morning. Most of the offices she passed were empty and in one a secretary was reading the morning paper.

The former cabinet minister rose as Abigail was ushered into her office. She was in her mid-sixties and well known for her ability to ease tensions wherever she held office. This was a quality soon to be stretched to its limit by a growing leadership struggle in the party. The older woman had been redeployed from the Cabinet to Luthuli House, where she now filled the position of the party's deputy secretary-general.

She came round her desk, both arms outstretched, smiling warmly. "Abby, my child. I've been hearing such wonderful things about you. Your parents would have been proud."

"Thank you for seeing me, mother," Abigail said.

The deputy secretary-general waved an impatient hand that seemed to indicate that she could never refuse to see Abigail. "I saw you at the Black Management Forum banquet with your husband. That was your husband, wasn't it?"

"Yes, that was Robert."

"He's the famous editor. Am I correct?"

"That's right. At least, I think of him that way."

"What a clever couple. You are going to have clever children. Are there any yet?"

"No, not yet."

"Don't wait too long. You're in your thirties already, I think." The former minister was so obviously concerned and well-meaning that her unasked-for advice and rather prying ways never met with a rebuff from anyone. "All the uneducated rural people are having dozens of kids. We need our highly educated people to have the kids who will lead us in the future."

Abigail was one of the many who loved her. She smiled at the older woman. But now can we get past this? she was thinking. What if we get on to business now? Is that possible?

"Is it you or Robert who doesn't want babies?"

"No, we both want children."

"Then the time has come to get on with it." She frowned at Abigail for a moment, but immediately the smile reappeared. "But there's something on your mind. Let's talk about that first. You can allow an interfering old lady to question you later."

Abigail started reminding her about the raid in Maseru twenty years before, but the deputy secretary-general did not need reminding. Her face, that smiled so readily, was stern now. "Yes, child, I remember. Your parents . . ."

"The night after that we were rescued in Ficksburg."

"Yes. It was a wonderful achievement."

"A man by the name of Michael Bishop was there."

"Ye-es . . ." It was said slowly, the vowel sound extended beyond its usual length. "I'm told he was there."

"A meeting was held to honor him in our offices a few days ago."

"I had heard that. I have to say that I was surprised to hear that he attended such a meeting."

"He didn't attend. Our minister was there and made the speech, but Michael Bishop didn't come."

She nodded. This was clearly no surprise.

"I wondered if you knew where he is and what he is doing now."

"Your minister wants to know?"

"I want to know."

"Abby, my child, I must ask you why."

"Mother . . ." Abigail felt very young, talking to this woman who had been a mentor to her mother and whom she knew would do almost anything for her. "Mother, I want you to believe me that this is important, but I don't want to make my problems your problems."

The deputy secretary-general thought about this for so long that Abigail was beginning to see it as a refusal. "Very well," she said at last. "To the best of my knowledge he holds no position in the party. And I only met him a few times during the struggle days. I don't know where he is now, but I'll take you to a male colleague who may be able to help."

She led the way out of her office, but stopped in the corridor as if she had just remembered something. Turning to Abigail, she spoke very gently. "It would be better if you had as little dealing with this man as possible. He is not someone you should be having contact with."

"I will be careful," Abigail said.

The male colleague was not educated, a former soldier in the liberation army, who had been given the job of handyman as a reward for his loyal service to the movement. They found him installing a lock on a storeroom door on the ground floor. He rose and dusted off his hands before folding them in front of him. It was the gesture of someone who was among superiors. The deputy secretary-general introduced Abigail and told him that they were looking for Michael Bishop.

Although he was about the same age, he addressed her as respectfully as Abigail had. "Mother, I fought next to him in the struggle, but I know nothing about him now."

"Did you ever work with him in October?" Abigail burst in suddenly.

"October, what year?" he asked.

"Any year in the month of October."

The handyman looked helplessly at the deputy secretary-general. "Mother, I don't know this."

"That's all right, Ephraim," she said. "Do you know who can help us?"

"Yes, there's a man in Diepsloot who was his commanding officer."

"Is that Jones, Jones Ndlovu?"

"Yes. He was Michael Bishop's commanding officer."

After receiving instructions on how to get to Jones Ndlovu, the deputy secretary-general accompanied Abigail toward the building's entrance. "I don't know how wise this is. Jones Ndlovu is no longer the man he was. They say he's a drug addict now."

"I'll go. I need to talk to him."

They had reached the lobby, but Abigail took the older woman's arm above her right elbow and drew her gently into a decorative alcove. "Mother, do you remember that while we were in London, a South African businessman was murdered there? It must have been in the early nineties."

The deputy secretary-general's eyebrows rose in surprise. "That was a long time ago, but yes, I believe there was such a case."

"Do you remember his name?"

"I think I do, but only because of his surname. It had racial connotations and, at that time, everything seemed to have racial connotations. His name was Whiteman."

"Whitehead."

"Yes, that's it. Whitehead."

"He was in the squad that raided us in Maseru that night."

The older woman's head jerked back as if she had been slapped. "Are you sure?"

"Quite. Do you remember, would Michael Bishop have been in London at that time?"

"He may have been. He was back and forth at times, between London and different parts of Africa. But, my child, what are you suggesting?"

"And could Whitehead have died in October?"

"I don't know." The deputy secretary-general was trying to

remember. "You know, I think it was some time in the English autumn."

Abigail released her grip. "Thank you, mother," she said. She tried to leave, but now it was her turn to be held.

"Wait, my child. What are you suggesting?"

"I'm not suggesting anything. I'm only suspecting."

"Wait a moment." The older woman paused to gather her thoughts. "I need to say something." Abigail saw a trace of pain in her face. "The struggle was a war. You know that?"

"Of course, mother. I was there."

"You were. And you, as much as anyone, know how many of our finest people were murdered by the regime." Abigail could not bring herself to answer this. "In a war you cannot always choose your weapons or methods. You have to use what is available. We used plenty of people in those days that we would like to be rid of today, but they were good comrades in the struggle and now we can't just throw them away. We have killers from those days in high positions today, some even in law enforcement. Some of them undertook operations that resulted in the deaths of civilians, which the leadership did not approve. But the masses and other activists see them as heroes. I was in Lusaka when this man arrived there for the first time. There were immediate disagreements over whether we should use him at all. At first we didn't trust him, this young white man who came from nowhere, and later, when he had shown that he really was on the side of the movement, I still did not want us to use him."

Abigail already knew where the older woman was leading her, but every moment of the first twenty years of her life, everything she had learned during that time, compelled her to listen without interruption.

"Michael Bishop was available. We did not choose him, but he was there and he was effective. My God, he was effective. But, as far as I was concerned, his motives were wrong. He was not fighting for freedom. He was fighting for something else entirely. I don't know how well you knew him . . ." This too was something Abigail could not answer. "If you find him, and

I don't believe you will, I don't want you going to him alone. Do you hear me?"

"I promise, mother."

"I would also prefer it if you did not conduct this search of yours for long. I don't want him to know that you are looking for him. Remember this—that the struggle was a war, in which the other side had all the guns. We had to use what we had. One of the things we had was Michael Bishop. That is the only reason we used him."

"I do know this, mother."

The older woman seemed still to have a need to warn Abigail, but there was nothing left to say. "And October, my child, any October? What does it mean?"

"I must hurry," Abigail said. "I must see Ndlovu, then get back to the office. Thank you, mother. And I will be careful."

"Do not go to Bishop alone. Never go to him alone."

15

Diepsloot was a settlement on the northern extremity of metropolitan Johannesburg. It had been created to absorb the torrential influx to the city of Africans from impoverished rural South African communities and those who had slipped across the border illegally from even poorer African communities. Diepsloot had started as a sudden explosion of wood-and-iron shacks on the open veld, without sanitation, electricity, running water or any coherent road plan.

Abigail had tried to contact Robert to tell him where she was going, but both he and his PA were out of the office and no one seemed to know where they were. She left a message on the voice mail of Robert's mobile phone, knowing at the same time that if she did need him urgently, he was too far away to help her.

By the time she turned at the traffic light on the artery that passed next to the township, it was beginning to take on the form of a suburb. The authorities had, in just a few years, created roads, built tiny, low-cost houses and provided basic services to residents.

Despite the obvious poverty, Abigail's was not the only nearly-new car on the streets of Diepsloot. Although most of the people were poor, there were some who had jobs that did not pay badly, but who preferred the very low cost of government-subsidized living. And there were the gangsters, the pimps and some traders who either did business in the township or used it as a refuge. They lived either in shacks or the subsidized cottages, but they dressed well and drove good cars.

Abigail had to ask directions twice before she found the opening, not quite a street, where Jones Ndlovu lived. It lay between a neat row of yellow-painted township cottages on one side and a ragged row of corrugated iron shacks on the other. She turned the corner and entered a thoroughfare that was surprisingly empty. Such township streets were usually dotted with cars, both serviceable and unroadworthy; children, both ragged and well-heeled; adults, both angry and resigned; and chickens that fled squawking in front of your car.

Today, this street, like all the others she had passed, contained the unroadworthy cars and the chickens, but very few people. She had already moved too far down the thoroughfare to turn back when she realized that she had a problem. A group of teenage boys had appeared from one of the shacks lining the narrow dirt road, deliberately blocking her way.

Abigail had never been part of the rough-and-tumble of township life. She had not been exposed to the regular robberies, muggings and holdups or the desultory killings and rapes that were a part of township life. South Africa's black townships had, during the latter years of the apartheid regime when resistance was most intense, become the most violent social system on Earth. Now, after the revolution had come and gone, the violence had declined only marginally. It had largely metamorphosed into crime and expanded from the black townships into the walled and burglar-protected white suburbs.

Because of her upbringing, Abigail did not possess that peculiarly African fatalism that made living under the continual threat of violence at least manageable. Most of her formative years had been spent outside the country. Much of her schooling had taken place in the protected environs of an expensive private school in Swaziland. During the nine years between the raid in Maseru and the country's first democratic election, she had lived first in London, in the home of another exiled

South African family, then in Boston where she completed a degree in public administration, then back in London where she worked for the movement. She had returned immediately after the 1994 elections at the age of twenty-four and had, since that day, lived in comfortable suburbs, insulated as far as possible, like her white countryfolk and the rest of the rising black middle class, from the excesses of the townships. While she loved her country and was wholly dedicated to the task of helping to rebuild it after the destruction surrounding the liberation struggle, her reactions were in many ways those of a citizen of a modern first-world city. She would have been seen by many in the township as being a "coconut," someone who is brown on the outside, but white on the inside.

Now, as the gang of young men closed around her car, she was aware that their motives could be anything from the politics born of unmet expectations, to simple criminality or sex. No gainfully employed young woman who lived in the township ever avoided these gangs entirely. Few of them had not been mugged. Few rapes ever came to the attention of the police. Even missing persons often went unreported. In a country in which more than half the men between fifteen and thirty-five were unemployed, those men and women who had employment ran the continual gauntlet of the disaffected and violent. Losing a mobile phone or a small roll of banknotes was so minor in the range of possible losses that they were considered let-offs.

In the next few seconds every type of violent township death presented itself to her, a quick unsolicited catalog that she would rather have ignored: the simple knife between the ribs; the panga with its meter-long blade made of cheap steel and sharpened on any cement slab till it had the edge its owner desired; the *kapmes,* somewhere between a panga and a knife and more effective than the others, but rarer; the AK-47 assault rifle and the 9mm Makarov pistol. These had originally been smuggled across the country's borders in apartheid days for raids on police and military installations, but were now being used for other purposes.

The teenage youths were swarming round the car, but at least Abigail could see no knives, pangas, *kapmesse* or Makarovs—and an AK-47 was not easy to hide. But the apparent absence of weapons was small consolation. The kids blocking her way were looking at her with undisguised hostility that, to Abigail's eyes, seemed like sexual predation.

What are you doing, Abigail Bukula? she asked herself. Coming to this damned place to search for a man you really do not want to find. And, if you get through this afternoon intact, and you find him, what then? What are you going to do with him? What is anyone going to do with him? What might he do with you?

One of the gang of young men, wearing T-shirts, jeans and sneakers, knocked on her side window and gestured for her to open it. His face showed that the gesture was a command, not a suggestion.

Abigail rolled the window down. "Can I help you?" she heard herself ask.

"Can she help us?" He mimicked her to his friends. Most of them were dressed like him, but some wore shorts and a few had no shoes or only plastic sandals. After a brief round of derisory laughter, he spoke to her again in a language of which she only understood the occasional word. She thought it may have been Setswana.

"I'm sorry. I can't understand you." She was trying to keep her voice even.

"So, foxy woman, where do you come from that you can't speak our language?"

"I grew up in exile."

"Political?" This was a surprise to the entire troop. "Don't you know you not supposed to be driving around here while the people are holding a march?"

"I'm sorry. I'm not from here. I didn't know about the march."

"Oh, yes?" He was shaking his head. "We are the township detectives. It's our job to see that no one stays away from the march. How are we going to get government to listen, if people don't join the march?"

This is all I need, Abigail thought, a gang of young, jobless firebrands saving the country. She had not heard of a march taking place anywhere, but sometimes these things arrived suddenly—spontaneously according to their organizers. "I work for the Department of Justice now," she said, knowing that she was taking a chance by this admission, but needing badly to establish at least some measure of authority.

The leader stared at her through half-closed eyes. It was clear that he needed to think about what the Department of Justice meant to them, if anything. "Government?" he asked eventually.

"Yes."

Already the gang members were edging out of her way. Their leader was not finished yet. "The government does nothing for us."

"So, you want to go back to the white boss?" It occurred to her as she was saying it that none of them could have been more than four or five when Mandela was released from prison.

"I'm not saying that. But government doesn't listen to the voice of the people."

"Today, I'm here to listen." Abigail was starting to think that, despite the bravado, they were impressed by her accent, as much British as suburban South African, her BMW, the Department of Justice connection and even the fifteen or twenty years she had on them. "I've come to listen to Jones Ndlovu. Perhaps you can show me where to find him."

"Jones Ndlovu?" The voice again had a derisory sound. "He's nothing. He lies in his shack all day. He waits for a woman who brings him food."

"He was not always nothing. Once he was a great man. Can you show me where to find him?"

At last they seemed to be satisfied. "All right, sister, but next time don't come when there's a march."

Two of the gang members ran ahead of the car, passed a few shacks and stopped in front of one that looked even less secure than the others. A rough wooden framework of old, worm-eaten planks supported a roof made of a few sheets of corrugated iron. Two sides had walls made of the same planks, nailed roughly to the frame. One of the other sides was covered with black plastic bin-liners. The last side served as the doorway. A door made of hessian bags and bin-liners was hooked back to allow light and air inside.

"Hey, Jones," one of her escorts shouted. "There's a foxy lady here who can't speak Setswana. She wants you." The attempt to impress her with their authority and toughness had disappeared and all of them, the leader included, had caught up to Abigail and were gathering excitedly around the entrance to Jones Ndlovu's shack.

Abigail had to force her way through the gathering to get to the shack. She hesitated in the entrance. She could see only the vaguest shapes in the deep gloom inside, but nothing that could be a human being. "You can go in." The leader of the detectives was standing next to her. "Go in. It's all right."

Abigail took a step forward and something moved on what seemed to be a mound of cotton waste products, perhaps factory off-cuts. Now she could see that it was a man, slowly rolling over and then struggling into a sitting position. He wriggled backward until he could rest his back against one of the plank walls. Once sitting up, he blinked in the direction of the doorway's brightness, trying bring his visitor into focus.

"Hey, Jones. Here's the lady who wants to see you."

Some of the light from the door fell directly onto Ndlovu's face and he closed his eyes. Abigail saw a deeply lined face that had not been shaven recently. It was the face, puffy around the eyes and loose around the mouth, of a heavy drinker. He held up an unsteady hand in an attempt to shield his eyes.

"Jones, my man," one of the young voices crowed. "You got a foxy lady visiting you from the Department of Justice." They seemed eager to get the message through, as if they were the ones responsible for producing so singular a visitor.

Four of them had crowded into the shack around Abigail. The rest were clustered behind her.

This was simply not going to work. She had to take charge and do it now. She turned suddenly to face the young men crowding behind her. "Listen, guys. Listen to me." Almost immediately their babble died down. "Listen, guys. You brought me here. Thank you for that. Now, I need to talk to Mr. Ndlovu alone. If you can just give me a chance to be alone with him, I'd thank you for that." They fell silent, but no one moved. "Come on, guys. The movement needs me to meet with Mr. Ndlovu. Give me a few minutes alone with him while you go back to your detective work and look after the march." She was making little shooing movements with both hands and they started to give way, a herd of sheep being guided by their shepherd.

They were soon outside. Their leader regained a little dignity by pointing to two of the youngest members. "You, Sello, and you, Sizwe. Look after the lady's car. The rest, come." With a final glance at Abigail, a look that told her that he too possessed authority, he set off in the direction from which they had come. The rest followed.

She turned back to the shack. Ndlovu was sitting upright when she again stepped inside. "Mr. Ndlovu . . ."

"So what does the Department of Justice want with Jones Ndlovu now, after all these years when our new government didn't need him?" The voice was firm enough, but it rattled with loose phlegm. He coughed loudly without raising a hand to shield his mouth, and spat onto the dirt floor of the shack. "I didn't think anyone in government still remembered Jones Ndlovu." He pointed a shaking finger at her. "They needed me once. I can tell you that." As her eyes became used to the dark, Abigail could see that the whites of his eyes were bloodshot. His lower lip curled over, the force of gravity having greater effect than whatever facial muscles still functioned. "Never mind," he shouted at Abigail. "The more things change, the more they stay the same. Have you heard that? The more things change . . . do you see any changes here? We had no proletarian revolution." It was not often he had an audience, and he was going to use the opportunity Abigail provided. "Do you see anything different? Tell me that."

"Mr. Ndlovu . . ." Abigail tried again.

"Do you see anything different here from apartheid days? First tell me that."

There was no avoiding him. If she wanted him to answer her questions, she would have to answer his. "There have been many changes," she said, "but not here. This looks like a township from the old days."

"Thank you. Thank you very much. The more things change, the more they fucking well stay the same." Suddenly there was an unexpected, less-than-elegant gesture toward good manners. "So what are you standing for? Would you like to sit down?"

The object closest to being a chair that Abigail could see was a small wooden packing case. She sat on it carefully. After her experience in Yudel's study she thought that it may be better not to dust it first. "How are you?" she asked tentatively. It was the standard African greeting. Anything less would have been impolite.

"As you see me," he said. "And you, sister, how are you? And who are you?"

"I am well," Abigail said. "And my name is Abigail Bukula. I think you may have known my parents while we were in exile."

"Tom and Bernadette Bukula? You are Tom Bukula's daughter? I remember seeing you in London, when you were this high." He held a hand, cupped as if he were holding water in it, at about knee level. "Your father was a good man. Your mother was also a real worker for the revolution."

"Thank you." And enough of introducing ourselves, she thought. "I am looking for someone you knew. I was hoping that you may be able to help me."

"Name?"

"Michael Bishop."

The expression that had started to become genial, suddenly hardened. "Why? Why do you want him?" Abigail imagined that even the alcoholic fog had dissipated, leaving him suddenly sober.

She had already decided that this was not a man to whom

she could entrust the whole truth. "We had a meeting the other day to honor him. He was invited, but he never came. We have a token of respect that we would like to give him."

"And you want to find him to give it to him."

"Yes," she said.

"Forget it, young Abigail. Forget Michael Bishop. You don't want to find him."

"I've met him," she said. "I'm not a stranger. He saved my life long ago . . ." Now he was searching her face in the darkness, clearly waiting for more. ". . . in Ficksburg," she finished.

"And what did he take in return?"

Much of my life, she thought, but said nothing.

"Go home, young Abigail. Go home. Forget about Michael Bishop."

"If I promise not to go near him alone, will you tell me?"

"Alone or with others makes very little difference." She saw in his face the signs of genuine concern. "But I truly do not know where he is. I have not seen him for fifteen years and I will be happy never to see him again. Perhaps if I had never met him my life would have been different."

"I gather he is a strange man."

"He is a man like no other and I do not mean that as being complimentary. Go home, young Abigail."

But Abigail was not yet ready to listen to his advice. "Where did he come from? Did you know his family?"

Ndlovu shook his head, as if trying to rid it of some inner obstruction. He wished that this girl, Tom Bukula's daughter, would go now and leave him alone. "No family. He turned up at the headquarters in Lusaka one day and said that he wanted to work for the movement."

"So he got a job in the movement?"

"Not so fast, young Abigail. He told us what he could do and he wanted us just to give him the targets. I said, fuck this—excuse my language. I didn't trust him. Many of us thought he was a spy."

"But you learned to trust him?"

"We gave him an assignment that, if he didn't fuck it up,

would demonstrate his loyalty and we did our best to monitor him. The assignment was to kill a farmer. This old bastard had murdered one of his workers and was given a fine of only a thousand rands, no jail time. Within a month the farmer was dead. We had a man in the local police station and so we know that they never had a suspect."

"So from then on he was in?"

"Yes, he was in, God help us." Ndlovu reached under his makeshift bed and pulled out a bottle of cane spirits. He took a quick swallow and waved the bottle in Abigail's direction. A quick shake of the head indicated her refusal and the bottle was again tucked away. "I never wanted him. He was not a soldier. I don't know what he was. He never asked how the movement worked. He never asked about our policies or our goals. He came for his assignments and, as far as I know, he worked alone. And there was another thing . . . Christ, I don't want to talk about this again. I'm finished with all that."

"What other thing? What was the other thing?"

"Leave it alone, young Abigail. Go home and leave Michael Bishop alone."

"The other thing?"

"To my knowledge, he never failed once, but once or twice we sent other men out with him. He came back alone each time, but the job got done."

It took a while for Abigail to absorb this. When she turned her attention back to Ndlovu, he was drinking from the bottle again.

"You never really got to know him then?"

"No one did. He worked alone and he had no need for comfort. Once, when we sent him on an assignment, he lived for six months in an old roofless ruin in the Magaliesberg hills to the west of Pretoria. It must have been the mansion of a rich farmer long ago. It was in the old Cape Dutch style, one of the first buildings to be put up by a settler in the Pretoria area. Bishop wouldn't sleep in the ruin of the main house. He said it reminded him of bad things from those years. I never believed that though. He slept in one of the little cells where the farm laborers, our people, had to live. Even that only had part of the roof left, but he didn't care. And he did nothing to close the hole in the roof because, he said, someone might notice. If it rained he just slept on the side where there was still some roof."

"Will you show me where it is?"

"I'll draw you a map, then I want you to go. You hear me?"

"I hear you."

"Good. There are also other hideouts he used. I know five of them. None of them provided a decent roof over his head. Discomfort was nothing to him." His head shook angrily. "Now you go. You go and don't come back."

But Abigail was not yet finished with Jones Ndlovu. "Will you draw me a map so that I can find the old house?"

"It was on what was left of an old farm called Vyefontein. If I draw you a map, will you go?"

"Yes, I'll go. Please draw me the map. And can you draw me maps to the other hideouts too?"

"I'll draw all the maps you want, but rather you go home. I knew your father and mother and I don't want to hear from you on this matter again. Your hear me? Don't look for Michael Bishop. You don't want to find him."

"One last thing. Were there any relationships? Girlfriends?"

"No relationships, no friends, no human loves, no pleasures. He never spoke about himself or his past. In fact, he never spoke much at all. There was no woman. I think he went to the whores in Lusaka, but I'm not even sure of that."

"No human loves?"

"Go, young Abigail. Why have you come here to fuck me up?"

"What other kind of loves did he have?'

"No loves, not any sort of loves. But he could handle animals. He could make them do anything he wanted." He was stopped in mid-stride by a returning memory. "He did seem to love European classical music, especially opera."

"He loved Italian opera?"

"No, I don't think it was Italian. It was English—music of the composer Handel, I think. There were some old LP records of his that I kept for him. Sometimes when he was in Lusaka he would play them. He played Handel often. His favorite was *Samson*, the one from the Bible. There were others too, but I don't remember their names."

When she left, the two young township detectives were still standing guard over her car. Now they looked like a pair of poor township kids. The threat she had seen in them an hour earlier had disappeared. She tipped them each five rands.

16

Leon Lourens had left the door of his workshop open, just as he did on most days. It was a warm day and he wanted to let in as much natural light as possible and also allow the air to circulate.

The car he was working on had run its right front wheel-bearing, a condition that was not surprising since, as far as he could see, the bearing had never once been lubricated. There were even traces of rust along the edges. The owner of the car, a landscape artist, had told him the car was making a funny rumbling sound. He had suggested hopefully that it was probably just a small fault, not likely to cost much, perhaps a tiny hole in the exhaust.

"If you bring it in for a service regularly, it'll cost you a lot less," he had told the artist.

The night before, he had moved his family to his wife's half-brother's home and he would be sleeping there too for another five nights, until the twenty-third, when it should be safe to come home. But there was no avoiding coming to his workshop every day. There was not much money and the oldest of the kids had started high school. Taking a week off work was out of the question.

Leon had no doubt about what was happening. He did not know who was doing it, but he assumed it must be someone in the government. That some others had died was sure and so, for his family's sake, he had to take precautions. He had gone to see Abigail Bukula. She was an important person now and she felt indebted to him. He had been relieved that, when he visited her, she had been friendly to him. If it was someone in the government, she would surely be able to stop them. She was a good person. He could see it.

But, after all, why would they come for him? He had never mistreated any blacks. His parents had been poor. They had made no money from the black man's labor. They never even had a domestic servant. His mother had done the housework herself, and he and his brother had chores they had to do. His father did the garden, growing vegetables for the family and mowing the lawn with an old-fashioned mower you had to push.

It was true he had been in the police for years, but he had always tried to do the right thing. After the Maseru raid he had been called in by his commanding officer to a meeting at which Captain van Jaarsveld was present. When he saw van Jaarsveld he thought he was going to be court-martialled for what had happened, but the commanding officer only told him that he was being transferred to the workshops in Pretoria. "Commando work is not for you," he had said, looking down at his hands while he spoke. Before he was out of the room, Captain van Jaarsveld had said, loud enough for him to hear, "That one hasn't got it."

That was good, as far as he was concerned. He didn't want whatever it was Captain van Jaarsveld had. He would do his job in the workshops and that was that.

And he had done just that. He had never fired his gun at anyone, black or white. The closest he had ever come was when he pointed his firearm at Captain van Jaarsveld himself. There was no reason they should come for him. And Abigail Bukula would help.

The new bearing went in quite easily. He greased it well, knowing that whatever the artist said, he would probably not service the car as often as he should, probably not at all.

He had just put away the grease gun and was wiping his hands on his overalls when the shadow of a man cut across the light from the door. In a moment the tire lever that he kept in his overalls for emergencies was in his right hand. If they were coming for him, he was not going to make it easy for them.

The alarm only lasted a moment. Then he saw that it was a white man, not very big or strongly built. Also, he was wearing a police uniform. Leon relaxed and slipped the tire lever back into his overalls.

The note that waited for Abigail on her desk was from the deputy director-general. It said that she should contact him the moment she came in, by the minister's order.

Just like him, she thought, to find someone else's authority to make use of. "He looked very pleased with himself when he came in here," Johanna had said. "I think you should go."

"How's the conference getting on?"

"Making progress, but I can't sign authorization for the suppliers."

"Where are the requisitions? I'll sign them now."

"I've got them." Johanna's hands had been massaging each other. "I'm doing it all alone, you know." The reproach in her voice was unmistakable.

Abigail put a hand on her shoulder. "I know, but what I am doing is so important. If I'm not successful someone may die. I have to rely on you for the conference."

"But what if I mess it up?"

"You won't."

"How do you know? Please tell me how you know."

"I know because I know you and you will not let me down." Johanna did not look convinced. "Now have the requisitions on my desk for signature when I come back. Will you do that?"

Abigail started to move away. "Aren't you going to help me at all?" Johanna's voice had burst out as if, having been forcibly restrained, it was suddenly freed.

"Not much," Abigail said.

"Oh my," Johanna said. "And my cousins have been phoning all afternoon."

"Your cousins?" Abigail reacted absentmindedly.

"It's because of my car. It's the first time that anyone in our family has had a car and my mother has been phoning all seven of her sisters to tell them how hopeless their children are, because none of them has a car like me. Now they're all cross with me."

"Be glad that you have cousins," Abigail said. "I don't have any."

"But they're all angry with me."

"We all have a cross to bear."

Johanna remembered the deputy director-general. "You'd better go to see what the little man wants."

Yes, everything has limits, Abigail told herself. In the civil service, any civil service, you could only take ignoring your immediate superior so far. She left her office to face the inevitable.

The inevitable turned out to be more a nuisance than a disaster. The deputy director-general wanted her to take a visiting Canadian dignitary to lunch. The visitor had arrived early for the conference so that, in her own words, she could get a feel for the country.

After little more than an hour, Abigail excused herself on the basis of all she still needed to do for the conference. Back in her office the requisitions were on her desk as Johanna had promised. Abigail signed them without reading their contents. Johanna had also left her a note to say that she had gone to the conference venue to check that everything was in order.

Another attempt to see Mandla Nyati to try to enlist his aid proved fruitless. "He's still in Cape Town," his assistant said. "I think there's something big going on there."

Then a beep from her mobile phone told her that a message had come in. It was from Robert. "I won't be home tonight, sweetheart," the familiar voice said. "I've been called to Cape Town to be briefed on something. Something big, I'm told. I'll call you from there."

She wondered if Robert's "something big" was the same as Mandla's something big. Their work had nothing in common, unless perhaps what Mandla was there for was such a news-making event that the editors of newspapers were gathering near the action. And yet Robert did not know what it was all about. Had he known, he would surely have told her.

17

One of the reasons that Yudel was sitting opposite Rosa in the Le Rendezvous Restaurant was that, although progress had been made on the stove, it was not yet functional. Rosa had decided that the only way to spur Yudel into decisive action was to insist on eating out until the stove, every part of it, was working again.

Yudel had forgotten the fuses until late in the afternoon. Their local hardware store had promised to have them by lunch the next day. "It can't be a very new stove," the assistant had said. "It's some time since they last used these. You should think about a new stove."

"I will," Yudel had said.

"Your wife will love you for it. Women love the latest in stoves."

"Just get me the fuses."

The chairs and tables of the restaurant were arranged around the trunks of two palm trees in a small courtyard. By ordering the prawn cocktail hors d'oeuvre at 35 rand, veal piccata at 65 rand, tutti-frutti delight at 24 rand and a bottle of Kanonkop dry red wine at 230 rand, Rosa was making a point about hurrying the repair of the stove. Yudel had ordered calamari, a small portion for the just-peckish at 30 rand, and coffee at 15 rand.

The waitress, a soft-eyed young woman, had told him, "We

usually only do the just-peckish portions at lunchtimes, but I'll see what I can do."

Yudel was an unusual man in many ways, not least in the sort of female attributes that he found stimulating. For more limited men, their admiration of the female body never gets beyond a discussion of breasts and legs. Others, marginally more perceptive, include such obvious characteristics as hair, lips and eyes. Yudel was a third kind of man who appreciated in a woman such subtle signs of sexuality as softly rounded balls of the feet, elegantly sculpted fingertips, well-upholstered thumbs, the gentle filling of the groove between ankle and Achilles tendon, even the soft pink lines at the back of her knees.

By far the greatest part of Yudel's excitement at these attributes had been enjoyed resentfully, at a distance. During the many years he had been married to Rosa she had only once caught him in an act of unfaithfulness that had disturbed the harmony in the Gordon home. He had arranged to meet her at a music shop and, while he waited, had listened to a Toscanini recording of Beethoven's Ninth Symphony. Business was quiet and the shop assistant, a girl of eighteen or nineteen, had fetched a second set of earphones and joined him. When Rosa entered the shop they both had their eyes closed, in a state of transport, coupled together via the electronic circuitry of the amplifier and Beethoven's Ninth. It took her a month to forgive him.

The waitress's attraction, for Yudel, rested principally on two features. First, he noticed her downy upper lip. Immediately after that, his eyes came to rest on her concave temples. To Yudel, although he could not recall the association, this was a sign of uninhibited sexual energy. She also had a sun-washed skin color and lean, but nicely padded fingers and thumbs. More than any other attribute, her forearms fascinated him. They were light and well-shaped, puffed out tantalizingly just below the elbow. The sudden, neat swelling of muscle had drawn his attention as she handed Rosa the menu, her arm passing within a few centimeters of his face.

"The Sephardic congregation is getting a new Torah," Rosa was saying. Lately, after an absence of many years, she had taken to attending shul again and was trying to interest Yudel. "Rachelle has invited us to the induction ceremony." Yudel used a small part of his faculties of attention to listen to what his wife was saying. He wondered where it was leading and whether there was any possible way he could reply intelligently, or at all, without upsetting her. "It has been written on scrolled parchment. A special silver and gold case has been made for it. The Rael family sponsored its manufacture."

"Do you know what the Torah is?" Yudel asked. He had given up the idea of replying intelligently.

"Don't be facetious, Yudel. Of course I know what the Torah is. It's the law. And it's high time you started taking an interest in such matters. I know at least as much about the scriptures as you do."

"How many books of the prophets are there?"

"You're trying to annoy me. You can take that supercilious expression off your face. I won't be drawn into your silly games. You don't know how many books of the prophets there are either."

It was true. Yudel did not know. He was saved from the need to reply by the return of the waitress. She had Rosa's 35 rand prawn cocktail and, probably out of pity, a few slices of Melba toast for him. Again that lovely, light forearm—lean, but swelling beautifully, passed just below his nose. He watched its progress as it came past, carefully positioning the toast in front of him, lingered unnecessarily for a moment, then withdrew. He looked up into her face and she smiled warmly at him in anticipation of the tip to come. Light reflected on a tiny, barely perceptible, golden line along the down of her upper lip.

Perhaps it was some memory awakened by the sight of the waitress's young hips rolling as she skipped between the tables on her way back to the kitchen, or perhaps it was only the warmth of an early summer evening or most probably the two glasses of wine she had already consumed, but Rosa's mood changed. "I'm glad the stove broke," she said. "It's too long since we last did something like this."

With the disappearance of the waitress Yudel's thoughts

turned to the sort of things that usually occupied them. He thought about the conversation with van Jaarsveld, if you could call it that. There were things that van Jaarsveld had said that, of those present, only Abigail had understood. This was a problem to Yudel. He wanted to understand. In everything, all his life, he had wanted to understand. This was no different.

Rosa was still talking. He tried briefly to follow the direction of her conversation. "What a wonderful night. Look at the stars through the palm fronds. I have the feeling, the exhilarating feeling, that nothing bad can happen on a night like this. Just feel this air."

Her remark directed his thinking to many nights, much like this one, each on October twenty-second when death had come suddenly via a wire garrotte. He wondered about the killer, and he had no doubt that the killer was just one person, a man, no longer young, and obviously skilled in his frightening art. He also wondered how it was that two people as different as van Jaarsveld and Abigail would know the killer's identity, and why Abigail would not tell him. His thoughts moved on and he wondered what thoughts, on this lovely night, were occupying the minds of van Jaarsveld and the murderer that Abigail was seeking.

"Yudel, say something. Don't just sit there. I try to make this marriage work. I've always tried, but you don't communicate with me. I never know what you're thinking."

It was true. He did not communicate with her. It had always been his belief that she did not want to know what he was thinking. She thought she did, but on the rare occasions when he had tried her with a little sample, she had usually seemed distressed. Did she want to know about these killings? Or about the real reason for Abigail's visit? Or about the mind of Marinus van Jaarsveld?

"Can't you say anything about the night?" Rosa was almost pleading. "About the stars? Or about the palm trees?"

"Bush pigeons like to nest in them."

"What?" Rosa asked.

"Bush pigeons like to nest in palms."

"That's very interesting." Her voice had acquired a sardonic edge. "I had no idea you were an expert on birds."

"Just something I picked up." Rosa was looking at him with the exasperation that comes with hopeless dejection when the waitress returned. Rosa had not quite finished her prawns, but the waitress already had her veal piccata and Yudel's just-peckish calamari. She placed the veal on the edge of the table for Rosa's future consumption and leaned forward to slip Yudel's calamari onto the place mat in front of him. Her arm, the same slender, gently swelling arm that had held his attention before, pale on the underside and brown on the outside, trimmed with fine golden hairs that you could see only when the light caught them, passed close by his face again as she positioned the plate of calamari. He tried not to follow it with his eyes, but she leaned forward a second time to do something to the plate. Whatever it was, Yudel's mind did not register the action. He saw only the softness of flesh, the subtle change of coloring where the pale underside met the brown outside, the light leanness and the compellingly elegant shape of the muscle. He leaned forward and bit it softly.

For much of his childhood Yudel had lived alone with his mother. Whatever self-confidence he possessed he owed to those years when he had been the center of her life. She had given him no scoldings, no hidings and only showed displeasure with one simple remark. "Yudel, you've done a naughty thing," she would say.

In the moment, the small fraction of a second, in which his teeth held the waitress's arm, Yudel knew that he had done a naughty thing. He released it to look into the girl's blushing, not entirely displeased face and Rosa's round, horrified, utterly disbelieving eyes.

Yudel sat in his study, trying to think about Abigail's matter and what it all meant. This was not made easier by Rosa's rather noisy presence in the kitchen. Judging by the loud clanking of metallic objects, she could be destroying it.

Between the clanking of pots and cutlery, Rosa was doing something that could not accurately be described as crying. It was more a kind of hyperventilating. She seemed to be drawing in great lungfuls of air, as if she was struggling to take in enough oxygen, and in the process making loud mezzo-soprano wheezing noises. He had tried to comfort her, but had been driven off by a furious denunciation of his lascivious nature.

What a fuss about a little bite, he thought. She had fled the restaurant, leaving him to pay a puzzled management and to tip a still-blushing waitress. Instead of waiting at the car, she had set off for home on foot while he followed, driving slowly, like a curb crawler, trying with excessive persistence to make a pickup. After a kilometer's determined march she had weakened enough to accept a lift. Her weakening had extended no further than that. Yudel's stopping along the way to buy a newspaper did nothing to improve her disposition.

To hell with it, Yudel thought. He opened the unread newspaper on the desk before him and tried to absorb the lead item on the front page. If nothing else, it might allow him half an hour in which to avoid whatever confrontation with Rosa the night still held.

Reading the newspaper did not work. Yudel had read the headline four times without understanding it before he came to that conclusion. He would have to deal with the Rosa matter.

He found her washing a few dishes and pots that had stood over from earlier in the day. In her anguish she may have been a little heavy-handed, but she had not been destroying the kitchen. When she turned to face him her eyes looked darker than usual and her skin had taken on a pale, waxen appearance. "You're going out," she told him between the wheezes. "Yudel, I'm only going to ask this once. Please give me a direct answer. Are you going to meet that waitress?"

"No," Yudel said. "And I'm not going out either." Despite the complete accuracy of his answer, he was aware that it sounded untrue, even to his own ears. "Rosa." He tried to bring more conviction to his voice. "I don't even know the name of that girl or where to find her."

"You seemed pretty intimate this evening."

"It was a momentary aberration." Yudel was seeking a way to strengthen his protestations. "She was so slow. I bit her arm in annoyance." As soon as he had said it, he wished that he could have withdrawn the words. To lie successfully sometimes caused a few guilt problems, but to lie so transparently created problems of every imaginable variety.

"Oh, Yudel." Rosa looked deeply distressed. "You're lying to me, you rotten man."

"The truth is . . ." Yudel looked for a format within which to frame the truth. "The truth is that I'm a fool."

Rosa did not need to think about this before nodding. "That is the truth," she said.

The darkness in the apartment was softened by lights in the garden and in the street. Abigail did not know why she felt safer in the darkness. Perhaps, she thought, because this was her home turf. She knew the doors, the obstacles and hiding places, even in darkness. She could also not be seen, at least not readily.

Michael Whitehead had been just one of many recent surprises. The boy who had been trying to get closer to her at the time was a junior crime reporter. In his desperation to impress her, he had taken her to the place where Whitehead's body had been found.

It had lain spread-eagled on an allotment, one of the tiny patches of earth which some Londoners used to try to stay in touch with mother earth, getting their hands pleasurably dirty with the soil from which we are so alienated. The patch of allotments was surrounded by rows of narrow, terraced houses. Perhaps a hundred houses had windows looking down on the place.

The one where the body was found had belonged to the British fiancée of a military attaché at the South African Embassy. Scotland Yard had questioned the attaché at length before deciding that he was not their man. To the best of Abigail's knowledge, the case had never been solved.

Her young escort had brought her to this entirely blameless part of the city and presented it to her like a magician drawing a rabbit out of a hat. "What do you think?" he had said.

By that time the owner of the allotment had removed every trace of the incident. "Of what?"

"Of the place where this Whitehead's body was found."

To Abigail, it had not looked like the sort of place where you would find the body of a murder victim. But what did such a place look like? Even to the community of exiled South Africans it had simply been a chance incident, a businessman who had the bad luck to run into the wrong man at the wrong time and in the wrong place.

She remembered one more thing her young crime reporter had said. "Had his throat slit, from ear to ear."

She doubted that he had got that from Scotland Yard. That had no doubt been his own analysis.

Abigail shivered. The place was so empty without Robert. This was the worst possible time for him to be away. She could not imagine a worse time. So suddenly and without warning. And with the twenty-second coming closer by the moment. The next day would be the nineteenth . . . just three days left.

She would go and see Leon in the morning. Until some sort of finality was brought to the matter, the only solution was for him to remain out of sight, and out of harm's way.

She stood for a while at the French windows, looking down into the neighboring garden. The white bull terrier she so hated had appeared out of the shadows and padded its way through the garden of the adjoining property. Almost immediately a man in ragged dungarees, riding a bicycle, by the look of him a manual laborer, had come down the road, stirring the dog into a frenzy. It charged the iron latticework of the gate, clawing it, trying without success to reach the cyclist.

The phone rang, taking Abigail away from the window. She paused before answering. God only knew who it could be. But then she realized that it was probably Robert.

"Hey, sweetheart," her husband's voice said, "how are you

this evening?" There was some anxiety in his voice. She could hear that he was really not sure how she would be.

"I'm okay. And you? What happened? What's it all about?"

"The briefing's tomorrow morning. I still know nothing. I'll be back tomorrow evening. My flight lands at ten past five. I'll get a cab home."

No, she thought. I'm not waiting that long. I want you back now. "I'll pick you up at the airport," she said.

"You'll have to slip away from work early."

"I'll be there."

"Okay. I really just wanted to hear how you are. You sound a little strained."

"Oh, God, Robert, please don't stay away any longer. Be on that flight."

"I will be. You don't sound good."

"Just be on that flight."

"You can depend on it. Is it this thing with Leon Lourens?"

"Just be on that flight."

"Yes, I will be."

After she hung up, Abigail returned to the window. The bull terrier was lying down on the lawn in a patch of light, its head resting on its front paws, the slit-like eyes closed. Repulsive creature, Abigail thought.

The animal seemed to fall asleep. Abigail remained at the window without moving, looking in the direction of the dog, without seeing him or even the garden. What have I been doing? she asked herself. I know him. How could I influence him, let alone stop him? And who could I involve? The police? My own department?

Abigail became aware of the presence in the shadows near the gate before the dog did. It was little more than a movement of deeper shadow in the already dark outline of the shrubbery. She stared at the place where she had seen the movement until it came again. For a moment the figure of a man was outlined against a narrow section of white wall that was visible between the bushes. He was moving down the side of the house next door, separated from the building where she lived by only a two-meter wall and the electric fencing along the top of it.

Then the dog saw him. The animal rose suddenly and started forward. Even through the closed window and across the intervening twenty or thirty meters she could hear its snarling. Then the dog charged, his stocky body held close to the ground.

Abigail had seen him attack once before. On that occasion the animal's victim had been badly bitten and had only been saved from more serious injury by the arrival of the dog's handler from a security company. Now there would be no handler to come to the intruder's aid.

The dog swarmed into the shadows of the shrubbery, a pale ghost-like form in the darkness, its feet slipping on the paving of the path as it drove itself forward. Later Abigail remembered hearing her own breath racing and feeling a sharp pain in the palm of her right hand as she gripped a protruding hinge on the French windows.

Then, as suddenly as the dog had charged, there was stillness in the shadows. She could still see the pale patch that was the animal, but he seemed to have stopped moving. Something inexplicable had happened. The dog was there, but not attacking, not even snarling. Could it be that he was not alive?

Then she heard the yelp, a single soft, plaintive sound, the kind of cry that did not seem possible from a bull terrier. And he was moving again, slowly this time, back into the light, reversing, his tail wrapped tightly between his legs. He dropped to his belly, facing the shadows he had just left. His head sank to his paws. Abigail saw his tail slowly twitching in apparent friendliness.

The man in the shadows moved again. Not a large man, he seemed to be coming toward the light, but turned back into the shadows, moving down the garden wall that passed below Abigail's window. The dog turned its head to watch him go.

Without pausing to think, she slammed closed the heavy wooden anti-burglary doors that closed off the French windows, and latched them. Then she ran for the front door and wrenched the steel security gate closed, hearing the latch snap into place. From room to room she fled, checking on the bur-glar bars on every window, but none had been interfered with. Back at her own front door she rang security. "This is number ten," she told the guard who answered. "I think someone may be trying to break into the complex under my window."

After the guard had assured her that he had contacted the company's armed response unit, she stood indecisively for only a moment in the center of the living room. Then she fled to the shower, closed the door behind her and locked it. Sobbing, her back pressed against the wall, she slid down to a sitting position, her head between her knees.

Oh, God, she thought, and I am searching for him. What could I possibly do if I found him?

18

To all who knew them, the four Bishop boys were an unremarkable group. None of them had ever achieved anything approaching significance, either in the classroom or on the sports field. None were so badly behaved that their teachers would comment on that either.

If all were unremarkable, the two youngest, Michael and Samuel, were possibly noticed even less by those who came in contact with them. They were not unusually shy, but by the time Samuel was twelve and Michael ten, they simply never offered anything about themselves to anyone. It was not so much that they withheld anything, merely that contact with them was impossible.

Neither seemed to have any ability to express himself. Since their mother had died nine years earlier, a month before Michael's first birthday, the home they lived in had become almost completely silent. Their father worked the farm the same way he had done when his wife was alive. But he worked it because he had always done so, rather than for any rational purpose. He knew how to produce crops, so he produced them. He took away the cattle gate that allowed easy access by cars at the entrance to his farm and replaced it with a heavy motor gate that stayed locked day and night. In a farming community where there was little canned entertainment and people visited back and forth between the farms, the neighbors soon started to avoid the Bishop home. Even the school principal looking for donations for the new gymnasium, the clergyman hoping for help with renovating the church hall, or the member of parliament searching for votes, left the Bishops off their schedules.

Bishop bought the boys what he felt they needed without apparent resentment. In return he expected unquestioning obedience from them. Any disobedience was met with the sort of brutal response that could have put him in prison forty years later. Even in a conservative Calvinist community in which punishment was an indispensable part of life, the other farming families were shocked at old man Bishop's treatment of his sons. After a particularly vicious incident, one of the mothers went to see the dominee about it. The next day the dominee's wife encouraged the other ladies at the women's weekly prayer circle to pray for the Bishops. "It's not right that he punishes his children the way you punish kaffirs," she said to some of the ladies afterward.

The obedience he expected from his sons was no different from what he expected from his farm workers. Although he never discussed it, it seemed to be a point of honor that he punished his boys in the same way he punished his workers. He was equally ready to use his leather *sjambok* to leave stripes on the backs of either. If a farm worker was held down by his fellow workers and whipped for some minor negligence, so too were his sons. The one to be punished would usually be held down by his brothers, but if none were available at the time, farm workers would do.

On more than one occasion at school, teachers had seen the marks left by whippings. Most had not approved, but a man's sons were his business and you did not tell him how to control them.

If there was a single civilizing influence in the home Bishop created for his sons, it was the piano that his wife had played while she was alive. And he insisted that his sons, rough and carrying the stripes of his attention as they were, take piano lessons.

There were those in the community who said that his treatment of his wife had something to do with the cancer that killed her. Whatever his reasons and whatever he felt about his wife's death, Bishop ordered them to play. Every evening they all took a turn at practice. Of the four, only Samuel showed any affinity for the music. There were times when his father ordered Samuel to play and would lie down in his bedroom to allow the music to calm him. Any of the few visitors to the farm who heard Samuel's young interpretations of Schubert, Liszt or Lehar melodies often commented on how well he played. The school's music teacher even suggested that Samuel be sent to a music academy, but Bishop replied that a farmer did not need that much music training.

As for Michael, he struck the notes in the prescribed order, but without any sense of their meaning or the emotion they represented. There were no louder or gentler passages, no thoughtful pauses and no reflection on the music after he got up from the piano stool.

Bishop and his sons ate at the long wooden kitchen table, served by a barefoot woman who cooked what Bishop brought back from town and what grew in the vegetable patch next to the house. There was also the occasional contribution from the chicken-run or the pigpen. Bishop sat at the head, his *sjambok* at his side, with the boys on either side, the two eldest on one side and the two youngest on the other. Michael sat farthest from him. No one sat at the foot of the table. The eldest boy had tried it once, but the leather tip of the *sjambok* had found him before he could duck, cutting the skin of his left cheek deeply enough to leave a scar. "That's your mother's place," his father had snarled.

At the table the only conversation had directly to do with the farming in which the boys all had a part to play. What they said was limited to what was essential. It was safest to be silent and keep your eyes on your plate. This was the policy of all Michael's brothers. It had been his too, until a singular incident when he was ten.

Bishop himself, Samuel, Michael and the two elder brothers had been out, fixing fences at a pasture they rented from a family where the father had died and all farming had come to a temporary halt. Bishop's herd of cattle had been growing, and the new calves would mean extra feed. More pasture was essential.

It was already dark as they arrived at the unlocked cattle gate at the entrance to the farm road that their farm shared with two others. The two younger boys were on the back and the others were in the cab with their father. As the headlights fell on the gate they could see a black boy of perhaps eighteen or nineteen in a gray suit that was a size or two too small for him. He had started to open the gate, having just dismounted from a bicycle that he had obviously spent hours shining. When he saw the truck he swung open the gate and saluted. His white teeth stood out against the darkness of his grinning face and the nocturnal landscape.

Instead of driving through, Bishop stopped in the open gate and got out. "Who are you?" he demanded in Afrikaans. "And where do you think you're going?"

In his response, the boy made three serious mistakes. First, he answered in English and, second, he did not address Bishop in a sufficiently servile manner. Finally he told Bishop what he intended to do instead of begging his permission. "Excuse me, sir," he said. "My name is Matthew Baloyi. I'm going to visit my uncle. He works for Mr. Bishop."

Bishop kept advancing on the boy. He continued in Afrikaans. "What's this English, and what's this 'sir' business? You call me *baas* if you want to go on breathing." The anger that underlay Bishop's devotion to his home language was all the stronger because of his English surname. Surrounded by van Dyks, van der Merwes and van Schalkwyks, he had always felt like an outsider.

The boy with the bicycle did not expect to be attacked. "Sir . . . *baas*, I . . ." The first blow caught him in the solar plexus and he doubled over like a rag doll. Before he could recover, another blow connected with the side of his head. He went down to his knees and Bishop kicked him, his heavy farm boots digging first into his left side, then his groin.

Michael had been watching, not showing compassion or even concern. If anything, according to one of the older brothers, his expressionless face showed nothing. Only the eyes seemed to reflect something akin to curiosity.

Suddenly there was something else to stir up his curiosity. Without warning Samuel appeared, running fast. He threw himself at his father, the boy upsetting the balance of the man. Bishop went down on one knee and his attention shifted from the African boy in the suit to his son.

Samuel retreated before the blows, dodging and ducking to avoid them. "Catch him, catch him," his father was screaming. The older boys' entire lives of obedience to this man had removed any possibility of refusal. They caught Samuel and brought him back to their father. "Hold him. Bring him." Bishop got back into the truck and his brothers dragged Samuel onto the back. Michael sat quietly, pressed against the cab, offering no opinion and making no movement.

Bishop pulled away with a jerk, his foot slipping off the clutch. Matthew Baloyi's bicycle was still where he had dropped it, next to the gate, and Bishop swung the steering wheel toward it, the weight of the truck crushing it and leaving it shattered, the wheels grotesquely buckled. Away to his right on land that had recently been plowed, Michael could just make out a faint white smudge in the darkness. It was a moment before he realized that it was Baloyi. His white shirt was all that was visible. Perhaps he had lost the jacket of his suit.

The drive to the farm house took only seconds. Samuel showed no resistance as he was stretched over a two-hundred-liter oil drum and held there by his brothers, waiting patiently while his father fetched the *sjambok*. No one there was later sure how long the beating lasted. What was clear from the police report—and this was the only time Bishop had ever been reported—was that the skin of Samuel's back was no longer visible under the cuts and the blood.

A mother from a neighboring farm, alerted by a servant who had run all the way from the Bishop place, had called her husband to investigate. Bishop had only stopped when he arrived. When he reported back to his wife, she had called the police. Their report never got beyond the local police station, but the sergeant had come to the farm and warned Bishop that, if it happened again, he would find himself in court. "He's your son, man," he said, "not a dog."

Through it all, no one had noticed young Michael, watching from the darkness, too far away to draw his father's attention, but close enough so that he would miss nothing.

As for Matthew Baloyi, he had not been seen around the farm since the evening his bicycle had been destroyed. What remained of the bicycle had found its way to the farm's rubbish dump.

Samuel's body healed, but his soul did not. A little less than two years later he went into the tobacco shed, knotted a rope around his neck, tied it to a beam and kicked away the drum he had been standing on. He did it one evening when his father and brothers were still in the bottom lands at other end of the farm. No one ever suggested that Samuel Bishop's death was a cry for help. He was simply killing himself.

At the sight of his body, his two elder brothers and his father shed real tears. Whatever they felt about their own role in his death, the agonized release of emotion in all of them was real. Michael too had bowed his head and wiped at his eyes. He knew what was expected. When the others had cut down the body and left the barn to call the police, for a long time he had stood over the physical remains of his brother. Now there was no wiping of his eyes.

After Samuel died, the piano lessons tapered off. Even the boys' father realized that the farm no longer had a player worth listening to. The older boys with their crude thumping and Michael's mechanical pressing of the keys could not satisfy even the least discriminating listener. In the last year of his life, he allowed the lessons to stop altogether.

By the time Bishop's murder startled the community, the killing of farmers by the forces of liberation, as some believed, along the northeastern border where the Bishops farmed, were no longer unusual. Guerrillas would slip over the Mozambican border, do their business and be back the same night.

Unlike other farm killings, Bishop had not been blown to bits by a landmine or sliced up by a volley of AK-47 bullets. He had been garrotted, and the apparent murder weapon, a length of heavy iron fencing wire, covered in blood, was still conveniently around his neck. If any of the officers noticed that the cut around his neck was much thinner than the cut fence wire would have made, none of them ever reported it. Nor did anyone notice that the wire that produced the low C was no longer present in the family piano. The day Bishop died was October 22, the same date on which Samuel had died. Bishop had outlived Samuel by exactly three years.

Michael's brothers all testified that they had seen a worker near the farm who had been beaten, then dismissed by their father, just a month before. There were always such workers, and finding one to pin the murder on was not difficult. The court found mitigating circumstances and shocked the farming community by not imposing the death sentence. The worker, whom the court saw as obviously guilty, was sentenced to life in prison.

Michael was just fifteen and his older brothers twenty and twenty-two. The older boys decided that they knew only farm life and would go on working the farm and that Michael should finish his schooling. Both had already found the undemanding country girls they wanted to marry and who were happy to marry them.

The morning after the farm worker had been sentenced, Michael's brothers found that he was gone and that his bed had not been slept in that night. A missing person report was made at the local police station, but he was never found. His brothers never saw him again. In fact, there was no record anywhere of Michael Bishop until he walked into the ANC headquarters in Lusaka five years later.

19

A weary Abigail drove to the office. The night just past had been another bad one. It had taken three hours and two more calls to security before she left the shower and went back to bed. She slept in short spells for perhaps a quarter of what was left of the night.

Commuter traffic into the city center was not heavy by the standards of bigger cities. It took Abigail, on average, some thirty minutes from the time she got into her car until she drove into the Department of Justice parking garage.

It was a time enough for reflection and informal planning of the day's activities. It was short enough not to frustrate her with the thought that she would be wasting her day. It was also a good time to make an early morning call on the car's mobile. She got Robert at the first attempt. "You are coming home tonight?" She still needed reassurance.

"Yes, I'm coming home tonight. What's wrong? Has something else happened?"

"No. I just want you home."

"I'll be there. Are you sure nothing has happened?"

"I'm sure. Just come . . . please come."

———

A woman was sitting opposite Johanna when Abigail came in. As soon as she stepped into the office, Johanna rose quickly, wringing her hands, followed somewhat uncertainly by the visitor.

Johanna's hands released each other for long enough for her to gesture quickly in the direction of the other woman. "This is Mrs. Lourens." The words seemed to chase one another out of her mouth. "Mr. Lourens was arrested yesterday. He's gone. Mrs. Lourens doesn't know where he's being held."

Abigail reached out both hands to the white woman. Leon Lourens's wife was a slender woman in her late thirties, pretty but showing the signs of living with too little money. There were lines around her eyes and across her forehead caused by worry. She had made no effort to color her hair to hide the gray that had already replaced most of the original brown. Her shoes had been worn too long and she was wearing her best dress, a knee-length cotton frock printed with yellow daisies. She was holding her white patent leather bag in both hands. Seeing Abigail's gesture, she immediately put down her bag, and took the offered hands in hers. "Mrs. Bukula?" she asked.

"Abigail," Abigail said.

"I'm Susanna Lourens." Her voice was soft and restrained, the voice of someone not used to asserting herself. "I'm sorry. I didn't know who else to come to. Leon told me about you. I know he came to see you."

"Come into my office," Abigail said, now holding Susanna by the arm. Over her shoulder, she added, "Johanna, you'd better come too."

Abigail led Susanna to the same chairs at the window where she had sat with Leon three days before. "Leon was arrested?"

"He moved us to his mother's house until this thing is over, but he went back to his workshop every day . . . to work." Abigail could see that Susanna was studying her face, no doubt looking for some sign of hope. "The neighbors said a policeman came and took him away. They arrested him."

"For what?"

"The neighbors didn't know. They stayed inside and just watched from the windows."

"All they saw was the police taking him away?"

"Yes, a policeman took him away."

"One policeman?"

"Yes. The neighbors said there was just one."

"Was the policeman a white man?" Abigail asked. Tell me no, she thought. Tell me the policeman was black.

"Yes, he was a white man." This did not seem important to Susanna though. She hurried on. "I'm sure they will tell you why they arrested him."

"Have you called the police?"

"All the police stations in Pretoria. They all say they didn't arrest him. But, if you phone them, they'll tell you the truth."

"Was he handcuffed?"

"Yes, I think they said he was handcuffed."

"Did the neighbors tell you about the vehicle they took him away in? Was it a police van?"

"No. I think they took him in an ordinary car."

Abigail did not know how much of what she was feeling showed on her face, but she saw the sudden widening of Susanna's eyes.

"Oh, God. Oh please, God. You think it was *not* the police."

"We'll find out if it was the police. I don't know for sure."

"But you don't think it was?"

"I don't know. I really don't know." But the other woman's eyes held the plea for the truth. Allow me that dignity, they seemed to be saying. "No, I don't think it was the police."

"Oh, Lord." She had been sitting upright on the edge of her seat. Now she sank back, like an inflatable toy from which the air had been leaking.

Johanna, whose eyes had opened so wide that the whites showed all the way round the irises, was already getting up. "Shall I try to find out if anyone knows where he is?"

"Yes," Abigail said. "Immediately, do nothing else."

"But the conference . . ." Johanna started.

"Do this first." Johanna opened her mouth to add something,

but Abigail had already turned back to Susanna. "Listen, I don't know for sure."

Susanna had been doing her own thinking. "Leon told me you said the government was not doing this." Abigail did not reply. "You did say that?"

There was no avoiding Susanna. She was a woman in real danger of losing her mate of almost twenty years. "I don't know who is doing it," Abigail said.

"But you don't believe it's the government?"

"No."

"But if it was those people who have been killing the others, it wouldn't have been a white man who came, would it? There wouldn't be a white man doing that, would there." Again Abigail was too slow to answer. "Oh, Lord," Susanna said. "Oh please, Lord. Oh please, Lord Jesus."

20

The grandmotherly woman who Abigail had seen in the prison parking area walked slowly along the gravel path into the pleasant gardens of Magnolia Dell. She was carrying a galvanized iron bucket of the sort used in South African prisons. She was early, so there was no need to hurry. Besides, her feet hurt. The work she did in a private hospital kept her on her feet for most of every day and her feet were rarely free of pain these days.

Annette van Jaarsveld found the bench where they had said it would be. You had to watch out for it as you came around a bend in the path. It was set back and partly obscured by the shrubbery.

She sat down to wait. The place was ideal. It was Friday morning and she had passed no one on the path. The only sounds were made by the traffic on Queen Wilhelmina Drive. Almost as a reflex her right hand again dug into a deep pocket in her skirt to ensure that the envelope was still there. She maneuvered the skirt until the pocket was between her knees, then clamped them together so that she could feel the presence of the money. It had been collected among her husband's supporters. There were not many of them now, but those who remained were more passionate than ever.

She had only ten minutes to wait before the man that she

expected came down the path from the opposite direction. She heard the sound of his leather-clad feet well before he came into view. As they had agreed, he was not in his prison warder uniform. The gray slacks and blue shirt that he was wearing were as inconspicuous as she could have hoped.

He stopped as soon as he saw her and looked down the path in both directions before he came to join her. He sat down next to her, his hands shaking as he reached for the bucket. The bastard, she thought. He doesn't even remember the password.

Then he did remember. "Have you got the bucket for the eggs?" he asked, his voice as unsteady as his hands.

She passed him the bucket without saying anything.

"And the eggs?"

She took the envelope from her skirt, but did not offer it to him. "Remember two things. Number one, this is the first five thousand, as we agreed." The man nodded. "The other thing is this—my husband has many friends on the outside who feel just the way he does. If he does not receive this by tomorrow afternoon five o'clock or if anyone else finds out about this, you and your eldest son will be dead in a week."

The warder tried to retain a little dignity. "Are you threatening me?" The effect was ruined by a quaver that had crept into his voice.

"Yes, my friend, I am threatening you," she said, speaking as softly as before. "And if you want to go on living and you want your five-year-old to go on living, you will pay attention to my threat." His eyes were on the envelope that held the money. She held it away from him for a moment longer before suddenly extending the hand that held it.

The warder slipped it into an inside pocket and rose, the bucket in one hand. "I'll go now," he said.

"Good-bye, my friend," Annette van Jaarsveld said.

In a moment he was out of sight, the sound of his footfalls on the pathway fading quickly. Then even that was gone.

No wonder they could be dominated for so long, the woman on the bench thought. If it had not been for the outside world interfering, we would still have been running our country. Ten thousand rand for his soul. They have no character and no standards.

Then she thought briefly about her own people who had been part of the negotiations that had brought some measure of peace to the country. Sellouts, she thought. They are no better. But Marinus was different. He was a rock. He was still true to his people.

Abigail spent the better part of the day visiting four of the sites of Michael Bishop's hiding places. Jones Ndlovu's maps were less than accurate, the lines wavered a little with his unsteady hand, but the essential details were there.

She found the place where the first one should have been, a few hundred meters from the main access to OR Tambo Airport, the country's main link with the outside world. Ndlovu had described a decrepit wooden shed of indeterminate age, but now a gleaming steel hangar stood on the spot. As Abigail watched, a bright new, smaller commercial airliner was being towed into the hangar.

Her second stop was at a rundown block of just six apartments in the Johannesburg suburb of Yeoville. There she spoke to five of the residents and all swore that they had never once seen a white person so much as visit the place, not since they had been living there.

After that, she visited a culvert that allowed flood water from a nearby seasonal stream to pass under a suburban street to a broader concrete watercourse. Early summer rains had filled the stream to the point where no one, no matter how immune to physical discomfort, could have spent ten minutes, let alone a night.

At the fourth site a shed, no more than shoulder height for someone as small as Abigail and exactly as described by Ndlovu, was still standing. A screen of trees sheltered it from the road. It was only by standing on the car's bonnet that she could see it at all. She could see how Bishop could have crept into it to sleep.

For his purposes, it was an unlikely place to have found a human being. But now the ground on which it stood had been incorporated into the zoo and was surrounded by an electrified fence. Two rhinoceroses grazed in the enclosure. Certainly the likes of Bishop could get in and out, but the rhinos would simply be too much trouble. And there would be visitors gazing into the enclosure at odd times throughout the day.

By mid-afternoon when Abigail got to the office, Johanna had exhausted every branch of every government agency that might have arrested Leon. No one had admitted to it. Abigail was not one to close her eyes to any violation of rights, whether in the name of the new South Africa or any other cause, but people being arrested and simply disappearing was not one of them. If the police, the secret service, or anyone else had him, she believed that they would not have hidden it.

A gloating little e-mail from her boss, the deputy director-general, had informed her that she had to report to the minister at 2 P.M. on the progress they were making with the conference preparations. It was the sort of minor crisis that reminded her once again of the many reasons that she appreciated Johanna.

She found Johanna at her desk. "I've done nothing for nearly a week," she told her PA. "I don't suppose I've given you much opportunity to work on it?"

"I've managed to do some of the work," Johanna said.

"What have you done?"

Johanna had organized the venue, including the sound system, both well within budget; she had quotes for the transport, the flower arrangements had been approved, the catering had also come in within budget, the speakers had all confirmed attendance, as had most of the delegates, and accommodation for speakers and delegates had been spread across ten hotels, none of them more than fifteen kilometers from the venue. She offered her notes and all documentation to her boss.

"How am I ever going to thank you?" Abigail asked.

"I thought I'd better do it with all the other matters on your mind."

"Thank you so much," Abigail said simply. "I want you to

come to the meeting with me. I'm not going to pretend that I did all this."

"It's okay," Johanna said. "I don't mind."

"You're coming with me."

At five to two the deputy director-general's PA phoned down to say that the meeting was already assembled and waiting for Abigail. When she arrived with Johanna he tried to turn the younger woman away, but Abigail had directed Johanna to a seat and sat down next to her. From the grim look on the minister's face and the unsmiling faces of a few other deputy DGs, it was clear to her that her boss had already briefed the assembled group on the likely lack of progress from Abigail's office. The minister, who had always looked for the good in Abigail's work, went straight to the heart of the matter. "So, let's have your report, young lady," he said.

Abigail, who was an extremely fast study, had been through the arrangements Johanna had made, continually referring back to her for details and precise amounts. By the end of the presentation the grim look had left the minister's face. He nodded in obvious satisfaction and turned to look at the deputy director-general as he spoke. "That seems to be in order. That seems like excellent progress to me. I cannot imagine why anyone would have doubts about the success of the conference. Good work, Abigail. And you too, my girl," he added in Johanna's direction.

"Thank you," Abigail said, her voice sounding sweet and altogether guileless, even to her own ears. "Most of the work was done by Johanna."

"Well done, my girl," the minister said to Johanna. "And, Abigail, I like people who share the credit."

"Thank you, Mr. Minister," she said. Now let me go, she thought. I have more important issues to attend to than this damned conference. For a moment she considered the possibility of raising the Leon Lourens matter with the minister, but the thought of trying to discuss it with his personal assistant, only to be promised an interview in perhaps a week, was too much to bear.

As for the deputy director-general, his jaws were clamped so tightly that a little muscle on the left hand side was twitching furiously. Abigail tried not to let her delight show. Well, little man, Johanna has certainly spoiled your party, she thought.

21

It was clear to Abigail that Jones Ndlovu's map, drawn with a quivering hand, was probably not accurate. She remembered that at the Black Management Forum's annual banquet two years before she had sat next to a young Indian woman from the Tshwane town planning office. But her name was a problem. Robert had also been at the banquet, but when she tried to reach him on his mobile she had only got his voice mail.

Then she remembered that Johanna had also been there. It had been her first banquet and she had not been able to stop talking about it for weeks. She called Johanna in and put the question to her.

"Lou-Anne Hamid," Johanna told her. "We have lunch sometimes."

"Have you got her number?"

"I'll get it from my desk."

"Good girl."

Johanna came back from her desk, glowing with new virtue, even if she did not fully understand its source. Abigail dialed the number and introduced herself. "Yes, two years ago at the BMF dinner. No, no, I'm not from Eskom. We sat next to each other. No, no . . ." A suitable description of herself for someone she had met once in the twilight of a banquet was not easy, then she found it. "I'm Johanna's boss."

"Oh, Johanna's boss. How is she?"

"She's fine. Listen, I need a favor."

"Sure."

"There's a farm on the northern road between the city and Hartebeespoort dam, called Vyefontein. It's up against the hillside."

"Yes, I know those farms. They're just bush really. You said the farm's name is . . . ?"

"Vyefontein. You know, fig fountain or fig spring."

"What do you want to know about it?"

"Just exactly where it is."

"I'll look it up. What's your number, so I can phone you back?"

You're not getting away from me that easily, Abigail thought. "I'll hang on," she said.

"It may take a while."

"That's okay. I'll hang on."

"You sure?"

"Absolutely."

Abigail found the locked farm gate nearer the road than she had expected, but otherwise the map that Lou-Anne Hamid had faxed through to her had been exact. She could just see the ruin from the place where she left the car. A thin screen of brush, most of it unruly eucalyptus scrub, imported generations before from Australia, sheltered the gate from the road and made it unlikely that she would be seen climbing it. She was deeply grateful for that. Pretoria was not a big enough town to be seen undertaking undignified activities.

That Abigail, as always, was wearing one of her trouser suits made the conquest of the gate a lot easier than would have been the case in a skirt. The track between the gate and the remains of the nineteenth-century farmhouse was by now barely distinguishable from the dry veld that surrounded it. It gave the appearance of not having been used for many years. She picked her way through the rough grass, trying to limit the number of abrasive seed pods lodging in the material of her pants. It was a task that demanded concentration.

She was brought to a stop by a straggling hedge. She looked up to find that the ruin was no more than thirty or forty paces away. Suddenly the exertions of climbing the gate and tramping up the old track both disappeared. There was the house, close enough to throw a stone through one of the windows from which the frames had long since disappeared.

This time there was no questioning herself about the reason for her presence there or what she would do if suddenly confronted by the man she was looking for. There was only the cold, unwavering compulsion to go forward, to see if Leon may just be somewhere in this old ruin.

Discomfort was nothing to Bishop, Jones Ndlovu had said. And if he had once used this place as a base, and used it successfully, was it not likely that he would return?

Abigail found an opening in the hedge. The house had been a comfortable farmhouse in its time. The outbuildings, a crumbling line of smaller buildings, were a further twenty or thirty meters down the track. A broad porch extended along the front and down one side of the house. Most of the walls still stood as they had been built, but the roof was almost entirely gone, corrugated iron sheets having long since been removed, probably to reappear in one of the region's many shack townships. Window frames, electric geysers, doors, door frames, flooring and ceiling boards had all gone the same way.

Between herself and the house was a strip of sandy ground. Anyone entering or leaving the house would have left tracks in it. She stopped to study the sand, slowly walking its length, but there was no sign that anyone had been there. The only tracks had been made by birds and insects, little scratchy indications of their passing.

Abigail moved slowly from room to room, the intensity of her concentration dispelling, at least for the moment, any thought of danger. A sudden rustling to her right, under the last remaining piece of roofing brought back her vulnerability. Her head jerked in the direction of the sound, a violent, painful movement. A pair of owls, disturbed by her sudden arrival in their domain, swirled into the air and were gone.

The sudden appearance of the owls had changed everything. Now the place that had been the terrain of her search had become a threatening den that was somehow waiting for her. Whereas she had been the hunter, now suddenly, because of two frightened owls, she was the prey. Inadvertently, she remembered what the deputy secretary-general of the party had told her: "Do not go to him alone. Never go to him alone."

Abigail knew that she had a choice. She could turn and hurry back to the car. And perhaps she could even do it without looking back. Or she could stay and concentrate on what she had come to do, search every room and do it slowly and thoroughly. A part of her said that it would not only be safer to flee back to the car, it would be more sensible too. What good would it do Leon if she were no longer alive to search for him?

There were good and rational reasons to leave. But staying had to do with her own view of herself. She would have to finish what she had come to do and she would have to do it properly.

Abigail moved slowly through the ruin, examining every corner for signs of human presence, every exposed piece of sand for tracks, no matter how slight the signs may be. When she had finished searching the house she went to the outbuildings, a shed, the remains of a six-vehicle garage, the foundations of a barn and a small bunkhouse for the farm workers. Again, there was nothing, no sign at all that anyone had for years been inside what remained of a family's home.

Jones Ndlovu had been wrong about one thing though. The house was not built in the Cape Dutch style. Either Ndlovu did not know what the Cape Dutch style looked like or else the years in between or the substances he used to dull the pain of living had confused his memory of the house.

She started back toward her car, still not allowing herself to hurry. She had done the job she came to do, and she was damned if she was going to panic at this late stage.

From somewhere behind her there was a new sound, a brief

rustling in the grass. It's an animal, she told herself, a mongoose or a hare. To turn to see what had caused the sound would have been to yield to the panic and she was not going to do that.

When she reached the gate she would still have to climb it, getting herself into the most vulnerable position of all. Then there was the last little stretch between the gate and the car.

It was only when she reached her car that Abigail turned back to look at the house, the scrub surrounding it and the brown Highveld grass obscuring the track. Whatever had made the rustling sound had gone to ground. As far as she could see, the owls had not returned.

Then she felt his presence. Somewhere from the scrub above her, he was watching. A ragged, intermittent breeze was blowing from the southeast and the only movement came from its effect on the grass and scrub. Even that was slight. But he was there, watching and waiting.

No, Abigail thought. I am imagining this. Whether I like it or not, my fear is controlling me. There's no sign at the house. It can't be so.

She got into her car and started the engine.

22

As Yudel Gordon neared the café where he was expected, his driving slowed, the result of being deep in thought. Rosa sometimes referred to it as his absent state.

In Yudel's view, the city was in the grip of a mild melancholia. The great anxiety of the years immediately after the first democratic elections had dissipated. He was grateful that no black mobs had expelled white suburbanites, like himself, from their homes. It was a relief that the rumblings that had been felt underfoot for decades had resulted not in the cataclysm of a Pompeii, but in a much gentler rearranging of influence and earnings.

There was something of the resentment of the excluded in Yudel's thinking when he allowed his mind to dwell on the desperate rush of the previous regime's politicians and senior civil servants to squeeze what they could from the country when they saw that they were losing all influence. He had been just as excluded from the equally desperate stampede of the new regime's senior functionaries to extract what they could from a changed country.

This was Yudel's Pretoria, the seat of the nation's government, a place that in the closing years of the apartheid era had lost whatever innocence it once had. There seemed little chance of that quality being restored any time soon.

The café was in one of the many arcades that weave a north-south network through the center of the city. When Yudel arrived the others were already seated at one of the bright yellow plastic tables that spilled out of the doorway and along the front beside plate-glass windows. A stream of people, big earners and small, eddied back and forth along the arcade and past the café. Most men wore jackets and ties. Women wore their hair styled, the older ones kept theirs in place with lacquer, and skirts were knee-length and shorter.

After leaning across the table to give Rosa the requisite perfunctory kiss, Yudel shook the hand of Freek Jordaan, deputy police commissioner for Gauteng Province and Yudel's friend of many years. He smiled at Freek's wife, Magda, who filled the last seat at the table as he sat down on the only vacant chair. A glance at Rosa's face showed that she looked reasonably relaxed. She may not yet have forgiven him, but at least she was not openly hostile. You could hardly expect more. After all, the incident at the restaurant was not even twenty-four hours old.

Freek was a big man, tall and broad in the shoulders. His face was tanned, the result of being out with his men whenever there was a law and order crisis of any sort, and the country still had too many of those. His hair was almost completely gray and thinning fast. Magda was a good-looking woman in her mid-fifties who spoke her mind on all occasions with an almost complete disregard for the consequences. "So, Yudel," she said. "I understand from Rosa that you are trying to help an attractive female government official in the spirit of reconciliation and so on." She raised an eyebrow archly. "Or has it got more to do with the way she looks?"

Damn it, Magda, Yudel thought, not now. "I am no longer assisting her," Yudel said primly.

A sudden roar of laughter from Freek, suppressed until that moment, was accompanied by a slap on the back, heavy enough to rattle Yudel's teeth. "Never mind, Yudel. We all have to do our bit for reconciliation."

Even Rosa seemed amused. That, at least, was something. "Has anyone ordered?" Yudel asked.

"I ordered you a Greek salad," Rosa said, "And I told them to add bacon, but they seem to be a little bit slow in the kitchen."

"Where do you find a place that isn't slow in the kitchen these days?" Magda asked.

"Anything is better than eating at home." Rosa looked meaningfully at Yudel. "Only one plate of my stove is working and we are having some difficulty replacing the fuses."

"The fuses shouldn't be too much of a problem," Freek said helpfully. He glanced uncertainly at Yudel, wondering if advice on the matter might be the last thing that was needed. Recent years had complicated the relationship between the two men. Under the old government, Freek had risen quickly to become the youngest colonel in the force. But his career had stalled at that point, the consequence of too often following his own mind, instead of his orders. His career had started moving again after the new government came to power. The instruction had come down from above that the country must have at least one white commissioner or deputy commissioner. And, if possible, that officer should be an Afrikaner, a member of the group that had been running the country for the last half-century.

For Yudel, the new South Africa had left his career floundering. At least he had a job under white rule. As far as he could see, the main effect of the majority of South Africans gaining the right to vote was his retrenchment. He had not been acceptable to the old government and, until his meeting with the commissioner of Correctional Services two days before, his relationship with the new government had possibly been even worse.

The result of their diverging fortunes meant that visits that had once been regular had dwindled away until they had almost stopped altogether. Rosa had arranged the lunch in the hope of restoring something of the past friendship. She felt that Yudel was becoming increasingly isolated and needed it.

As for Yudel, he looked across the table at Freek, resplendent in his uniform, looking as relaxed and confident as always, no matter who was in power, and thought, Fuck him. Everything works out for him. It always has.

Freek caught his glance and tried a forced smile. "So, Yudel, how are things?"

The question only irritated Yudel further. Did Freek really expect an answer to it? Well, fuck him, if he did. He was not going to get one.

"Did you hear about Yudel's contract?" Rosa asked, trying to lighten the mood. She was wondering if the lunch had been a good idea. She could already see that Yudel was in one of what she called his black hole moods.

"We did," Magda said. "Congratulations, Yudel."

"They realize they need somebody who can get the job done," Freek said.

Yudel looked grimly from one to the other. He was determined to show no sign of pleasure or even interest.

At none of the other tables had the patrons received their orders. Usually a continual stream of waitresses, dressed in the same bright yellow as the décor, flowed in and out of the kitchen to serve the patrons. Today, there seemed to be none at all.

Inside the café, a young manager was hurrying back and forth behind the counter with quick, light movements. Blocking the entrance to the kitchen, the waitresses had gathered in a tightly packed, discontented knot. Yudel noticed the face of one, lips pursed in indignation, cheeks puffed up as if by inner pressure. As he watched they started moving through the entrance to the kitchen, leaving the young man to flit frantically about his duties alone. A few moments later he arrived at their table and leaned forward apologetically. "I'm terribly sorry, people." He blinked as he spoke. "We have a small difficulty. If you're prepared to wait a few minutes, I'll have your order with you."

Freek looked heavenward, a gesture of supplication. "What's the problem?"

"The ladies who wait on the tables are staying away until three o'clock." He glanced uncertainly at the curious faces of his patrons at the other tables. "Management did a survey and found that the waitresses get good tips, so they reduced their wages."

"There you have it." Freek waved a disgusted hand. "No one is interested in doing a job properly anymore."

"Well, management pulled a rather sharp trick there," the manager said. "They have reason to be unhappy."

Freek was about to pursue the matter when Magda laid a restraining hand on his arm. "It's all right," she said. "We'll wait." After the young man had left, she spoke to Rosa. "Isn't it wonderful when they sound so middle-aged?" She mimicked Freek. " 'No one is interested in doing a job properly anymore.' "

A moment later the waitresses were streaming out of the front of the café, joining the passing throng until they were no more than a few bright patches in the rest of the foot traffic.

"There goes lunch," Freek said soberly.

"It's a long time since things were so tense," Magda said. "Freek has been called out nearly every night for the last three months. Armored car heists mostly. He's only been sleeping two or three hours a night."

Yudel and Rosa both turned inquiringly to Freek. For the first time Yudel noticed how the other man's face was tinted with gray and seemed more lined than usual. Red veins showed in his eyes. "But why?" Rosa asked. "Freek has so many men he can send."

"Not when you're the only one who can do things properly," Magda said. "If you want something done right, you have to do it yourself." She was mimicking Freek again.

"Is he doing this apart from his ordinary duties?" Rosa was awed.

"A man's got to do what a man's got to do," Magda said.

Freek patted Rosa's hand in a brotherly way. "The problem is that there is too much crime and too few experienced policemen. Some ordinary constables have been on duty sixteen hours a day. It's not going too damned well, let me tell you."

The young man of the café was back at their table, massaging his hands fretfully. "Will four tuna salads be in order? I know that isn't . . ."

Freek interrupted him. "Yes, the Lord knows. Four of anything, so long as we can eat it."

They watched him dash back to the counter, squeezing between a standing patron and a table. "Not Freek's kind of man," Magda suggested.

"He didn't do too badly there with the staff a few minutes ago," Freek said. "Not badly at all." But another thought had entered Freek's mind. "Yudel, do you remember a political by the name of Simon Mkhari? He spent time on death row, I think. I don't know why."

"He burned an old woman alive," Yudel said. "Yes, I remember him."

"Yudel remembers all these awful things," Rosa said.

Freek nodded. He had not needed that piece of information. He also knew Yudel well. "Mkhari was killed yesterday. You heard about the firefight in Marabastad between a gang of robbers and some of our men?"

"I read about it in the papers."

"Mkhari was one of the robbers we killed. It looks like his crimes may not have had only political motivation."

"They didn't," Yudel said. "I remember him well."

23

As Yudel turned the corner, entering the street where they lived, he recognized the car blocking the entrance to the driveway as belonging to Abigail. She was standing next to it, looking both tense and determined. It was a look that Yudel was beginning to recognize.

"It looks as if Abigail needs to speak to you again," Rosa said.

Yudel and Rosa got out of the car together. "Leon's missing," Abigail started without any preliminaries. "He seems to have been abducted."

"And now?"

"Now, we have to find him."

"There are things you need to tell me," Yudel said. "You'd better come to my study."

Abigail glanced at Rosa, as if asking permission. "Run along, my dear. I'll make coffee afterward."

"There were eighteen of us living in the house outside Maseru at that time." Abigail was again in Yudel's study. This time they were seated on the same side of the desk, Yudel's eyes never leaving her face. "I was the youngest in the house. I was just fifteen. Usually I was at boarding school, but I had been sick. If they had waited another day I would have been back at school. My parents were there and most of the others were couples. All of them were youngish people, under forty."

Abigail was leaning forward, her hands clasped in her lap. Yudel was surprised by her transformation as she started speaking. The confidence that was so much a part of her disappeared. She gave the appearance of being no older than the fifteen she had been at the time. The words poured out of her, as if she had been waiting for the last twenty years to tell someone the story. "I don't know why we thought we were safe. The house was no more than five kilometers from the border, as the crow flies. It seems so naïve when I think about it now. To have assumed that the apartheid regime would have respected the borders of little Lesotho seems crazy. And to have assumed that they did not know about our house seems equally crazy. In those days the movement was riddled with informers in the pay of the security police.

"I remember clearly that evening before they came. It's as if the later events etched even the earlier part of the evening in my mind—as if they were also part of that night's horror.

"I had been outside with a young married woman, Julia. We were batting a ball back and forth with wooden paddles, the kind you take to the beach. She had just come back from a stint in Lusaka. The movement had deployed her there as a teacher in the ANC school. There was a small lawn in front of the house and the ball kept escaping into the overgrown flower beds whenever I missed it. I've never been good at that sort of thing.

"It was a lovely late spring evening. When it got too dark to play anymore, Julia and I sat down on the grass. I remember telling her about my ambitions. At that age I wanted to be an actress. I suppose most fifteen-year-old girls want to be actresses. The stars were as bright as they can only be on the Lesotho highlands. It seemed that if we reached up we would be able to gather handfuls of them. On such nights there always seem to be more stars in the Lesotho sky than anywhere else on Earth.

"Through the open window of the living room I could hear my father and one of the other men talking. They were arguing about the sort of government we should have in South Africa after the revolution. The other man was a Trotskyite and he wanted a government that would follow Trotsky's thinking. I was never sufficiently interested to try to understand what sort of government that would have been. My father was a social democrat and wanted a government like Sweden's. The doors and windows stood open, no curtains were drawn. And none of us gave a thought to the possibility that there could be men on their way to kill us. Oh God, Yudel, and there *were* men on the way to kill us." The flow of words stopped as suddenly as it had started. "Must we do this? Must we really?"

Yudel could see that this was not just an idle question. Abigail would rather have done anything other than tell this story. He doubted that, without the disappearance of Lourens, he would ever have heard it. "You are not doing it," he said. "You're telling me about that evening, but you are telling me everything except what is really important. If I am to help, I must hear about the important things, not the stars and the bat-and-ball game or Trotskyite plans."

Abigail's eyes were begging him to find some other way, but she nodded. "I will tell you. It must have been about ten o'clock before I went to bed. I had a small room off the kitchen that had probably originally been the pantry. I heard some of the others moving around for a while as I lay in bed. Then everything was quiet.

"I don't know how long I slept, but I heard later that they came at about half past three. I don't remember how I woke up or exactly what happened and in what order things happened. I do remember being on my hands and knees next to the bed. The noise was deafening. There was shouting and heavy boots on the wood floor and what sounded to me like explosions. My door was open a bit and through it I saw the figures of men in camouflage. They all seemed to be moving."

While telling this part of the story, she did not look at Yudel.

The memory of that night so long ago absorbed her completely. Now she turned her attention to him. "Yudel, you have to understand. Until then I had been a schoolgirl in a comfortable private school. My main challenges in life were being accepted by the in-crowd at school and staying out of the way of our awful English teacher."

"Just tell me," he said. "Tell it in the order in which it happened."

"I don't know in what order anything happened. I do remember that I was out in the living room at one point. There was a terrible pain in my right side and I was rolling on the ground. Some of the men in camouflage were in the room, but none of our people were there. I heard the explosions coming from the bedrooms and from the kitchen. At one point I was looking out of the open door and seeing more soldiers on the dirt road outside.

"I was in the hallway, trying to get to the closed door of my parents' room, but the pain in my side was terrible. There was a loud crash against the door from the other side, as if something big had been thrown against it. Then I think the door burst open and one of the soldiers fell headlong into the hallway. His rifle was on a shoulder strap. It clattered to the ground next to him. He was young and I saw him raise a hand to his forehead, then suddenly my father was there and trying to take the rifle from him. That was the first time I saw Leon. Of course, I didn't know who he was at the time.

"You have to understand, Yudel, that while my father was a member of the armed wing of the movement, he was not a soldier. He was a medical doctor, deployed by the movement to any area where his skills were needed. The young man was still stunned and I thought my father was going to be able to take the gun from him, when suddenly he was struck by the stock of a rifle. He fell to the floor, holding his shoulder where the blow had landed. Immediately one of the men was standing over him. That was the first time I saw that man."

"Van Jaarsveld?"

Abigail had started weeping. Until this moment she had not

been able to hide her distress, but her control had been complete. Yudel saw that now the story had reached the point that had, until now, made telling it impossible. "What happened to your father?" he asked.

"He . . . he . . ." Continuing suddenly seemed impossible.

Had she been a patient, Yudel might have waited to hear the rest of the story. But she was not a patient and Leon Lourens had been taken from his workshop. Waiting was out of the question. "You have the strength to tell me," he said, speaking slowly. He reached out to take one of her hands in his.

"My father . . . my father . . . he and Leon were on the floor . . . I was crawling . . ."

"Crawling? Where were you crawling to?"

"Toward my father. I was crawling . . . toward my father. He was unarmed and injured, but to me he had always been the place I could find safety. Then . . ."

Yudel knew what happened then, but he had to hear it from her. Inserting his own assumptions into her memory could do no good. He waited for the weeping to stop. When it did she was again in control and the words again came pouring out.

"I was almost touching him when van Jaarsveld killed him. I never saw where the bullet entered. I only saw him fall backward onto the floor with his eyes closed. He could have been asleep, but I knew he wasn't.

"There was terrible screaming. I was sitting up and I remember the room swaying as I rocked myself back and forth. I could not immediately tell where the screaming was coming from, only that every time I gasped for breath it stopped. Van Jaarsveld hit me across the face and the back of my head. I was flat on the floor again, but my screaming continued. I could do nothing to stop it. I heard him shouting at me. He pointed his rifle at me and for the first time I could make out words in all the surrounding noise. 'If this doesn't stop, I'll kill the kaffir *meidjie* too.' I understood enough Afrikaans to know what he was saying. But I had no control over the screaming. He lifted his rifle to his shoulder and said something about shutting me up permanently.

"Then there was another voice, telling him to put down his weapon. It was Leon, and he was pointing his rifle at van Jaarsveld. Van Jaarsveld shouted something at him about obeying orders, but he kept his rifle pointed at van Jaarsveld. I heard him say that if van Jaarsveld shot me, he would be the next to die. I don't think this was what van Jaarsveld expected. I remember startled faces of young men around us. Van Jaarsveld was shouting an order at him, but Leon kept his rifle pointed straight at him.

"I don't know how long it went on like that, but I remember van Jaarsveld saying that he did not have time for this. He said he had work to do, and he turned and left. As he went I heard him shouting orders at the others. Even then I realized that he was trying to save face. There was something about Leon. I believe he would have killed van Jaarsveld if he tried to shoot me. I think van Jaarsveld believed it too." The torrent of words that had been pouring out of Abigail stopped abruptly and she fell silent.

"Of the people in the house, how many survived the night?" Yudel asked.

"Just six of us."

"And you were taken to cells in Ficksburg?"

"Yes. At the police station."

"And something happened there?"

"We were freed by the movement."

"How?"

"The three policemen on duty were killed, all in the same way. And all in the way that these apartheid policemen have been dying over the last twenty years."

"And the date of the incident in Ficksburg was October 22?"

"Yes."

"And you know who killed the policemen in Ficksburg?"

"His name is Michael Bishop."

"You saw him that night?"

This time Abigail did not answer, nor could she look at Yudel. There was a desk calendar on Yudel's desk. He turned away from Abigail to look at it.

"It's the nineteenth," she said.

"And this man who saved your life in Maseru was abducted today?"

"Yesterday."

"If it's any consolation, Abigail, you can be sure that Bishop, or whoever is doing this, will wait till the twenty-second. Where is Bishop?"

"No one seems to know. Will you help me find him?"

"And if we find him, what will we do with him?" he asked.

She was looking helplessly at Yudel.

"We need the police," Yudel said.

"I can't even interest my own department."

"Tell me about Bishop."

He believed her and he wanted to help. Abigail could see that. It seemed to her that there was more than a desire to help in Yudel. He needed to help. Perhaps, she thought, he needed to atone for the fact that throughout the bad years he had worked for the apartheid government. "Why, Yudel?" she asked.

"So that I can try to understand . . ."

"No, not that. Why did you stay in the service of the apartheid government all those years?"

"I'm a criminologist," Yudel said. "They had the criminals in their cells. There was nowhere else for me to work."

"Is that all it was?"

"That's all."

"And private practice?"

He shook his head. "No. I wanted the real thing."

And now we are here, Abigail thought. Me from the movement and you from the old prison system. And will you really be able to help me?

"Tell me about Michael Bishop. Tell me everything you know."

Abigail told him what she was able to and everything Jones Ndlovu had told her. In the telling it all sounded pitifully thin to her own ears.

"And Ficksburg? Tell me more about Ficksburg."

"I have to go," Abigail said.

"Did Michael Bishop kill the policemen in Ficksburg?"

"Yes."

"Tell me about it."

"I must go."

"Don't do this," Yudel said. "Don't run away again. I need to understand."

"I'm not running away and I will tell you everything, but I have to fetch Robert at the airport."

"Before you go—surely the thing is to find Leon, not Bishop."

"If we find Bishop, we will find Leon. I know it."

Yudel stood outside in the gathering twilight and watched Abigail drive away. Will you tell me everything? he wondered. What is it that happened in Ficksburg that still cannot be approached after all these years? Whatever it is, right now you are fleeing from it again. How many times in the past have you fled from it?

24

"Why?" she had asked Yudel. "Why did you stay in the service of the apartheid government all those years?"

They had the prisoners, he had replied. Yudel sat at his desk, crouched forward, his eyes directed to the floor between his knees, but he was seeing nothing. His hands were on his thighs and his shoulders were hunched tightly together. He was rocking slightly.

Why? was indeed the question. He had often explained it to himself by remembering that the government had the prisoners. But the truth was that Yudel was ashamed of those years. He had often told himself that he was doing some good and there were times when he *had* done good. He had tried to bring sanity to situations in which sanity was in short supply. But there was no avoiding the fact that he had been part of the apartheid apparatus. If Abigail was fleeing from something, then so was he.

Perhaps that was part of his resentment of Freek. It all seemed so easy to him. He seemed to suffer no self-doubt. What Freek Jordaan did was the right thing to do—unlike Yudel Gordon, who was never entirely sure what the right path looked like.

Now there was Simon Mkhari, whose final chapter had been written in the dirt of a dusty Marabastad backyard the previous day. There had been many like him.

Yudel was not one to harbor hatred, but there were classes of criminal to whose cases he had been unable to bring objective detachment. Foremost among these were those who killed for political reasons. The self-righteousness with which they explained the burning alive of an old woman or the blowing to unrecognizable fragments of late-night revellers in a beachside bar was more than he had ever been able to digest. In recent years he had come face to face with some of them, now dressed in the respectability of senior government positions. They repelled him still.

Mkhari had not been one of those that the new government either needed or wanted. He disgusted Yudel, but not as much as those who had profited from their past homicides, under the cloak of liberation. This afternoon at lunch he had felt no regret at hearing about Mkhari's end. It had seemed a fitting one.

Despite all this, there had been a few minutes he had spent in Mkhari's company that would stay with him always. It had been to his shame, not Mkhari's.

Mkhari had originally been sentenced to death for the burning of the old woman and Yudel had visited him on death row. The prisoner had asked for the visit. He had heard the story that occasionally did the rounds on death row that no one was ever really executed. They fell through the floor of the gallows to an underground passage that led to the mint, where they made money for the rest of their lives. The theory was that the government could not allow people to go free who knew how to make money. So those who were sentenced to death went to the mint instead.

Yudel had been telling him that this was not so, and Mkhari had started to interrupt loudly when he suddenly stopped speaking. Something had happened down the passage toward the entrance of the block. Yudel had also heard it, but had not immediately attached any importance to the single word that now hung in the air like a sharp lowering of the temperature. The humming of voices that was always a part of death row had all but stopped. Within seconds, there was complete silence. The skin covering Mkhari's face had become taut. His pupils had dilated until the brown of the irises had all but disappeared. His nostrils flared with a sudden intake of breath. He had forgotten what he had started to say and even seemed to have forgotten that Yudel was with him in the cell. Like everyone else in the entire community of some 130 condemned prisoners, he was listening.

Yudel was listening too. That one word had been submerged below conversation level, yet it clung to the edges of his memory, an anonymous intrusion. The double row that made up the death cells had been reduced to a single, quivering sensor, straining to pick up whatever more there might be.

The door of a cell closed. Yudel heard steps in the passage and the sound of another door opening. Then the word he had heard before, but had not been able to hold on to.

"Pack."

Mkhari's eyes were set, unblinking. There were other words too, but it was that one for which all were now listening. Again a door closed, the steps came closer and another opened.

"Pack."

That was three. Yudel knew that there was not a man who was not counting. To know the number meant nothing in itself. It was only a statistic on which to hang their wondering. Again the man who had spoken was in the passage. The sound of his footfalls and those of his entourage was sharp and clear, leather heels clicking on the concrete surface. He stopped, just a few doors away. The heavy steel bolt slid clear and the hinges creaked briefly as the door swung open.

"Pack."

And that was four. They were close enough for the other words to be audible. "I want jacket and address now."

Again the footsteps in the passage. Just a little way and they would be level with Mkhari's cell. Yudel saw the expectancy with which the prisoner's eyes were fixed on the door. But this was fear, not excitement.

Then the sliding of steel against steel was coming from the solid steel door of Mkhari's cell. With a jerk it swung open and Sergeant Paulsen, senior warder in charge of the block, came in. He stopped at seeing Yudel. "Mr. Gordon . . . I didn't realize . . . I have to . . ."

Yudel nodded. Unconsciously he had taken a step back, so that he would not be between the warder and prisoner. There was no avoiding what had to be done. Paulsen stepped aside to let the sheriff come through.

"Pack," the sheriff said. He was a pale, balding, nondescript man of middle age. "Give me jacket and address now." Jacket and address. They were everything in the world that a con-demned man possessed. Jacket stood for his personal effects. He would be moving to another cell, and they needed to go with him. The address was needed because his status would be changing and his next-of-kin would have to be informed.

The others had all complied silently and without resistance, but Mkhari rushed to the farthest corner of the cell that was only just big enough to contain a narrow bed and room to move around it. Paulsen gestured and two more warders came in. "I need you to wait outside, Mr. Gordon," he told Yudel.

From outside the cell, Yudel heard Mkhari's deep grunting protest. "No, leave me." He was speaking Afrikaans. "I stay here, I'm telling you, I stay here." There was a scuffling of feet and a muttering from the warders. The struggle was brief and they soon appeared with Mkhari between them. He was taken down the corridor in the direction of the lawyers' room at the end of the block.

The sheriff stopped at four more cells, making a total of ten. After he too had left for the lawyers' room, death row returned to such life as it possessed. Someone down at the far end laughed; a thin, piping tenor, an uninhibited release of tension. A second voice, deeper and coarser, joined the first, while close at hand, Yudel heard someone sobbing. "God save the queen," another shouted with comic irrelevance. Loud talking, laughing and whooping sounds of joy echoed from walls where the win-dows were uncurtained and floors uncarpeted, as every man who had been bypassed regained his voice.

On his way back to the entrance Yudel had to pass the lawyers' consulting room. He knew what he would find there. He had seen it all before and knew the form it took.

Despite himself, he slowed as he approached it. Nine of the prisoners were queuing at the door, watched over by two warders. Mkhari was the first man in the queue. He had given up the struggle and was staring in front of him through unseeing eyes. Immediately behind him was Peanut Setlaba, a bodybuilder who had often boasted to the others on death row that they would not be able to hang him, his neck was too thick for the rope. It was a boast that was soon to be proven empty. He had been found guilty of killing his wife in a crime of passion. Behind him stood Bernard Kanasi who, in an act of revenge, had killed his former mistress's nine-year-old son. The faces of the men, all of whom had been the center of hideous killings, each in its own way reflected a state of deep shock.

Inside the room the sheriff, looking excessively solemn and dignified, was seated at a table. A third warder stood next to him. As Yudel watched, Mkhari was ushered into the room and positioned in front of the sheriff. "You were convicted of murder," the sheriff told him. "You were given leave to appeal by the trial judge. Your sentence was upheld by the Appellate Division. You petitioned the state president, but clemency was not granted." The voice was flat and unemotional, reciting the prisoner's history from the time he had been taken into custody. Among death row prisoners the sheriff was called the storyteller. "Accordingly, the date for your execution has been fixed for O-seven-hundred hours on the morning of . . ."

Every man on death row passed this way. Without any exceptions they took their turn in this queue and waited to hear whether they would be going to the pot, so called because you stewed there, in which no one was scheduled to spend more than seven days—or down the hill to the main prison and life.

But Mkhari had not been destined to die that way. Before his seven days in the pot were up, the old government had granted a moratorium on the death penalty. Reconciliation talks with the liberation movement had started, and would have stopped as suddenly if the apartheid government had continued executing the movement's activists. Once the new government had come to power, Mkhari's murder of the old woman was seen as a political act, furthering the aim of liberation, and he had been freed. Yudel had filed a report, outlining the reason for his opposition to this prisoner's release, but the man who turned out to be the last white commissioner of correctional services was trying hard to keep his position. He had no intention of opposing the wishes of his new masters in even the slightest way. He granted Yudel an interview, but from the first moment it was clear to Yudel that he was speaking to a man who was not listening to him.

The new South Africa had been no more accepting of Simon Mkhari than the old one had been. Yudel felt no pleasure at having been right about him. Hearing about his death in the Marabastad firefight left him with nothing but the emptiness of failure.

Mkhari was just a small part of Yudel's memory of those years. How did I stay so long? he asked himself. How was it possible? Little by little, perhaps. One day at a time.

But he knew that it was not that simple. The state of the country was a tragedy, perhaps the world's most significant tragedy of the time. And he was at the center of it.

The truth is that I was fascinated by it, he told himself. I loved being at the center of it. I loved it. No, let me not admit to that. I was fascinated by it. That's enough.

25

Abigail's anxiety to get away from Yudel and an even greater anxiety not to be late for Robert saw her reaching the airport half an hour early. She did not want to spend another night alone in the apartment.

She found a seat in a café from which she could see the board that would show her when Robert's flight landed. She had ordered coffee when she remembered Susanna Lourens and what she would be feeling. She had saved her number on her mobile, and now she called it.

A man answered in Afrikaans. *"Dis Van Rensburg wat praat."*

Having spent most of her formative years outside the country, Abigail knew little Afrikaans, but had followed enough of his reply to realize that his surname was not Lourens. He would probably be the half-brother Leon had told her about. "Abigail Bukula here. May I speak to Susanna?"

"Why? What do you want?" The switch to English had been immediate, but the voice was hostile.

"I'd like to speak to Susanna. She came to see me yesterday."

"Have you found Leon?"

"No."

"Then what do you want to say to Susanna?"

"Look, she came to see me. I want to tell her what I've done."

"She's asleep now. The doctor's given her a sedative. But if you haven't found Leon, I don't think you've got anything to say to her anyway."

After Susanna's timidity and pleading, Abigail had not expected this. "I don't know what to say to you."

"Don't say anything. You people have said enough. It's people like you, people with influence, who are always making speeches attacking white people, who cause this sort of thing to happen. Perhaps it's time for you to say nothing."

After he hung up, with twenty minutes before the flight was due to arrive, she finished her coffee and made her way to domestic arrivals. Leaning against a pillar, she waited for Robert.

When news that the flight had been delayed for twenty minutes flashed onto the board, she barely reacted. Abigail told herself that she was not going anywhere without Robert. If it was delayed all night, she would be there, waiting.

It turned out that an all-night wait was not necessary. The flight was only ten minutes late and the familiar figure of Robert, tall and loose-limbed, a briefcase in one hand and a light traveling bag in the other, his tie absent and the top button of his shirt undone, came casually through the exit. He looked like a man who had never had a problem of any sort in all his life.

If Abigail did not fully realize how powerful her need of her husband was at that moment, he realized it even less. He staggered back a few paces with the force of her welcome. "Whoa," he said. "Take it easy. I'm just a little fellow." She tried to laugh at his joke, but it was not easy when she could not see him for the tears filling her eyes. "With a reception like this, I should go away more often."

"Don't you dare. Don't you ever go anywhere without me ever again."

By this time Robert could see that this was no longer a laughing matter. "Let's get to the car," he said. "You can tell me there."

The highway between the airport and Pretoria was broad,

had only slight bends and few of those. But that early evening a number of flights, international and local, had landed within minutes of one another and the road was busy. Despite the privacy in the car, Robert felt the need for a quieter road. He took the Olifantsfontein turnoff, a road that led through pastoral surroundings and quiet residential areas where the doors of houses were already closed and the streets were uniformly still. He slowed the car to give his attention to Abigail. "So, tell me," he said. "Tell me quickly."

"Leon's gone. I believe he's been abducted."

"Are you sure?"

"A single white man in police uniform took him away. We've phoned everywhere, but no government body has him."

"Tell me everything."

She told him everything, how she had met Yudel, her visit to Jones Ndlovu, her search of the house in the Magaliesberg hills and, most of all, how she had been unable to raise any interest from anyone. "I know Mandla Nyati would try to help, but he's gone to Cape Town too."

Robert brought the car to a halt in an avenue of pines, entering the village of Irene. He turned to her. Uneven light from a street lamp, filtered and interrupted by the pine branches, fell on his face. She could see in his eyes how serious he was. "I don't think there will be any help from senior people."

"Why? Just because he was a hero . . ."

"It has nothing to do with that. No one will be able to help."

"But why not?"

"The deputy president is going down. The head of the National Prosecuting Authority believes he has a case of corruption against him."

"My God. That's why you had to go to Cape Town?"

"This was just a briefing from our chairman. I expect in the next few days to be called, with other black editors, to a briefing by the man himself."

"I can't believe it. Does the president know?"

"The word is that he does."

"My God." The abduction of the man who had saved her life did damage to Abigail's view of her country in a singularly personal way. Now the possible guilt of the deputy president on charges of corruption, just eleven years into the new South Africa, did damage to that image in a much broader way. If this were true, the vision of a joyous future beyond apartheid had been sullied. "Is he guilty?" she asked Robert.

"I'm the wrong person to ask," he said. "I can't stand the machine-gun song he sings at every rally. I know that I don't have a rational view of him. I always hoped that he wouldn't be around long, but it looks as if the NPA wants to try him in the press because they don't have enough on him. That's just not right."

"All this in just a few days," Abigail said.

"One thing you can be sure of—all of those in your department, who are high enough to help you, will be running around like headless chickens. They won't even be able to hear what you're saying, let alone do anything about it."

"But Leon . . ."

Robert interrupted her. "Leon is just one apartheid soldier . . . not much in the broader scheme of things."

"Then we're alone in this." She sounded like a small child. Robert had never been able to resist it.

"I do have something, though." He reached into a pocket of his suit, brought out a photograph and passed it to Abigail.

It was a reproduction of an old color photograph. In the light from the car's ceiling she saw that it was slightly out of focus and taken from behind. But the subject had turned his head, as if to see what was happening behind him, to give almost a profile view of himself. The face it revealed was an undistinguished one. The nose was small and featureless, the mouth also small and framed by thin, colorless lips. The face was almost unlined and the dusty-brown hair straight and cut short.

Abigail stared transfixed at the photograph. It was not a face you would normally notice, but it was the one she would never be able to forget.

Robert was driving again. "If another picture of him exists, the media do not have it," he said. "I believe that's the only one, and it's possibly twenty years old." He glanced at her. To his eyes, she seemed to have shrunk back into her seat.

Abigail laid the picture down on the only place that seemed available, Robert's left thigh. He put it back in his pocket. When she did speak it was in an attempt to break free of the subject that was again consuming her. It was also an attempt to show that she really was interested in matters that were important to him. "Your empowerment deal?" she asked. "Has anything else developed?"

"No, no," he said absently. "No. Bigger matters have got in the way of that, at least for the time being."

Yudel Gordon sat behind his desk in his study. Without moving from the chair, he reached out and took a book from the bottom of a pile on one of his many cluttered bookcases.

The state of his study, which both Rosa and the domestic worker were forbidden to enter, made it all the more surprising that Yudel invariably went straight to the book he needed. The book he now opened was a biography of the composer, Georg Frideric Handel. It was troubling to Yudel that he shared some aspect of his taste in music with this Michael Bishop, this killer that Abigail so feared.

Yudel read a few pages, but the book was a lifeless thing. He put it back on the shelf. It was not this that fascinated Bishop. It was the music itself. Handel was about music, not the words in a biography.

Abigail had heard from Bishop's old comrade that *Samson* was his favorite. Yudel went in search of his own recording and found it on a shelf where he kept CDs, in a small lounge looking out on the garden. He loved to sit there, listening to music. He had to pass the door of the room where Rosa was watching television. She looked curiously at him, but in a way that seemed quite friendly. That's something, he thought.

He took the recording of *Samson* back to his study, where he had a small portable player. After closing the door so that the music would not interfere with Rosa's program, he put the first disc into the player and sat down as the music began.

Yudel closed his eyes to listen. As the overture started, a deep relaxation came over him. It was the effect that Handel usually had on him. Especially at times like this when his nervous system seemed stretched to the limit, the lovely flowing rhythms of the music worked their magic on his soul. To his senses the efforts of orchestra, chorus and soloists blended into a wonderful wholeness. Even Michael Bishop's love for this music could not diminish the peace Yudel felt.

The recording featured Yudel's favorite singer, the American tenor Jan Peerce. Yudel had heard it many times before, and its effect had always been the same. As song followed song the sense of peace deepened. He slipped back in the chair, his legs stretched out in front of him.

Time itself almost ceased as the music consumed every part of his consciousness. Then suddenly the warmth and relaxation were gone. Peerce was singing softly and melodiously, but the words forced themselves upon Yudel's attention.

. . . pains intense oppressed,
That rob the soul itself of rest.

Yudel reached out toward the player to replay the piece, but he hesitated for a long moment and the music continued. The melodious wholeness of the music was suddenly farther away and Bishop much closer. Then Peerce was singing again. The great tenor's voice filled the room, rising and falling with Handel's glorious music, but again the words that Handel had borrowed from Milton were shutting out everything else.

Total eclipse! No sun, no moon,
All dark amidst the blaze of noon!
Sun, moon and stars are dark to me.

Yudel switched off the music. In his desk pad he found the telephone number of the only classical music store of any consequence in the city. He recognized the voice that answered. "Gary," he said. "Yudel Gordon here."

"Hi, Yudel, what are you looking for tonight?" The voice had the cheery note of a salesman with a regular customer. "I've got a great new recording of Gregorian chants, some monastery in Europe . . ."

"Handel. How's your trade in Handel going?"

"Trade in Handel's a bit slow. We've got a new CD with some bits and pieces you might like, kind of a highlights package, Carreras and others."

"What about the oratorios?"

"Got nothing in stock at the moment."

"What I was wondering is—have you sold anything lately?"

"No, but I'll get you anything you want."

"But have you sold anything lately?"

"No. I could've though, but I didn't have what the guy wanted. He came in looking for Handel's *Samson*. I doubt that more than five copies of *Samson* are sold every year in the whole country. I said I'd order it for him, but he wasn't interested." The salesman's voice took on an enthusiastic note. "You looking for *Samson*? I'll get it for you from the States. It'll cost a bit."

"Listen, Gary, this man . . . do you know his name?"

But Gary was still in sales mode. "Any particular recording ?"

"Listen to me, Gary. Do you know who this guy is?"

"He was just a guy off the street, a little guy, about your size."

"And he wanted *Samson*?"

"It looks like there's a sudden interest in *Samson*. I better get a few copies. I'll let you know when they come."

"Thanks," Yudel said absently. "Appreciate it."

"This sometimes happens when there's a live performance."

"Say that again," Yudel said.

"Tomorrow night. Jo'burg city hall."

"*Samson?*"

"*Samson*. But it's just local singers. You want something really good, I can get you the best."

"Did you mention this performance to your customer?"

"Sure. I told him."

"Did he say he'd go?"

"No, he didn't say anything. But listen, Yudel, I got to go. A customer just came into the shop. I'll phone you when I get those copies of *Samson*. I got to go see what the customer wants."

"So long," Yudel said.

After he hung up, Yudel went back to the recording. By the time the last notes of *Samson* had died, his attention was no longer with the music. He looked up Bukula in the telephone directory. There was only one and the initial was A. He dialed the number and a male voice answered. "Yes." The single syllable was clipped still shorter.

"Is that Mr. Bukula?" Yudel asked.

"It's Robert Mokoapi here," Robert said. "If you're looking for Abigail Bukula's husband, you're speaking to him." Yudel was not accustomed to married people having different surnames. He thought about this for a moment. "Hello," Robert was trying again. "Are you there?"

"Yes," Yudel assured him. "I'm here."

"What do you want, friend?" Despite the mode of address, the voice did not sound friendly.

"I had hoped to speak to Abigail."

"She's asleep. Do you know what time it is?"

"No," Yudel said truthfully. He glanced down at his watch to find that it was just after midnight. "Five past twelve," he told Robert.

"I wasn't asking what the time is. Don't you think it's a bit late to be calling people?"

Yudel considered the question. "Well, I suppose . . ."

From the background Yudel heard Abigail's sleepy voice, asking, "Who is it?"

"Who is it?" Robert demanded.

Yudel knew the answer to that one without thinking. "Yudel Gordon," he said.

A moment later Abigail was on the line. "Yudel? Has something happened?"

"I think so. I think something has just happened. I think I may possibly have found your man."

After he told Abigail what he had found, that it was only a possibility and that she should not place too much hope in it, he hung up and got up slowly from his chair to go to the window.

No sun, no moon—he remembered the words. All dark amidst the blaze of noon! Sun, moon and stars are dark to me.

Did the words speak to Bishop in a way that only he could understand? Or perhaps he did not understand, but felt only the darkness in which he lived, the void where his soul should have been. All dark, Yudel thought. But if darkness was all Bishop had ever known, he would not recognize it as that. At some point there must have been light; some moment, perhaps some person, that was not part of the darkness of his present being.

And tomorrow night's performance of *Samson*? he wondered. Is it possible that he might be there? Could it be this easy after all this time? Or this hard?

26

Thursday, October 20

Abigail and Yudel waited for twenty minutes in the office of the assistant to the deputy police commissioner for Gauteng before they were called in. Freek rose and smiled as they entered. He held Abigail's offered hand in both of his for longer than necessary. "Miss Bukula," he said. The way he said it, her name may have held a more profound meaning than any other word in any language, ever. There was a warmth in his eyes that Freek reserved for members of the opposite sex.

"Forgive me for intruding," Abigail said. She too was smiling warmly.

"There's nothing to forgive," Freek said.

With Freek still holding her hand, as if it were a precious possession, Yudel looked from one to the other, wondering vaguely whether he could be getting in the way of something. He cleared his throat. "Ah, Yudel," Freek said, as if noticing him for the first time. "Good morning."

Seated around the table in the meeting room that adjoined Freek's office, it took all of an hour for Abigail, assisted by Yudel, to explain what had been happening and how they wanted him to help. When she was finished, he turned to Yudel. "Do you accept this thing about the twenty-second of October?"

"It's not a matter of accepting it. This is what has been happening."

"And a man in police uniform took this Lourens away?"

"Yes," Abigail said. "And we can find no official body that has done it . . . certainly not the police."

"And this Bishop?" Freek was talking to Yudel again. "I've never heard of him."

Yudel looked at Abigail.

"Few people, even senior police officers, have heard of him," she said.

"And tonight he's going to be at a concert in Johannesburg?"

"Maybe," Yudel said.

"Maybe," Freek said thoughtfully. "There are no guarantees here."

"How many times have you picked up criminals in their favorite haunts?" Yudel asked.

"Once or twice. It happens."

"One or two hundred times is more like it. How many times have you found a fugitive watching a movie that features his favorite actor or at a sporting event where his team is playing?"

"All right, Yudel. Not every day, but it does happen. I get the point."

"The real point is that there are hundreds of movie houses and sports fields, but I doubt that Handel's *Samson* has had many performances on this continent. But tonight it is being performed, and this man, for whatever reason, has a special affinity for it."

Freek nodded thoughtfully. Then he turned suddenly to Abigail. "Let me explain something to you," he said to her. "I am the highest-ranking white police officer in the country. I am the only survivor among the senior police officers from apartheid days. And I am only here because the present administration needs experienced officers and in the old days I refused to be transferred to the security branch. In fact, I refused to cooperate with them. To say that my position is insecure would be an understatement. But this is what I am—a policeman. All my life I have been one. I can do nothing else. I want to do nothing else. If I set off on some adventure to arrest a former hero of the liberation struggle without authority and without any real evidence to back me up, how long do you think I will last?"

"If you don't, Leon will die the day after tomorrow," she said simply.

"You believe this, Yudel?" Freek asked.

"I believe that if he is in the hands of the man who has been doing these killings, he will certainly die on the twenty-second."

"The man? One man?"

"This thing is a compulsion," Yudel said. "Only individuals behave compulsively. And it was just one man who came to pick up Lourens. Any official body would have sent more than one."

Freek looked from one to the other. This was not something he wanted to hear, but everything in him, all his life, prevented him from turning away from it. "Is there a photograph of this man?"

Abigail took the one, grainy, partly obscured picture from her bag and handed it to Freek. "This is not going to do much good." He looked at Abigail.

"Are you prepared to be there?"

Looking at her, Freek could see that she would have preferred being almost anywhere else tonight. Her response was not immediate, but eventually she nodded. "Can Robert, my husband, come?"

"He's the newspaperman?"

"I'll tell him he's coming for me, not the story."

"Okay. We'll try to keep you hidden."

"I also want Yudel to come."

"Don't worry about Yudel," Freek said. "If we try to keep him away, he'll just buy a ticket."

Yudel was looking from one to the other, listening to them discussing him.

"Yudel has instinct," Abigail said.

Yudel nodded in agreement. It was always good to be appreciated.

"I know he does," Freek said, grinning briefly at him.

"So you'll do it?"

Freek raised a hand that was clearly intended to stop her getting ahead of where he was prepared to go. "What I'll do is interrupt the national commissioner, who is at this moment having a private meeting with associates. And he doesn't like being interrupted when he's busy with important matters. I'll interrupt him and ask his permission. That's as far as I'll go." He rose suddenly. "Let's go back to my office."

Abigail and Yudel followed Freek to his office. "Will you let me know what he says?" Abigail asked.

Freek was already dialing. "I'll do better than that. You're coming with me to see him."

"Is he in his office?" Abigail asked.

"No, but I know where to find him."

They drove in Yudel's car, with Freek in the passenger seat next to him and Abigail in the back. Freek was right about where to find the commissioner. The club was outside the city, shielded from the road by a dense screen of trees and shrubs. The lawns and flowerbeds were beautifully kept, and the cars in the parking lot bore names like Mercedes, Lexus and Maserati. Few would have cost their owners less than half a million rands.

The building itself was low and wide, glass-fronted across a reception and restaurant area. A few couples were seated at tables or on couches, drinking expensive spirits mixed with various soft drinks to limit the effect.

The commissioner was at a table overlooking a pool filled with sparkling water, but empty of humans. Three of his companions were prominent white businessmen who needed influence in the right government circles and were prepared to do what they had to, to get it. The fourth was a young black man, the only one wearing a suit and tie. He was taking notes.

The commissioner looked only vaguely annoyed at the appearance of Freek, Abigail and Yudel. The young man, who since graduating in law had been the commissioner's personal assistant, leaped to his feet and came to meet them. "If you'll wait in the restaurant, the commissioner will join you shortly," he told them.

They went back into the building and found a table that looked out over the lawns. "The great do not like to be disturbed while they are deciding our fate," Freek said, then added after a moment's thought, "or should it be fates?"

"Either will do," Yudel said.

"The complexities of the English language confuse me sometimes."

A waiter came unsmilingly toward them. "The car we came in gave us away," Freek said. "He must have seen Yudel's Toyota. If we're going to frequent this place, you'll have to buy a Mercedes, Yudel. If we'd come in a Mercedes or a Lexus, still better a Jaguar, he would have been smiling."

The waiter arrived at the table, still showing no pleasure at their presence. "Would you like something to drink?" he asked, his tone not hiding his lack of interest.

"Yes," Freek said. "We would like something to drink, if it's not too much trouble."

"No trouble at all, sir," the waiter mumbled morosely.

An hour after the drinks had arrived and their glasses had long since been emptied, the commissioner had still not come. "His *boytjie* said he was going to be here shortly," Freek said.

"He needs to come now," Abigail said.

"He'll come," Yudel said.

"Freek needs to prepare," Abigail said. "He needs to come now."

"Take it easy," Yudel said.

But Abigail felt that she was too close now to take it easy. "I'll give him five minutes, then I'm going to get him."

"You stay put," Freek said.

"How can he treat us this way? I'm a senior government official too." Her chest was heaving with indignation. "So is Freek," she said to Yudel. "And you are an important consultant to the Department of Correctional Services. I come from a family with a history in the struggle. My parents died in the struggle. Who does he think he is?" Every argument she raised increased her indignation. She was on her feet now, the five minutes she was going to give him forgotten already.

"Sit down," Freek said.

"You sit down, if that's what you want," Abigail told him. She turned and started toward the courtyard where the commissioner was either entertaining or being entertained. In a moment she was out of sight, through the doors at the back of the restaurant.

"Why are women so difficult?" Freek asked Yudel. "And so different?"

"The Almighty has decreed it so," Yudel said philosophically. He liked the sound of his own wisdom.

"What do you suppose He was thinking at the time?" Freek wondered.

A minute passed, then another, and Yudel wondered aloud if they should go in search of Abigail, a sort of rescue mission.

"I have but one career to give for my country," Freek said. "Let's wait."

The doors through which Abigail had left swung open and she came in, followed by the commissioner. This time he looked more amused than annoyed. "It takes a woman," Yudel said.

Freek and Yudel rose and remained standing until both Abigail and the commissioner were seated, then they too sat down. "Freek," he nodded. "And Mr. Gordon, I think. I hope this is going to be worth messing up my meeting."

"I think so, sir," Freek said. "Abigail, you'd better tell the commissioner your story."

Abigail did as Freek had suggested, but unlike Freek, the commissioner stopped her after just a few minutes. "Come with me, Abigail," he said. "I want a word with you in private."

Freek and Yudel watched them go, once again in the direction of the courtyard. "And now? What's this all about?" Freek asked, not expecting an answer. "Is this an all-black thing that we are not allowed to know about?"

In the courtyard, the commissioner was waving Abigail to a seat. "You're Tom Bukula's daughter, right?"

"Yes, sir." Abigail tried to sound like a nice, humble African girl.

"I knew your father in the struggle days."

"I know."

"So what are you doing with these two old boys, these refugees from the old regime?" The smile on his face held a demanding element.

"They're the only ones who have agreed to help me so far."

"I'm not sure that it looks good, you traveling around with these two old white guys."

"Commissioner, this is more important than how anything looks." She was losing the humble African girl thing.

"The only reason that no one else is helping you is because there are serious matters facing the country at this moment."

"I know."

"What you don't know is how serious these matters are."

"I do."

He looked at her with an expressionless face. Even the smile had gone. "I doubt it."

Abigail wanted to shout at him that she knew about the deputy president and that no one in high office was able to think about anything else, but it was Robert who had told her about it and he had sworn her to silence.

"This is about Michael Bishop, isn't it?" So far she had not mentioned his name. The surprise must have shown in her face. "He's not just a problem to you," the commissioner said. "He could be an embarrassment to the entire movement. He has never subjected himself to the discipline of the movement. Tell me what you want."

"I want deputy commissioner Jordaan to set a trap for him tonight."

"You know where he's going to be?"

"We think we do."

"Where?"

For an instant Abigail recoiled from the idea of telling the commissioner. How do I know where your sympathies lie? she wondered. How did you guess about Michael Bishop? "In Diepsloot, with an old comrade of Bishop who lives there," she lied.

"And Gordon, where does he come in?"

"I met him by chance," she lied again, "and he led me to Jordaan."

"Jordaan's an effective policeman," the commissioner said. "He'll set a trap as well as anyone. And I'll arrange the warrant. There are still a few pliable magistrates who will take my word that this is necessary. Freek will have to pick it up. Let's go back to your new friends."

After they left the club and the commissioner had returned to further discussions with the business community, they traveled in silence for a few minutes. Then Freek asked, "And this Diepsloot business he was talking about?"

"I told him that's where we're setting the trap," Abigail said.

"You lied to the commissioner?"

"Yes."

"My God, woman. I'm on his staff. I'm only doing this because he agreed to it."

"I know." Abigail clamped her teeth together and clasped her hands tightly to keep them steady. "You can tell him later that the information I supplied changed during the afternoon. You have to understand that I don't know where his sympathies lie. Not everyone who was in the struggle will care about stopping this man from killing Leon."

27

The pain in Leon Lourens's back and shoulders had been growing throughout the two nights and one day since he had been abducted. He had been given enough food and water, but since he had been in this place he had been untied just three times, once for only seconds and that had ended in a loss of consciousness.

The first time he had been untied he had tried to remove the blindfold. Before his hands had reached it he had been seized from behind, an arm closing around his neck so quickly that there was no chance of resisting. The blood supply to his brain was cut off by pressure on the carotid artery, and in a moment all consciousness was gone.

When he awoke he found himself tied to the chair again. After being left that way for another ten hours and having urinated twice in his pants, he did not try to resist again. On the other occasions his hands had been freed just long enough for him to eat and perform the necessary ablutions.

The blindfold that covered his eyes had been taped to his face and forehead and had not once been removed in the time that he had been there. Not the smallest gleam of light penetrated the blindfold at any time. He was certain that the room was in complete darkness.

He was tied to a wooden chair, his arms drawn back tightly

by the rope and fastened to the backrest, his hands tied tightly together. His ankles were tied to the chair legs. Any movement was impossible.

The strangest aspect of his abduction was that he did not even remember seeing the face of the man who had taken him. When he had come into Leon's workshop, he had been silhouetted against a bright afternoon sky. When Leon was led to the car he had tried to see the other man's face, but it was turned away. It was as he slipped into the passenger seat that Leon lost consciousness. When he regained consciousness he was blindfolded and tied to the chair.

No one had spoken to Leon during the time he had been there. He could smell the food and hear it being put down on a second chair. The bucket he was to use for defecating was handed to him in silence.

At no time did he know how many people were in the room with him or if he was alone. Although he had listened for it, he had never heard a door open or close. But he had heard other sounds. He had heard breathing again, very soft, but clearly in the same room and only occasionally. Time had passed, often hours before he heard the breathing again, but whether his captor had left and returned or had simply moved farther away, he had no way of judging.

Once on the first day, after hearing the breathing louder than before, he had tried to reason with his captor, explaining about Abigail and how he had never agreed with the indiscriminate killings of the apartheid regime. He had tried to tell his captor that he had been moved to ordinary duties because his seniors had felt that he could not be trusted with special operations.

To none of it was there any response. When he had finished speaking he listened for the breathing to see if he was reaching anyone, but this time he heard nothing.

When reasoning failed, Leon's anger had grown. He had roared at the injustice of this imprisonment, shouting that whoever they were they did not know who their enemies were, that he had a wife and children, and could they tell him who would care for them? The roaring had only lasted a few seconds before a gag was slipped skilfully and firmly into his open mouth and part of the way down his throat. It was clear that more shouting would only dislodge it further, suffocating him.

The attempt at reason had failed and his anger had lasted only a few hours. The state of mind that accepted his own death as inevitable came surprisingly quickly. If he had been able to judge the time, he would have known that, after only twelve hours since he had first been tied to the chair, he had given up any thought of survival.

He had occasionally heard the wind in trees and more than once he thought that he had heard a car hooting. It was clear that he was not in the suburbs, but that there was road traffic not far away. It was also clear that he was the one chosen to die this year. He had been abducted on the nineteenth and, even without a view of daylight, it now had to be at least the twentieth. Leon Lourens had no doubt that he had less than forty-eight hours to live.

To Leon, the prospect of death had never been frightening. He was an uncomplicated man who believed that he had done the best he could in life and that he had done no wrong serious enough that atonement might be necessary. He believed that there was sure to be a life after death and that God was certainly good. He had nothing to fear.

Only one aspect of his approaching death caused him pain. Without him, Susanna and the children would suffer terribly. It was true that they had Susanna's half-brother, but he and his family were also not wealthy people. They would try to help, but they were probably also struggling to keep their own heads above water. He knew that the new South Africa was not a good place for those white people who were not able to look after themselves. His family was fairly secure as long as he was alive, but what would they do after he died? He tried not to think about it.

28

The city hall was an old building by the standards of Johannesburg, one of the world's youngest cities. It stood in the center of
the original part of the city. It was made of brown stone and
had the clock tower, the broad staircases, the intricate system
of passages, entrances and exits that reflected the architecture
of the early twentieth century. Besides the theater, the building also housed the city's main library and various municipal
offices. People attending the concert would be able to park in a
broad basement parking garage and enter the lobby from there.
It was not an easy building in which to set a trap.

Deputy commissioner Freek Jordaan, wearing the dress suit
and bow tie of the impresario's staff, was on site by three in the
afternoon, five hours before the start of the performance. After
the meeting with the commissioner, he had spent almost an
hour with Abigail trying to understand why she was so certain
that Bishop was the most likely suspect. Most of all, it was the
method of killing that persuaded him. Garrotting the victim
with piano wire was not a method of killing he had ever come
across in his career and it was certainly not a method in which
soldiers of the liberation movement had been trained.

Thirty of his officers, all wearing overalls and carrying furniture, posters, banners and equipment, trickled in during the
next hour. They all gathered in the theater: Freek, a captain,

four lieutenants, seven sergeants, some inspectors and the rest constables. Twenty years before, all the men for a mission of this sort would have been white. Now two-thirds were Africans. Ten of the officers were women.

Copies of the photograph of Michael Bishop had been handed to all of them. "Take a good look at it," Freek said in English. In years past he would have been addressing them in Afrikaans, but many saw that language as being part of the system of oppression they had endured for so long. "I know it's not much to recognize him by, but that's all we have. His name is Michael Bishop, and we will be arresting him on suspicion of murder."

He pointed to the rows of seats for the choir and spoke to Captain Nkobi. "Who will be in the choir?"

The captain gestured toward two of the inspectors. "Salaala and van Dyk, sir."

Freek took a few steps toward the two officers. "You've got to look like you're singing, understand?"

"Sir," Salaala said in a sharp affirmative. Van Dyk nodded.

"Have you ever heard this sort of music?"

"Yes, sir. I sing in our church choir," Salaala said. "Once a year we do a Handel concert."

"Not ever, sir," van Dyk said. "I don't know what it sounds like."

"Well, just look like you're singing."

"May I join in the singing?" Salaala asked. "I'm a bass," he added. "You need bass voices in Handel."

"Do you know this *Samson* stuff?" Freek asked.

"No, but I catch on quickly. I . . ."

A light, anxious voice broke in from the doorway. "No, no, commissioner, please." It was the impresario, a small man whose long gray hair fringed a neat, pink bald patch. "The choirmaster . . ."

"It was just a thought," Freek said. To Salaala, he said, "No singing. Keep your concentration where it belongs." Before Salaala could voice his disappointment, Freek, who had immediately forgotten the impresario, moved still closer until he was almost touching Salaala and van Dyk. His eyes seemed to have darkened and his face had taken on an angular look that forbade any possibility of humor. "From the stage you will have the best view of all. The lights above the audience will be at full strength as the audience comes in and, after that, they will not go down as far as they normally do. You should be able to make out faces better than anyone else."

His attention turned to the others. "Let's see the twenty who will be in the audience." Ten men and ten women, who would be attending as couples, stepped forward. "The seat positions are as planned?" he asked one of the captains.

"All except the two on the side aisle in row six. We had to move them back to row seven. There were people in those seats."

"Good enough. The other eight will be in the foyer and garage, dressed either in municipal uniforms or in the penguin suits supplied by the organizers." He scrutinized his team, one officer at a time. The senior men had all been chosen by him personally and the others chosen by them. "This man is very dangerous," he told them. "I am told that there isn't one of us who could deal with him one-to-one. I want no dead heroes among us. We have all been carefully chosen and we all know what to do. So do it—according to the book. I have complete faith in all of you." He paused for them to think about what he had said. "Are there questions?"

"The photograph, sir. It's not good." It was van Dyk speaking.

"I know. It's the only one there is. And another thing, it's at least twenty years old. Bishop will be pushing fifty by now."

"And this old guy will be too much for one of us to handle?" one of the younger officers asked.

"I'm told so. Let's not try it out."

"Can we know anything about the suspect?" van Dyk asked.

"Only what I've told you. He is highly trained and very dangerous in close combat." Freek knew that, despite their numbers, he was endangering all of them. "On no account draw attention to yourself by turning and surveying the rest of the audience. Each one is positioned to see part of the audience without turning. Don't try to do more than your share. As for communication, you can speak very softly and still be heard over the audio system. Only do it when you have to. The communications center is in a small office behind the theater. I will be in the foyer, greeting guests as they come in. I will try to shake hands with everyone. I hope that I will be able to spot him on the way in."

"Do we expect him to be alone?" The question came from the captain who had spoken earlier.

"Almost certainly. He is known to be a loner." He paused, again looking over the team for the evening's activities. "I believe that if he is here tonight we will surprise him. He has no reason to believe that we may be waiting for him."

"He will definitely be here?" The question came from a female constable.

Less than fifty percent, Freek thought, maybe less than a twenty percent chance. But he could not afford to have them relaxing with the idea that their target may not turn up. "Without question," he said. "Two more things: all the emergency fire exits will be locked in defiance of the fire regulations. The only way out will be through the front door. Also, we have one person who has seen him face-to-face before. This person will be seated in a box from which the whole theater is visible."

After he had finished, the team was dispersed with their orders for the evening. Those who would be dressed as staff were to be back by six and the members of the audience were to drift in between seven and half-past. Freek held back Captain Nkobi, who was to be in charge in the theater, and the lieutenant, who would head the team in the lobby and garage. "Spotting him will not be easy. Pick up every possible suspect. If we arrest six and let them all go with an apology, that will be better than missing him. I want him. If he is in this theater tonight, I want to bring him in. Do you understand?"

After Nkobi and the lieutenant had assured Freek that they understood, they too were sent away with instructions to be back when the time came. Left alone in the theater, Freek looked around. It was gloomy and shadowed, only a few lights near the stage left burning. He had done this sort of thing before, but never in a place like this and never with this many men. And, in the past, only with common criminals. Michael Bishop was something different—the circumstances were different and the venue was very different. It was going to be an interesting evening. He had a feeling that it may be more interesting than anyone could imagine.

29

The parking attendant examined the three tickets Robert Mokoapi offered him for only a moment before allowing them into the garage. To Abigail, he gave the impression of having done it many times before. On other days he was known as Inspector Nkomo, but he had mastered ticket-examining after just a few minutes of training.

She watched Robert as he followed the directions of the parking garage staff, another one of whom was also a policeman. She spoke to Yudel who was seated directly behind her. "How many men does Freek have here tonight?"

"Thirty," Yudel said.

"Do you know where they'll be positioned?"

"We've already passed two."

"How can you tell?"

She felt Robert lay one of his large hands on hers. "Relax," he said. "They know what they're doing."

"Freek described his planning to me," Yudel said as Robert parked the car and switched off the engine. "But let's wait a minute. It's still forty-five minutes before the advertised time. Let's wait a few minutes before we go in. Freek will be in the lobby and one of his men will show us to our box. We'll be safe. There'll be a guard just inside the door of the box."

It was ten minutes before they left the car, walked the length of the parking garage, climbed the steps to street level, crossed Rissik Street where more policemen, dressed in the impresario's uniform, were watching over the arrivals, and passed into the theater lobby. As Yudel had said, Freek, immaculate in his tuxedo, was shaking hands with two middle-aged women who had just arrived. "Delighted to meet you," Abigail heard him say. "Remember that there's a complimentary glass of wine, sponsored by Nederburg, in the upstairs lobby after the first act."

Behind Freek, in the entrance to the manager's office, a worried-looking man in a business suit, the impresario who had organized the performance, watched Freek's performance. He had tried to object to the presence in his theater of a squad of policemen, few of whom had ever heard of Handel. "Would you prefer a mass murderer and no policemen in your theater?" Freek had asked him. It had been a short discussion.

"Thank you very much. That's lovely," one of the ladies was saying to Freek.

"Very good of you," the other added.

The two ladies moved on and Freek smiled at Abigail. At the same moment a voice spoke at her shoulder. "Welcome to tonight's performance." The speaker was a tall man with dark, prematurely graying hair. He, too, was wearing a tuxedo. "Mr. Gordon's party, I believe. Let me show you to your seats."

Abigail followed him up the stairs to the higher level. She glanced back once to see Robert just behind on her left, and Yudel another pace farther back on her right. By the time they reached the box another policeman had joined them. When they entered, he followed and took up a position in the shadows next to the closed door.

The seat that been chosen for Abigail was in the box's back row with Yudel and Robert on either side. Her seat was in darkness, hiding her almost completely from the theater below. Down below there were only eight people in the theater, but others were starting to arrive, in twos, threes and fours. A few of the men were in business suits, but most were dressed casually, in turtleneck sweaters or windbreakers, with slacks and shoes that did not lace up. The women too seemed to have come to listen to the music rather than to display themselves. So far, everyone was part of a group. No one had come alone.

As Freek had promised, the lights over the stalls were brighter than usual. Abigail found that she could see the faces far more clearly than she had expected. A quick glance around the theater seemed to indicate that he could not yet be there. He would surely be alone. Yudel took a pair of opera glasses from one of his jacket pockets and passed them to her. She tried them and in the relatively good light of the theater she studied one face after the other. The glasses drew each face up close to her in distinct focus.

Twenty years is a long time, she thought. But if I see his face, I will know it. One clear view of him, no matter how much he has changed, and I will know it.

She felt Robert's hand on her knee. On the other side Yudel was moving restlessly, also studying the people below. She was suddenly very grateful to the two men, her Robert and this strange man on her other side. They were great guys. Neither of them were violent men. She knew neither would last more than a second or two with Michael Bishop, but here they were, shielding her on both sides. A couple of heroes, she thought, each a tough guy in his own way.

Yudel leaned across and fiddled with the bodice of her dress. "Take it easy there, fella, I'm watching you," Robert whispered so softly that Yudel could only just hear it.

"I'm just . . . I'm just . . ." Yudel struggled with the thin wire that was hidden in the front of Abigail's dress and managed to get her microphone switched on.

"I've got my eye on you, man," Robert murmured.

Despite the circumstances, or perhaps because of them, Abigail felt a giggle rising inside her and had to suppress it. "Now, now, boys," she whispered.

Yudel too had to stifle a chuckle. "No more talking," he managed to get out. "We're live to the communications center now."

The stream of people coming up from the parking garage

became a steady flow. In the lobby, Freek was still trying to shake every hand and look into every pair of eyes. He had the sure belief that if he looked into the face of this man, he would know him. His life as a policeman had schooled his senses so that now it was almost impossible to lie to him successfully. When the stream of arrivals became too dense and he missed someone, Captain Nkobi stepped forward quickly to welcome the person. He, too, studied the faces of each new arrival.

An athletic-looking man in his fifties entered alone from the parking area. Freek moved forward with outstretched hand. Before the man reached him a woman of about the same age, surrounded by three teenage girls, had caught up to him. One of the girls had him by an arm and was whispering something that made him laugh.

"Welcome to this evening's performance," Freek said. "Don't forget the free glass of wine at the end of the first act."

"We'll be there," the man said.

There were more young couples than Freek would have expected—some groups of ladies, a television actor that Freek recognized, middle-aged people, also in groups or couples, the city's mayor and others, drawn together by their love of the music. Another smallish man of about the right age and build entered the lobby. Freek moved forward and offered his hand. The man shook it and Freek looked searchingly into an unlined, blandly innocent face that squinted back at him through thick-lensed glasses.

The police couples in the audience had been in position half an hour before the start of the performance. They were all doing exactly what Freek had instructed them to do, studying everyone seated in their field of vision and the new arrivals as they came in, and all without turning around or making any noticeable movement.

Abigail watched as the members of the orchestra entered the pit and started making the discordant sounds that went with tuning their instruments. A little burst of violin music sliced through the other sounds, a foretaste of better things to come. With ten minutes to go, the arrivals had diminished to no more than a trickle. Only the occasional party was coming from the parking garage now.

So far, just one couple had come in directly off the street. All the other members of the audience had come in from the parking garage.

A man of perhaps eighty, walking with a cane and leaning on the shoulder of a young woman, perhaps a granddaughter, came in slowly from the parking garage and allowed Freek to shake their hands and study their faces. "Will you be able to find your seats?"

They would be able to find their seats, thank you, good of you to ask.

Captain Nkobi and two other men were in the lobby with him. He waved to Nkobi to come closer. He spoke softly. "Thoughts?" he asked.

"He's not here," the captain said. "Definitely not."

"Okay," Freek said. "To your post and believe that he is here. Above everything, let your men believe that. Remember that he's no ordinary criminal."

Something did not feel right to Freek. There was no logical reason for him to believe it, only the inner uneasiness that he rarely ignored. When he had, it had always been to his cost. He agreed with his captains that Bishop had not come through the lobby, and he knew that there was no other entrance. Or could there be? One of his lieutenants had entered the theater at the back to give himself a view of the entire place. Nkobi was in the lobby. Soon the choir would enter and the men in the choir would have a clear view of the stalls. The boxes had all been filled with private parties, leaving no room for anyone extra. Also, Freek's men on the upper level had searched the boxes earlier and watched the members of the audience entering them.

That left the emergency exits. Freek followed the hallway that encircled the theater on the lower level, checking again that the emergency exits were secure. Each one was solidly locked and did not yield a millimeter when he tried to budge it. Then he took the stairs to the upper level and did the same. The doors were as solid as those below.

Please, Lord, Freek prayed. Let us not have a fire tonight. Bishop or no Bishop, let's not have a fire. One of the lieutenants, who had been positioned on that side of the theater, had the keys for the emergency exits, but in the chaos of a fire they were unlikely to get more than one open in time.

In her seat, any small excitement Abigail may have felt, any amusement at Robert's murmured teasing, had fallen away. Now there was just a chill that went beyond ordinary physical coldness. It did not begin in the extremities, the way the cold of a winter night might grip you. This coldness came from within, a deep numbness somewhere in her chest and slowly spreading through her.

Through the opera glasses she had studied every face in the theater. And now she was no longer as sure as she had been earlier. Perhaps he could be the thick-set man, sitting alone in the back row. People changed. In twenty years they changed a lot. Then there were two others, a slight man with a woman, but he looked too young. There was also a dark-haired man of average build, with an older man.

Not impossible, she thought, looking at each of them. The microphone rested where Yudel had switched it on, just inside the neckline of her dress, but she remained silent.

I will know him, she thought. I will certainly know him when I see him. I am certain. Perhaps I am certain. If only I could get rid of this feeling of cold. She leaned against Robert, but the cold was everywhere inside her. There was no ridding herself of it.

30

The windows of the prop storeroom had been painted over many years before, covering the glass with a grimy, cracking coating that had once been cream in color. Despite the paintwork, the windows still let in some light from the street and surrounding buildings.

A row of figures, manikins dressed in the outfits of eighteenth-century pirates, vestiges of an ancient *Peter Pan* pantomime, would have been silhouettes against the dull glow of a window to anyone who came in at the door. No one did, so no one saw them or that one of the figures, this one dressed in the nondescript clothing of the early twenty-first century, moved from his position near the window toward the door.

Michael Bishop had been in the storeroom since early afternoon. He had waited without moving for almost six hours. Now he waited until, faintly in the distance, he heard the applause that marked the entrance first of the choir, then the soloists and, finally, the conductor. Then he waited still longer until he heard the overture begin.

Stepping out of the storeroom into a narrow passage, he closed the door carefully behind him. For a few seconds he stood quite still in the doorway, making sure that he was alone. The wariness he felt was something that never left him, no matter where he went or what he did. And he knew that at any time the authorities could decide that yesterday's hero had become today's problem. To Bishop there was no one who could be trusted and no set of circumstances that was entirely innocent.

The passage led into the broader one that surrounded the theater and off which a number of doors opened. Again he waited a long moment. A man in a tuxedo came out of the theater and moved away from him toward the lobby. Bishop watched him go, then started in the other direction, this time walking quickly, a patron who was late for the start of the performance.

The overture had ended and the tenor was singing, his voice light and clear. Bishop passed the doors at the back of the theater, knowing that they were too far from his seat. He stopped briefly at an emergency fire exit, tried the handle and found the door locked. Farther along the hallway, another emergency exit was locked. He wondered vaguely if this meant anything, or if it was simply incompetence.

He had reached the entrance to the theater that was closest to his seat when he saw the last emergency exit and its door that was standing slightly ajar. He entered the theater opposite the fifteenth row where his seat had been booked and waited briefly in the shadow of a deep doorway. The theater was brighter than he had expected, but it made little difference. The lights would be going up between the acts anyway.

The seat number on his ticket gave him the last seat in the row. But next to his seat were two empty ones and then a young couple who were clearly entranced by the music. He moved quickly past his own seat and sat down next to the man, reached across and shook his hand. "Apologies for being late," he whispered.

Three rows back one of the police couples had seen him enter, a lone man, slight of build, possibly fiftyish, exactly what they had been told to watch for. But then they saw him take the seat next to the couple and shake the hand of the man, clearly a friend. The female officer looked at her partner, but he was shaking his head, a barely perceptible movement. This could not be their man.

Up in her box, Abigail had also seen him. She had seen the side door of the theater open and close, a barely visible movement against the dim light in the hallway. She had seen the quick, light way that he moved, and the sudden movement of his handshake. She knew that the handshake meant nothing. If you offered to shake the hand of a stranger, that person would usually respond. She knew who it was with as much certainty as she had ever possessed about anything, all her life. "He's here," she told Yudel, speaking so softly that he was not sure that she had spoken at all.

Yudel slid from his seat in a crouch, trying to stay in the shadows. He waited for Abigail and Robert outside the box. "Where's Freek?" she gasped as she reached him, with Robert close behind.

"Downstairs," Yudel said.

From the top of the stairs, Abigail could see that Captain Nkobi had his firearm drawn and was aiming it at a short, broad-shouldered man. One of the other policemen was cuffing his hands behind his back. She could hear the man's voice, menacing, but not raised. "Have you people gone completely fucking mad?"

"This way," the captain said. He had the man by the arm and was propelling him into the manager's office.

"You bastards are going to pay for this." The voice was raised a little higher now. "Consider this the basis for a front-page news story."

As Abigail reached the bottom of the stairs, the door to the manager's office slammed closed. One of the policemen in a tuxedo stepped in front of it to block the entrance. "You've got the wrong man," Abigail told him. "The man you're looking for is inside."

"The captain's questioning him," the sentry said.

"This is lunacy." Abigail had grabbed the lapels of the tuxedo and was trying to pull him out of the way. "Where's Deputy Commissioner Jordaan?"

"I don't know, ma'am. Let the captain do his work."

Yudel joined the discussion. "You'd better stand aside. This lady is the only one who's ever seen the suspect and she has just identified him inside the theater." The façade of complete assurance that is the territory of every police officer in charge of a situation began to crack and the first flicker of uncertainty crossed his face. "You're going to be in big trouble if he gets away," Yudel added.

The officer opened the door and turned to enter, but Abigail was already pushing past him. "Who the hell is this now?" The handcuffed man spat out the words in disgust. He was wearing a carefully tailored leather jacket over a silk shirt. It was not the sort of outfit you would have found on a poor man.

The captain had also turned toward the door. He looked determined. If this was their man, he was not going to release him easily.

"This isn't the man." Abigail tried to keep her voice down. It would be a disaster if the sound of the argument should reach into the theater.

"Thank you, ma'am," the handcuffed man said. "I don't know who you are, but it's pleasing, under these circumstances, to meet someone who is not a complete moron."

"I'm sorry," Abigail said. "This is just a mistake. I apologize."

"Then I trust I can be set free. My name is Lee McKenzie. I am the chairman of Gauteng Fiber Boards. We can still ignore this matter if it is resolved immediately."

The captain was looking at Abigail. He looked as uncertain as the man who had been guarding the door. "He's inside the theater. I saw him," Abigail told him. "This is not the man."

In the fifteenth row of the theater Michael Bishop was not enjoying the music. The choir was singing vigorously, but he had come to realize that two of its members were silent. They were both making a pretense of singing but, to his eyes, it was a poor pretense. He had noticed the one on his side of the theater first and then started examining the others. After that he studied the other members of the audience. A couple seated four rows in front of him were not touching each other and seemed to be watching the audience to their left and probably in front as well. As far as he could tell, they seemed to have no interest in the music. On the far side of the theater he found another such couple. They were looking across the theater toward the side where he was sitting, but ahead of him. As far as he could see, they never once looked at the stage. Five or six rows ahead of them another couple were behaving in much the same way. Bishop rested back in his seat.

Without turning his head he looked toward the doorway through which he had entered. It was empty and, beyond that, there was the emergency exit that he had seen where the door was open.

In the lobby, Lee McKenzie had been released and had accepted the briefest apology. "But don't go back into the theater, not yet," Captain Nkobi told him. "I don't know where Commissioner Jordaan is," he said to Abigail. "The last time I saw him, he was going upstairs toward the boxes."

"Christ," McKenzie said, sitting down on a couch against one of the walls. "What the fuck is this? I can't believe it."

Abigail did not hear him. She was again talking to the captain. "You can't wait, captain. I'll point him out to you."

The captain nodded. As he followed Abigail, he collected his men from their posts. "Two will go down the center aisle," he said softly, "to cut off that path. Two others will come with me through the side door to make the arrest."

Inside the theater, Michael Bishop knew that he had already waited too long. The signs were there. How they could have known was of no interest to him, only that it appeared they did know.

Some thirty seconds later the captain, Abigail and the two officers stepped into the theater. It took a moment for Abigail's eyes to become accustomed to the semidarkness. For a second she thought that she must be looking at the wrong row. But it was only a moment, then she realized that the seat he had been occupying was empty.

"Yes," the captain whispered through his teeth. "Which one is he?"

"He's gone."

"Christ, was he ever here?"

"Yes, he was there, in that seat."

"There was a man here." It was the voice of the man whose hand Bishop had shaken.

A male voice from one of the nearby seats sounded irritated. "Could you pipe down? Some of us came for the music."

Michael Bishop was pushing closed the emergency exit through which he had just passed, so that there would be no obvious trace of his flight. He went quickly down a single flight of a fire escape, but not so quickly that he might risk stumbling. His senses were tingling with the possibility of pursuit. He felt no sense of victory, only the animal fear that comes with the need to flee.

He reached ground level in a narrow alley. The street was no more than thirty meters away. Once he got there he would turn left, then left again at the first corner and disappear into the jumble of streets and alleys that made up the eastern part of the inner city.

He walked quickly, knowing that if there was a policeman at the end of the alley, it would be important not to run. There would be other people on the pavements around the city hall, and they would be walking. A running figure would only draw attention.

Ahead, and partly hidden by a corner of the city hall, was a street lamp. It was close enough that he held up a hand to shield his eyes. A ragged street urchin, probably a homeless child, ran past the entrance to the alley. He was followed by another, almost as ragged. Bishop's eyes followed them for only an instant, but it was too long an instant. In front of him something flashed in the light from the street and his consciousness exploded in a shower of sparks.

Freek Jordaan stepped away from the wall, massaging the knuckles of his right hand. He bent over and handcuffed the unconscious body of Michael Bishop. Can't handle him one-to-one? he thought. Whatever gave them that idea?

From the main entrance to the lobby Abigail saw the growing

crowd of policemen around Freek in the mouth of the alley. For a moment the excited knot of men parted and she caught a glimpse of the figure on the ground. It looked limp, almost lifeless. And yet she could move no closer. She saw Yudel walking down the pavement toward the alley, but as she felt Robert's left arm around her shoulders, she moved closer to him.

31

It was just two hours after midnight in the Tshwane West police cells. Michael Bishop had been under interrogation for almost three hours. He answered all questions softly and politely and told his interrogators nothing.

The national commissioner of police had instructed Freek to contact him when the arrest had been made. Freek called him from the alley behind the city hall and listened to the commissioner's instructions. "Remember, he's not just anybody. Nobody touches him. I don't want to hear about bruises later on."

"Yes, commissioner," Freek had said.

"Nothing, you understand?"

"I understand. No one will touch him."

"If you've got nothing, you can still hold him legally for forty-eight hours. By that time it will be the twenty-third."

"I understand."

"Good, then do it."

"Of course, there's still the missing man—Lourens."

"I know."

Now Freek was interrogating Bishop in the police station's only room that was wired for sound. Abigail was with Robert, Yudel, Captain Nkobi and one lieutenant in a small room adjoining the charge office. They were listening to the inter-rogation. In the charge office, two constables and a sergeant, who had been told nothing about the night's activities or about the suspect who was being interrogated in their cells, did their best to look busy while the deputy commissioner was in the building. They had not expected this sort of thing. With luck they may have passed the night quietly, each man taking a turn to keep watch while the others slept.

Most of Freek's questions had concerned the matter of where Bishop had been on October 22 the year before, and the year before that, and still another year earlier and every year, all the way back into the 1980s.

To every question Bishop answered in the same polite, but evasive way. "You can't expect me to know the details of my whereabouts all those years ago, deputy commissioner. This was all long ago. I can't remember what happened on a partic-ular day last year, let alone all these other years you're asking about."

"You do know where you were," Freek said again and again. "And you know that I know."

"You're quite wrong, deputy commissioner."

Freek also explored at length his unorthodox arrival at the concert. He had already established that Bishop had a ticket for the seat he had occupied. "And yet you chose to creep in through some back entrance? Innocent people don't behave that way."

"I arrived early. There was no one at the ticket office. There's nothing unusual in that, is there?"

Freek had interrogated a great many suspects in a long ca-reer, but he had never before met one like Bishop. Every ques-tion was answered and every answer was unfailingly polite. He never once raised his voice or showed any sign of tiredness or irritation. Questioning him was like fighting someone who never struck back, but could absorb your punches in a way that rendered them ineffectual.

Of the people in the police station, most had never heard of

Michael Bishop, and only Abigail had ever heard his voice. She had heard it on one night long before and it had been as even and unemotional then as it was now. But she had heard it many times since then, at night, in the tortured corridors of her dreams. At any time, in all those years, she would immediately have recognized his voice, had she heard it. Alone or in a crowd, at work or at home, in darkness or the bright light of day, she knew that she would have recognized even a single word. Now she listened, transfixed, held by the hypnotic monotone that had been imprinted in her mind.

At the theater Freek had asked her if she would come close to identify Bishop, but although he was still unconscious she would come no closer than twenty paces. "It's him," she had said.

"Are you sure?"

"Yes, I am absolutely sure."

But that had been unnecessary. Bishop had not denied his identity. He had refused to give an address though, saying that he was currently a homeless person, living on the streets. "You are not a homeless person," Freek had said. "Your clothing is clean. You do not carry the marks of a homeless person."

"Nevertheless, I am one."

On the drive back to Pretoria, Yudel had traveled with Freek, following close behind the car in which Bishop was being transported. Abigail had asked Robert to fall back to let the police cars go ahead. "Let's just go home," she had said. "They don't need me anymore."

Robert had nodded in response without saying anything. But before they reached the city she had told Robert rather to go where the police were taking him.

"But you said you wanted to go home."

"Rather go with them."

"But why? They'll do the rest."

"I need to go."

"You need to get away from this."

"No, I need to be there. I must."

"Why?"

"Capturing Bishop was never that important to me. Finding Leon is."

"The police will do it. And Yudel will help."

"I have to go."

But now it seemed to Abigail that after three hours of interrogation, Freek was going nowhere. This sort of questioning would not even get past Bishop's outer defenses. For a moment on the pavement outside Johannesburg's city hall, lying unconscious in the alley, he had looked vulnerable. But it had been only until he regained his senses. Now he was again invincible. Freek was no more than a battering ram against the defenses of a castle that was hopelessly sound. His questioning was a blunt instrument when something far sharper and more penetrating was needed.

Yudel too had tried. After listening to Freek for a while, he believed that he understood at least some part of the puzzle that was Michael Bishop. "Who did it to you?" he asked Bishop.

Bishop looked closely at Yudel and then decided he would not answer any of his questions. "Who made you so ashamed?" Yudel asked.

But an impenetrable wall had descended around the prisoner. Yudel could not know it, but for just a moment the picture of his shame, in the form of the lifeless body of Samuel, hanging from a beam of the tobacco shed's roof, had returned to him with complete clarity. He could not allow Yudel into that part of his life. Now it was shut off from all access by the present. Yudel too was shut out. His remaining questions could have been directed at a statue and had as much effect.

Freek had come back and Bishop had slowly returned to the surface of present consciousness. He at least answered Freek, but to Abigail it seemed he controlled the exchanges. Before she could restrain herself, she had turned to Nkobi. "Let me try," she said.

"The deputy commissioner . . ." he started to say.

"The deputy commissioner is getting nowhere," she interrupted. "Call him out so that I can ask him."

"Do it," Abigail heard Yudel say. "Let Deputy Commissioner Jordaan decide."

It was the sort of suggestion that made sense to someone accustomed to obeying orders. The captain got to his feet and set off to call the deputy commissioner to let him decide.

When Freek returned with the captain, Abigail was on her feet. She did not know if she had a better chance of success than Freek, but she knew that she could never be free until she faced the man in the interrogation room. And then there was Leon. "Let me try," she told him.

Freek seemed to consider the suggestion. He was not accustomed to needing help under any circumstances, but he nodded and stepped aside to let her pass.

"One thing," Abigail said. "I want the sound turned down. I want privacy with him."

"Certainly," Freek said. But it came too quickly.

"Where's the amplifier?"

"Down there." Freek pointed to a metal box, mounted against the wall at ankle level.

"Can it be opened?" She had already found a hinged door and opened it. The components of the amplifier itself were mounted on a plug-in printed circuit board. Abigail extracted the board and slipped it into her bag.

"You're serious about this?" Freek said.

Robert was on his feet. "No, no, this makes no sense . . ."

Freek raised a hand that asked Robert for a moment in which to speak. "Just give me a few moments with the prisoner."

"What are you going to do?" Robert demanded.

"Shackle him. He won't be able to get close to her."

"I don't want him to feel . . ." Abigail was trying to object.

"That's the only way," Freek told her. "He's shackled or you don't go in alone and the sound stays on."

Abigail looked first at Freek, then Robert, before answering. "Shackle him then."

"And you stay on your side of the table," Freek said.

"Very well."

"Promise me that."

"I promise you that I will stay on my side of the table."

After she had entered the interrogation room, Yudel spoke to Freek. "He's the worst kind of psychopath. He will endure anything, suffer any pain, wait as long as it takes, to get his way. You could torture him, even kill him, he will tell you nothing. There is no breaking him, ever."

"I know," Freek said.

When Abigail opened the cell door her eyes immediately met Bishop's. He showed no sign of surprise. If he had not been expecting her, he was certainly not surprised to see her. His hands were cuffed and his ankles shackled so close that they were almost touching. A chain connected the shackles to a heavy bracket on the wall behind him. Freek was taking no chances.

Abigail's was the first to lower her eyes. Bishop's calm, un-blinking stare was just as it had been twenty years before and it was just as impossible for her to meet it for more than a few seconds. She closed the door and sat down on the chair opposite him. Neither had spoken.

Abigail slowly raised her eyes to meet his. Over twenty years, little had changed in the expressionless face that she had not been able to forget. The hair was thinner and beginning to gray, but the face was unlined. "Good evening," she said.

"Good evening." His way of speaking was seemingly without interest, but she knew that he had recognized her the moment she entered the room.

Abigail had to hold tightly on to herself. She knew that she could not afford to shrink for even a second. The Michael Bishops of the world, and thankfully there were not many of them, fed off any sign of weakness in others. Her face was less than a meter from his. She remembered seeing it closer than that, much closer. And even then the eyes had been as they were now, the voice showing as little interest.

Where are you? she thought. You must be in there somewhere, but where? "I did not expect to see you again under these circumstances." To her own ears her voice wavered uncertainly.

Bishop answered with only the faintest nod to suggest that perhaps their meeting this way was a surprise to him too.

"You missed the meeting to honor you last week." She was trying to give her voice a more confident sound, but with little success.

He nodded again, only a vague agreement. Perhaps some things could not be avoided.

"And now you're here, under these circumstances."

Again the little nod, a barely perceptible movement of the head. But this time he spoke. "Memories are short," he said.

She waited for more, but he was again silent. Abigail thought that she understood, though. "Everyone remembers," she said without sympathy. "That's what the meeting was all about."

He paused, apparently considering his response. "But now I am hounded and in chains, if only temporarily."

If only temporarily . . . He was not going to admit to being powerless. Nevertheless, Abigail knew that this was the moment. "Give me Leon and I will try to help."

Now she could see the smallest smile, devoid of humor, distorting the corners of Bishop's mouth. "Is this not just a little arrogant?"

"Arrogant? I don't understand."

"Remember who it was who dealt with the enemy in Ficksburg. Remember who your department was prepared to honor, just last week. Now you are the one who thinks you have the power to keep me here or let me go." The mockery in his voice was unmistakeable.

"You won't be able to escape from here," Abigail heard herself saying. Oh God, she thought, I'm letting him drag me into this.

"Escape will not be necessary. Do you think this apartheid policeman will be allowed to hold me? Do you know what I have done? Do you know who I have worked with?" The message was inescapable. "You were a child and I dealt with your enemies. I was the only one who could deal with them. As I remember, that oh-so-gentle father of yours was not very effective."

Abigail's face felt as if it was on fire. "My father. Don't dare mention his name." She could hear the quivering in her voice. "Someone like you cannot understand . . ." In her anger and confusion she lost the thread of her response. She was not even sure that she knew what response she had intended.

"Not very effective, was he? The idea of a revolution is to kill the ruling class, not to let them kill you. It's as well that he left his life's blood on the floor of that old house. He was the kind that I can imagine being raped by his guards in an apartheid jail."

Abigail was unable to speak. Holding on to consciousness was difficult enough.

"I saved you—I, a true hero of the struggle. Now you imagine that you hold my life in your hands? And you don't see what you are offering me as arrogance?"

I don't know why, Abigail thought, but he wants me to dispute what he is saying.

"You're fighting me now, but you did not fight me in Ficksburg."

He was goading her and it was working. Worst of all was that she felt she was no match for him. And the mention of her father had removed any ability she had to deal with this creature. She could not think of him as a man. Her father had been a man. Robert was a man. Michael Bishop was something entirely different. "Ficksburg was long ago." To her own ears, it seemed an empty response.

"I remember every part of it. I remember it clearly. I remember the little sounds you made and I remember that you did not resist."

"I was a child."

"You were a young woman. You could have resisted. It

would not have helped you, but you could have resisted. You did not though, not at all. You came willingly."

As he spoke, Bishop shifted on his chair, seemingly trying to ease the pressure of the cuffs on his hands. For a moment she saw one of his hands. They were big for a man of less-than-average size, hard and yellowed with calluses across the fingers. They were unlike the hands of any other man she had ever seen. She had forgotten those hands, but now she had a glimpse, less than a second in which she had seen just one of them. To Abigail that brief view was an obscenity, a view of some nakedness that was not for her eyes.

She tried to break free of the direction she felt him driving her. "Just give me Leon Lourens. He saved my life . . ."

The distorted smile was still present on Bishop's face. "I will walk out of here a free man, perhaps today, perhaps tomorrow. But Leon Lourens will die tomorrow. And there is nothing you can do to stop it. And nothing you can do to keep me here."

"I still have a day," Abigail said.

"And you believe you can find him?"

"We found you." Abigail thought she saw the slightest flicker of alarm in Bishop's face. She was aware that it may just have been a reflection of the light or just a muscular twitch that had nothing to do with what she was saying. "I found your old commanding officer and I've been to your old hideout in Magaliesberg." And there it was again, a spasm so small that under any other conditions she would not have noticed it. But perhaps it was nothing. "I'll find him," she told Bishop. "And I'll find him today."

Again he moved awkwardly in his seat and again she could see the hands, the same hard, callused hands that were too big for the rest of the man. "You will not find him. You are not as clever as you think."

Did the voice shake? Or was that also her imagination? And was it possible that this man could ever be unsure of anything? This was not a mind that could see possibilities that existed beyond his own desires. What element of uncertainty could there be in his thoughts? Or am I seeing and hearing something that I want? Abigail asked herself. "I'll find him today," she said, still watching Bishop closely. But this time there was only the emotionless stare of those unblinking eyes.

32

In the hours before sunrise most of Pretoria was still asleep. Only a few cars were moving. They belonged to those who would be unlocking the doors of retail outlets, police going to their posts and assorted insomniacs who had contrived to avoid the tyranny of their beds.

There was no traffic at all on the road to the smallholdings that were spread along the Magaliesberg's south-facing slopes. Yudel was driving and Abigail was in the passenger seat. They had left Freek at the suburban police station where Bishop was being held and had dropped Robert at his paper's local office. Before they left the police station a call had come for him: the deputy president matter had flared up again and it could be today that the head of the National Prosecuting Authority would call in editors for the briefing that was going to change the country. Yudel stopped the car at the place where Abigail had parked two days before.

"I found the old farmhouse that he once used for a hideout," Abigail was saying, "but there was nothing, and yet when I mentioned it I was sure that there was a reaction from him. I want you to help me search the place."

"If you were here earlier and there was nothing, there is not likely to be anything now."

Abigail got out and started for the farm gate that blocked the driveway. Yudel heard her voice faintly through the closed windows of the car. "If you won't come, I'll go alone."

There's no arguing with her, Yudel thought. Poor Robert.

The eastern sky was already brightening. In perhaps an hour the sun would be rising over Pretoria. For now, the hillside where the ruin of the house was located and faced south was still in complete darkness. Stumbling on the uneven surface, Yudel caught up to Abigail halfway to the ruin and grabbed onto an arm, bringing her to a stop. "If your friend is here, he could be under guard," he whispered.

"You keep saying that Michael Bishop must work alone. And we know where *he* is."

"No. I said the compulsion is his. He could have recruited helpers. Or at least one helper. Homicidal pairs who work together are not that rare."

"He came alone for Leon." There was no arguing with that. "Are you coming, Yudel?"

"Yes," Yudel said. "Yes, I'm coming."

Yudel had brought a torch from his car. Nevertheless, in the deep twilight of the early morning, the ruin that had been forbidding in daylight was a tangle of loose floorboards, shattered glass and occasional underbrush. Yudel followed Abigail from room to room, stepping carefully to avoid falling through an ancient, rotting floorboard, then along the broad verandas, into the crawl space under the house and finally through one outbuilding after another.

They had not gone far when she took the torch from him, shining it into every crack and corner. Not only was there no sign of any person, but he could also see no sign that anyone had been living there in years. The only footmarks on the loose sand around the house were those that Abigail herself had left two days before.

Eventually they found themselves in front of the house in an early morning that was still dark enough for the city lights in the middle distance to be bright points in the gloom. "He's not here," Abigail heard Yudel say. "I don't believe that he has been here at all."

"I know, but I had to come back. I had to make sure."

"That's all right."

But for Abigail it was not all right. During the last week, the days had passed for her as if she had an inner alarm, and the knowledge that time was running out was so much a part of her that no timepiece was necessary. Things were not all right. She was afraid that they might never be all right again. She knew that the bold front she had put on for Bishop, telling him that she would find Leon today, was no more than that.

She turned to Yudel, looking for some word of hope, but he looked as desolate as she felt. At that moment her mobile phone rang. She recognized the voice on the other end as that of Susanna Lourens.

"Abigail?"

"Yes. It's Susanna, I think."

"Yes, it's Susanna." Her voice was shaking. To Abigail it sounded like that of a much older woman. "I want you to know . . . I needed to speak to you . . ."

"Yes?" To Abigail's ears, her own voice was surprisingly soft and uncertain.

"My brother, you spoke to my brother on the phone."

"I didn't know who he was."

"He was angry."

"I understand."

"He was angry. I don't think like him. I . . ." Her voice trailed away.

"It's all right."

"It's just. I don't want you . . ." Again her voice seemed to lose momentum.

"It's all right. I understand. It wasn't you on the phone."

"It's just, please . . ."

"I'm not offended, truly."

"Just don't stop looking for him. Please don't stop looking for him." The words were gushing from her like water from a dam where the wall had just collapsed. "Please keep searching for him. Whatever my brother said, it wasn't me. Please don't stop looking for Leon. Please."

"I won't stop. I'm not stopping."

"Please keep searching. Let the police search, let everyone search."

"Susanna, listen," Abigail tried to interrupt. "I won't stop. I won't ever stop. I'm doing everything I can."

"Please, please, please. There's this thing about tomorrow, the twenty-second. Do you know about that?"

"Yes, I know about it."

"Will you find him?"

"I think so."

"Will you find him today?"

"I believe so. I pray so."

"I'm praying too. I'm praying every day. I'm praying all day."

"Pray for all of us," Abigail heard herself saying. "Pray harder than you've ever prayed."

"I am, every moment. Find him, please find him."

After she had ended the conversation, Abigail looked at the ruin they had been searching. The light was a little better now, but the ruin was still a gloomy, forbidding presence. Then she turned to look down at the city where the streetlights were still shining and the buildings were slowly becoming visible. The Union Buildings, away to the left, were a silhouette against the slowly lightening sky. She could now see some of the deep purple avenues of jacarandas that lined almost every street.

Suddenly there was a voice, a full-throated cry that seemed to come from a distance, but grew quickly louder. "Leon, Leon," the voice cried. "Leon, Leon." She heard it again and again, each time more loudly than the time before. She looked toward the car to see where it was coming from, then back at the house. "Leon, Leon." There was deep desperation in the sound.

Yudel had her by an arm and was drawing her toward him. She wondered why he was doing that. "Leon, Leon." She wondered too why the hinges of her jaw were aching. She raised a hand to one side of her face, searching for the pain. "Leon, Leon."

"Abigail," Yudel was saying. "This is not going to help."

The crying for Leon stopped and she was gasping for air in Yudel's arms. "Be calm," he was saying. "Please be calm." He had stopped himself from telling her that everything was going to be all right. He too was doubting it now.

In the place where he was being kept prisoner, Leon Lourens had heard what he was sure was a car, and that it was closer than the other sounds he had heard. But the car sound had stopped suddenly, as if the engine had been switched off. And it had not started again.

Now everything was quiet. It had been a long time since he had last heard the breathing. His captor had either left or moved to a distant part of this place. If there was ever complete silence anywhere, this was it.

Ever since he stopped hoping for rescue, he had been at a sort of peace. It was not a peace that held any sort of contentment. It was rather the peace that came with fatalism. Now the sound of the car threatened to disrupt that. He tried to dampen any thought of rescue. If it did happen, it would happen without his participation. He knew that he could do nothing to free himself.

Then he heard the sound. It was a female voice calling his name. She called again and again, the sound coming from a distance, or perhaps just muffled by the walls of his prison. "Leon, Leon." It was Abigail. He knew it. That he recognized it had to do with more than the sound of her voice. Something deep within the core of him told him that it was Abigail. And she was close by. "Leon, Leon."

In an instant the peace and the fatalism left him. He tried to cry out, but the gag was bound tightly in place and he could produce no more than a muffled protest. Instantly, and without his planning it, his limbs were straining against the rope. "Leon, Leon," he heard it again. The chair bucked and rocked with the power of his efforts. It swiveled for a moment, then fell to the left. Leon landed heavily on his side. He heaved his shoulders upward. Perhaps there was a rope that might slip loose.

There was always the possibility of his captor being there and again attacking him, but he could not think about that now. And it had not happened so far. He must be alone. "Leon, Leon." Where could she be? Lying on its side, the chair bucked and slid on the cement surface of the floor. He reached a wall and kicked against it, trying to achieve some leverage. His arms, shoulders and legs were aching more than before, but for now he could not feel the pain.

Eventually Abigail's voice fell silent, then exhaustion came and Leon lay still on his side on the cold cement floor. He heard the distant sound of the car engine starting and the sound fading as it moved away. The darkness around him again returned to silence.

33

In his cell in block D of C-Max, Marinus van Jaarsveld waited
for what he knew was coming. He sat on his bunk, his head
turned toward the cell door. Someone was moving in the corridor between the cells. He heard the clank of buckets and
stiffened expectantly.

Bringing buckets to the cells this early was not according to
the schedule. The prisoners did the cleaning of both cells and
corridors, but not until at least an hour later. Today the buckets
were being delivered early to avoid the possibility of inspection
by a senior officer.

Van Jaarsveld could hear cell doors opening and buckets
being dropped off. He had heard this many times before and,
by now, was able to judge the warder's progress perfectly. He
heard the door of the cell next to his open, heard the bucket
make contact with the concrete floor and heard the warder
speak. "Fifteen minutes," he said. Then the cell door closed
and a moment later the door of his own cell was opening. The
warder who appeared in the doorway was the same who
had met Annette in Magnolia Glen. "Fifteen minutes," he told
van Jaarsveld.

After the warder had left, van Jaarsveld fetched the bucket
and brought it to his bunk. It took heavy pressure on one side of
the bucket's false bottom before it gave and the opposite side

sprang open. Seizing the false bottom in a strong right hand, he jerked it upward and it came away. In the bottom was the 9 mm Makarov and twenty rounds, just as he had been promised. Under the gun, providing enough padding to stop it rattling, were a white T-shirt and jeans. He filled the clip and slipped the gun, the remaining rounds and the clothing under his mattress. The possibility of a cell inspection today was slight. That had also been arranged.

Van Jaarsveld was not in a hurry. He had been in prison for ten years and he was not going to act rashly now. He knew when the best time would be. Just after the early morning shift change, the gates would be lightly guarded and the minimum number of warders would be present. Most of them would still be in the shift room. It was also then that the gate of Block D would be left open for him. He would wait until the appointed time.

In his office near the only gate of the prison, psychologist Patrick Lesela was doing his paperwork. In the short time he had been at the prison, Lesela had impressed everyone with his attention to detail. He had made himself aware of every aspect of the way the prison operated. He was often seen walking the prison's corridors, filling one notebook after another with his observations. His activities were so thorough that on one occasion a senior warder had laid a complaint about him. "I am simply immersing myself in the working of the prison so that I can be more useful," he had told the prison's head warder.

While, according to the plan devised by Commissioner Joshua Setlaba of Correctional Services, Yudel would be driving the program nationally, Lesela would be in charge of the local prisons. It had been a surprise to Yudel when, the day after he met Lesela, he had tried to discuss the program with him, only to find that he had not yet read through it. "I have been too busy with routine tasks," Lesela had said.

"Routine tasks are not more important than this," Yudel had told him.

"I will start it immediately," Lesela had said. But he had still not opened the file. It lay unread in the top drawer of his desk. He did not anticipate the need ever to read it.

Sergeant William Tshabalala had, at thirty-two, moved up quickly after starting as an ordinary constable eight years earlier. He was happy with his progress in the force, but living off his salary was not easy. Fortunately, his wife was also an earner. She, like her husband, was a conscientious worker and she too had moved up from being a supermarket shelf-packer to her present position as credit controller for an engineering company. Between them they had been able to afford a modest suburban home and so get their two sons and a daughter away from the violence of the township in which they had both grown up. With careful budgeting, they had also been able to afford a decent suburban school for their children, and the car he was now driving on his way to work.

In recent years, an exodus of skilled policemen to private security companies had meant long shifts for those who had remained. Tshabalala did not expect relief much before midnight.

On the other hand, most days were quiet in the Tshwane West police station. At most, the cells would hold a few drunks from the night before and they could now be released. He would be the senior man on duty. If luck was on his side, he would have time to read the papers and to work on the plan he was trying to develop for the extra bedroom he would build himself, buying used materials from a demolisher as he needed them. As a child, he and six siblings had slept in the living room of the tiny low-cost house that had been home to five adults and seven children. The extra bedroom he was planning would give each of his children a separate bedroom. He was determined that they were not going to grow up with the deprivations that had been part of his early years.

Planning had always been important to William Tshabalala. Since he was a child he had been thinking about ways to advance in life. The addition to his home of an extra bedroom was only a small part of his planning. The day would come, he was sure, when he would be ready to start his own security company. That was a long-term plan though. But, he told himself, if he continued to work hard and plan, it was achievable.

34

Abigail had spent most of the morning listening first to Freek, and then to other officers interrogating Bishop. Every time Freek was relieved in the interrogation room, he had stayed in the office, listening to the efforts of the other officers. His eyes were red, his hair was uncombed and his skin was covered with a film of sweat.

He continued to follow the interrogation with complete concentration, watching for any response that could betray a weakness. By early afternoon, when Abigail left, he had still found none.

She made her way to the house in Muckleneuk, where Rosa let her in. The dark eyes of the older woman were even darker now, a reflection of the anger within. "I told Yudel to go back there to tell Freek what to do," she said to Abigail. "How can they let that monster get away with this?"

"I've just come from there. They've been interrogating him since midnight, more than twelve hours now."

"Freek should thrash him." Rosa's eyes flashed in indignation. "Freek should thrash him and thrash him and thrash him until he tells them where that man is."

"Yudel told you about it?"

"Not everything. He never tells me everything. But he told me enough to know that Freek should thrash him."

Abigail found herself nodding. If only it had been that simple. "Yudel hasn't been there all morning."

"He's in his study again, staring into space. He does that when he is faced with an insoluble problem. Sometimes he gets inspiration. Not always though. He told me he has a feeling about that place you took him to. I told him that this is not a time for feelings. This is a time for action. He said he doesn't know what action to take."

"I need to talk to him."

"Go in, go in." It was said with a brief, impatient shake of the head. "But afterward, you go back to the police station and tell Freek to thrash that monster."

Abigail nodded again. Rosa was not in the mood for a rational discussion.

In the study, Yudel was sitting behind his desk, but side-on, leaning forward, his head in his hands. He was clearly deep in thought, so deep that he did not hear her enter. Yes, she thought. My friend, you are not a man of physical action.

She was almost upon him before he became aware of her. He rose suddenly to face her. If Freek looked tired, she thought, Yudel looked close to collapse. There was an agony in his eyes that went beyond physical weakness. "Yudel . . ." she said, but never got beyond his name. Looking at him, standing in the chaos of his study, without the jacket and tie he had worn to the *Samson* performance, he seemed to have more gray hair than the day before. She knew what he was going to say before he spoke.

There was something in his look that drove away the possibility of any secrets between them. He spent a long time, framing the sentence. "You came here to tell me about Ficksburg."

"Yes."

"Would you care to sit down?"

To Abigail, the circumstances made Yudel's politeness seem absurd. She almost responded that she would not mind if she did, thanks awfully. But she said, "I've left it too late."

"Neither of us knows that. Tell me now."

"I don't think there's anything there that will be helpful, but I'll tell you."

"Everything?"

"Absolutely everything." She sat down on the same chair she had occupied two days before. For a long moment she seemed to be struggling to find a place to start, then she began, not smoothly or effortlessly, but in uneven snatches of memory.

"Only six of us survived the Maseru raid. They took us across the border through a place where they had already cut the fence.

"Leon got into the armored vehicle I was put into and sat down next to me. I hardly remember anything of the drive to Ficksburg, but I do remember van Jaarsveld shouting at Leon in Afrikaans, *Ja, go with your black whore.*

"At the time I never even thought about what a serious thing it was for Leon to stand up to an officer the way he had, even pointing his gun at him. I had just seen my father killed and I knew what Leon had done and all I wanted was for Leon to hold me, but there were other soldiers in the vehicle. I don't know whether he would have held me if they had not been there, but I thought that he would have. I know how strange it sounds, but that is the way I felt.

"What do you want to know, Yudel? Tell me what you want to know."

Only Abigail knew what she had to tell him, but he had to let her get there in her own way. "Where did they take you?"

"Ficksburg. The police station in Ficksburg."

"And what did they do with you there?"

"They took us straight to the police cells. I never saw Leon, or van Jaarsveld either, after that. They didn't put us in cells with criminals. I suppose they thought we might influence them for the worse, and turn them into revolutionaries.

"The four women went into one cell and the two men who were still alive in another. The woman, Julia, the one I had been playing ball with earlier in the evening, had also survived.

"People have asked me if that was the longest night of my

life, expecting me to say yes. But I don't think it was. I only remember bits of it. For me, the night may only have lasted an hour or it may have lasted a week. I have no clear memory of the passing of time or how I spent most of it."

"They put you in the cells for the night?"

"Yes. At one point all four of us were clustered together with our arms around one another. I also remember being alone at times. The cell was big, designed for many prisoners, twenty or thirty perhaps, and there were times when we were scattered around it.

"There was a lavatory in the corner with a screen around it made from board. It was high enough to give some sort of privacy, but you could see the feet of the person using the lavatory. I know it's bizarre, but I still remember the feet."

Abigail seemed to be struggling with the memory. Perhaps there was too much, or perhaps it had been suppressed for too long. "Was anything done to you there?" Yudel asked.

"Not by the police. The ordinary policemen in Ficksburg did not seem to be bad men. There was a white officer and two black constables. The white officer only glanced at us, then went back into the police station. The cells were in outbuildings in the police station yard, maybe twenty meters away from the main building. I suppose they didn't often have important prisoners in Ficksburg.

"I don't know if they thought of us as important. They had gone to enough trouble to attack our house, kill most of us and abduct the few survivors. Do you think they thought of us as important, Yudel?"

"I believe they did."

"It seems so strange. I never thought of us as important."

"But they kept you there that night?"

"Yes, and the next day. One of the two black policemen led us into the cells, then he unshackled us and locked us in without saying anything.

"It was the other one who made an impression on me though. I needed so for someone to be kind to me. Like Leon had been. And this man was. He was about fifty and his hair was gray in patches, rather like my father's. The night was hot and I remember him coming in a number of times with a jug of water. And every time the water had ice cubes floating in it. There must have been a refrigerator in the police station. But I'm sure ice was not usually offered to prisoners. It was a kind thing for him to do when you think how people like him were indoctrinated. We were communists and terrorists, as far as they were concerned. On one of his visits, he squeezed my shoulder and told me not to worry, that I was underage and they would have to try me as a juvenile. He was a good man and I remember the name he used was Jan. No doubt he had an African name, but during working hours he was Jan to both his colleagues and to the prisoners."

Abigail again lapsed into a silence that seemed to have more to do with the jumble of recollections she was struggling with than her emotional state. "It happened long ago," she said eventually. "I don't remember all of this part very well."

"You were there the next day too?"

"It must have been the next day, because there was daylight from the windows and it was unbearably hot. The cells did not have ceilings and with the sun beating down, the corrugated iron roof must have been too hot to touch. The only air came in through the window, where I had seen the stars, and a small inspection hole set in the solid steel cell door at about my head height. But the inspection hole only gave you a view into a narrow passage that had gray, unpainted walls.

"They brought us food. There was meat, but it was gray and did not taste good, but there was enough for all of us and we ate it.

"Most of my memories of that day, the night before, and the one that followed, are vague. The way we were rescued is the only part of it that remains clear in my mind."

She grabbed hold of Yudel's arm closest to her with both of her hands. "Michael Bishop was there. Isn't that enough?"

"No," Yudel said. "Help me understand. I need to understand."

When she started again, her voice was more even and the

picture she was describing more composed. "I think it must
have been close to midnight or even past midnight. I had not
slept at all. The image of my father dying was all I could think
about. From what I had seen it was not impossible that we
would never get out of Ficksburg alive. I also thought about
Leon. I thought about the way he had stood there pointing his
gun at that ghastly man. It seemed to me that, although they
were wearing the uniform of the oppressor, both Leon and Jan
were on my side.

"I remember a drunkard singing. His sang terribly, stumbling from one key to another, singing the same line over and
over. I even remember the line. It went, 'Down to the bar
room he staggered and fell down by the door.'

"At first it seemed to be coming from somewhere at the
back of the cells and I thought that he must be another prisoner, but the sound moved past the cells toward the police station itself. He must have run into one of the policemen, because
I heard one of them shout at him, saying that if he didn't shut
up he would spend the night in the cells.

"He argued with the policeman, then I couldn't hear them
anymore. I thought he must have been bundled into a cell,
because everything went quiet. Later I heard him farther away,
for a short time, then it was quiet again. I've often wondered
who that man was and what he would think if he knew what
was about to happen.

"I remember clearly how complete the silence was. There
was nothing at all, not even the sound of a car, and no sound
from the other cells. In our cell only Julia and myself were
awake. The other two were both lying on their backs, breathing through their mouths.

"And, Yudel, then the strangest thing happened. I was sitting
with my back against the wall when I saw the cell door open. It
swung slowly inward without a sound. But no one came in.
There was a long moment, more than a moment, perhaps a
minute or more, that I looked at it as if it were an hallucination.
Then I got up and started toward it. I remember Julia catching
me before I reached the door. Have you ever been in the cells,

Yudel? I mean, I know you've been inside many, many times, but have you ever been inside as a prisoner."

"No, never."

"Not once?"

"No."

"Well, the door opening and no guard there . . . this is the strangest thing of all. You don't expect it to happen that way."

"What did you do?"

"I don't know how long I looked at that open door, with Julia holding me. Eventually, I asked her to let me go, but she wouldn't. She was telling me not to go there, that it was a trap, that they were going to kill us as escaping prisoners if we went outside. That door was standing there, wide open, and I had to go. It took a struggle to free myself. She gave up eventually. I heard her starting to cry as I got to the door.

"The passage was empty and I followed it until it ended at a door into the yard, which was also open. If they had set a trap, they were well hidden in the open piece of ground between the cells and the police station. I walked across that open patch of dirt as if I were in a trance. If there were sounds, I don't remember them. As far as I remember, everything happened in complete silence.

"There was a flight of four or five stairs leading up to the back door of the police station. Why I went up the back stairs into the open door I will never know, but that's what I did. I did not even pause at the door. Like the cell door, it was half open.

"The light in the room was coming from the front of the building somewhere. By that dim light I could see the body of one of the policemen. He was on his back, as if asleep, but I knew immediately that there was no life in his body."

She stopped again, struggling with some, private part of the memory. Yudel tried to get her going again. "He was the enemy. You must have been glad to see him dead."

"You would think so. But to me it was a continuation of the night before. I did not see the Ficksburg policemen as my enemies. They seemed like ordinary men. And Jan had been a friend.

"I think that finding Jan was somehow the worst moment of both nights, even worse than my father's death. Perhaps the death of my father had driven me to saturation point. My threshold for brutality had been reached. I had no longer the capacity to deal with more of it.

"What looked at first like a pile of washing against one of the passage walls turned out to be Jan's body. I remember kneeling next to him and touching the graying hair that reminded me of my father's. I don't know how long I stayed in that position, but later I found myself in the charge office at the front of the police station. And there I found the body of the white sergeant. He was lying on his side behind the counter. The light was better there, and I could see a very thin cut across his throat. I thought at the time that it had been made by a very sharp knife. I have since learned that it was made by piano wire.

"The front door was wide open and I stopped there. I remember a hedge and a wooden fence made of round poles. By the light of a street lamp, perhaps half a block away, I could see a young white man. He was sitting on one of the horizontal poles of the fence. He seemed to be waiting for someone and he seemed completely unconcerned about the bodies inside the police station. I knew at once that he had killed them.

"He noticed me the moment I appeared in the doorway, and I believe he knew who I was. He never looked directly at me, but I believe he saw me in every detail. I was still standing there when he slid to the ground and started coming toward me."

Abigail was lost in her story now. Yudel knew that this was Michael Bishop and that it was this part of her story she had come to tell him.

"His grip on my arm felt strange. He did not seem to be holding me tightly, yet I was helpless. I thought someone that strong did not need to use his strength. When he led me back into the police station I cannot say that I fought him. There was a room with a couch. It had a hard coir mattress on wooden slats. Scratchy bits of the coir stuck out of the mattress and rubbed against me.

"I can't say that he used any force. That would suggest that I resisted. He also did not undress me and there was no foreplay. He only unzipped my jeans and pulled them down to my knees. He did even less undressing himself. I think he only unzipped his fly.

"I closed my eyes so that I would not see him and turned my head away, but he turned my head back and kissed me. I remember how hard his lips felt. They did not seem to be made of flesh at all. And I remember his voice. There was no expression in it. You are lucky, he said. You are blessed. Do you know that?

"I never answered and he never looked for an answer. That was all he said. I thought at the time that I was immune and that he was not touching me, but I have never been able to think about that time that started when I first saw Jan's body, and ended when Michael Bishop got off me and went away. Tonight is the first time since then that I have ever tried to remember it. If Leon was not in such trouble, I would still have closed my mind to it.

"To understand just how bad it was, you have to understand what the killing of my father meant to me, then the killing of all our other people—then, when it seemed to be over, the killing of Jan . . . and you also have to understand what Bishop was like. There was no fury in him, not even any lust, just a strange, cold desire. I can't describe it."

Abigail stopped speaking as suddenly as she had started. She slid off the chair until she was kneeling next to the desk. "I'm sorry, Yudel." To her own ears she sounded feeble, undone by the images that had been buried for so long. "I always hid it from myself. Forgive my weakness." She bent over her hands in a position of prayer.

Yudel knelt next to her and placed a hand on her shoulder. Slowly she lifted her head and he helped her back to the chair she had been sitting in. Then she was speaking again: "Bishop didn't use a condom, and I leaked blood and his semen all the next day. For years afterward I thanked God from the depth of my soul every night that it had not resulted in a pregnancy. It was my first experience of sex, and my last until I met Robert nearly ten years later.

"Julia found me zipping up my jeans and helped me. I remember her saying that they were bastards and they didn't need to do this. She took me to a minibus taxi that had come to take us away. By morning we were in a house in Johannesburg, having traveled on back roads all the way. Bishop sat in front with the driver, but to my knowledge he never even looked at me once during the drive. Within a week I was in Botswana and a month later I was at ANC headquarters in Lusaka.

"You see, Yudel. On one night in Maseru I was saved by a good man, defending an evil cause, and on the next I was saved by an evil man, fighting for a good cause."

"Nothing in life is ever without complications."

"I know that. And I also know that one of the complications is the way many people in the movement see Michael Bishop. To them, he is a genuine African hero."

"He's no hero," Yudel said. "He doesn't have the motives of a hero."

"Many believe that he is one."

"He's not a genuine African hero. You are."

"Why don't I feel heroic then?"

"I don't think heroes usually do."

"I think that Bishop felt heroic after every successful mission. He seemed to be using me to celebrate what he did to those policemen. I don't care whose side they were on, Yudel. They were human beings and he was exulting in the death of all three."

"You didn't see him again until this week?" Yudel asked.

"I did not even hear anything about him till last Thursday, when our department decided to honor him. I did not see him again until I saw him unconscious on the pavement last night. The first time I ever spoke to him or he to me—except for those few words—was early this morning in that interrogation room."

"What I don't understand," Yudel said, "is that I've never

heard of the Ficksburg thing. Maseru was all over every South African paper. Then, the next night, something as dramatic takes place less than a hundred kilometers away, but there's complete silence."

"I don't know for sure," Abigail said. "But I do know that the movement did not want to publicize Michael Bishop's activities. He was too clinical, too effective, even. The leadership thought that if people knew about him they might start to sympathize with the regime. As for the government side, they always tried to cover their defeats."

Yudel nodded. But there was something else. "This has affected your relationship with Robert," he told her.

"How can you tell?"

"It has though, hasn't it?"

"What does it matter, Yudel? When this is over we can get back to normal."

"It matters to Robert."

He could see her anger only in the sharp points of light in her eyes. "It's not your business. In any case, how can you know?"

"I can see it in him."

"Christ, Yudel, it was my first time. I was fifteen and till we came to Maseru I had been living a sheltered suburban life in London. My father had just been murdered. It was not a nightmare. It was real. It was beyond even torture. First my father's death, then Jan, then that. I can't describe what it did to me."

"It wasn't Robert," Yudel said gently. "He came to you long afterward in pure love. And he took all that away."

"How do you know?"

"He did, didn't he?"

"Yes."

"That is the true reality, the one you must hold on to. The other thing happened long ago, and it's over. Robert is here and he's not going anywhere. What he is to you is one pole of the human compass; Michael Bishop is the opposite pole. There is no similarity between them." He rose slowly.

Abigail rose too. "You're a good man," she told Yudel.

"Not everyone agrees with that assessment."

She stood where she had risen, without moving. "But Leon, where is Leon?" she asked.

Yudel moved away from her into his private thoughts. It was a tendency she had noticed before. She waited for his return. "Abigail," he said slowly, "something has been eating away at me all day."

"Yes?" Abigail found herself struggling for breath. She felt deep within herself that this strange little man may yet find the key to it all.

"Earlier today, you said that when you mentioned this place to Bishop there was a reaction. Do you remember that?"

"Of course."

"What form did the reaction take?"

"He shook."

"What part of him?"

"His faced twitched and his hands shook."

"But they were cuffed."

"He raised his hands and I could see that they were shaking. It happened twice."

Yudel retreated again into his thoughts. And again Abigail waited. "He wanted you to go to that house," he said at last.

"Why?"

"I don't know."

"How can you be sure?"

"People like Bishop are different from you and me. No matter what the urgency, his face will not twitch and hands will not shake. He knows that other people have these weaknesses and he showed them to you to convince you of something. It was an act. He wanted you there. But I don't know why."

"Is this what psychopaths do?"

"The term 'psychopath' is just a word. I'm not sure it has that much meaning."

"But isn't he what the books describe? One who is completely single-minded in achieving his goals and will do anything to achieve them, risk his own life—kill, if necessary."

"Yes, that is what the books say, but it's not enough."

"What would be enough?"

"It's not what he would do to achieve his goals that explains anything. The question is why does he have such goals."

"That is a terrible question."

"The answer may be more terrible than the question."

"Yudel?" Her voice held a new sharpness. This was something she needed to know now. "Will they get what we want from the interrogation?"

"No."

"Rosa says we should thrash him. What if Freek tortures him?"

"No. He will simply give us wrong information."

"Are you sure?"

"Yes."

"And Freek? Do you think he agrees with you?"

"Yes, but like us he does not know what else to do. So he will continue interrogating and hoping that Bishop makes a mistake."

35

Sometime around noon Freek's desperation got the better of him. It was a desperation that had been building almost since the interrogation began. Bishop's smug calm did not help much either. Freek lunged across the table at the prisoner, seizing him by the throat with a grip that few men would have been able to break. "You bastard," he grunted. "Have you got no decency at all? I'll fucking kill you."

Both chairs and the table were thrown across the room and the two men crashed to the floor. Bishop, his hands cuffed, was helpless.

Freek's attack lasted only seconds before he was being pulled off the prisoner by two of his officers. Captain Nkobi was one of them. "Stop, deputy commissioner," he whispered close to Freek's ear. "This will play into his hands."

With the return of sanity, Freek's grip loosened and he stumbled to the far side of the room as the two policemen re-arranged the furniture and put Bishop back on one of the chairs. It took a few minutes before Bishop could speak and then he could manage no more than a whisper. "Yes, deputy commissioner. This attack will play into my hands."

"There was no attack here." Freek still sounded out of breath. "Did either of you men see an attack?"

"We saw no attack," Nkobi said. "The prisoner needs to know that lying about us is not going to help him."

Bishop tried another angle. "You were pretty good there for a moment," he croaked. The traces of a mocking smile showed on his face. "Of course, it helps that my hands were cuffed. Perhaps you'd like to try it some time when my hands are free?"

Before Freek could respond, Nkobi had stepped between him and the prisoner. "Let me take over," he was saying. "Why don't you rest, deputy commissioner?"

It was good advice and Freek took it. But he went no farther than the front office, where the amplifier was working again and he was again able to follow the interrogation.

It was mid-afternoon when the call for Freek came through. The citizens of a township in a disputed zone had barricaded the road into the township and were burning heaps of tires in front of the barricade. Apparently they were protesting against the poor service they were receiving from their municipality. They wanted the provincial boundaries redrawn to move the township into the Gauteng province, where they believed they would receive better treatment. Refuse had not been removed for weeks, pensions were often paid months late and the township's roads were so potholed that traffic could move at no more than walking pace.

"I'm sorry to interrupt your Sunday, but I hope you can go personally," the polite voice of the Gauteng minister for local government reached him over the connection. It had the sing-song quality of South African Indian speech.

"I would be happy to go, but we are in the middle of a very important interrogation."

"This is far more important. I'd like you to go. Let me give you the number of my mobile in case you need to contact me." He read out the number. "Just in case you need me."

Freek allowed a pause to get the minister's attention. "I'm afraid this is a very important interrogation."

"Of one suspect?"

"Yes, but this is an important suspect."

"Look, one of our department's buildings is close by and could be threatened. I think you should go personally." The voice was less polite now.

"I'll send good men."

"I want you there. The premier wants you there. Do you want me to call the national commissioner?" There was nothing polite about the voice now. Polite threats rarely sound polite to the threatened.

"Not especially," Freek said, "but I'm not going on your authority."

"All right. If that's the way you want to play it. Expect a call from the commissioner." The connection was cut with more than a click as the phone was put down heavily on the other side.

Fuck him, Freek thought. He picked up the phone immediately though to start making arrangements for a suitable squad to go to protect government property. He hoped the politician would be able to reach the commissioner. That would simplify everything for him. He would either receive an order to stay where he was, or to go to what sounded like a fairly minor disturbance, as riots go.

It took the politician a while to find the national commissioner. His call reached Freek nearly an hour later. "I want you to do what he wants," the commissioner told Freek.

"I feel I might be getting somewhere with this prisoner," Freek said. It was not true, but to leave now for another job was unthinkable.

"He'll still be there when you get back."

"Commissioner, you know that's not the way interrogations work. We have to keep at him."

"Sometimes we have to make choices. I need you to go there."

"And of course, there is the time element in this matter."

"You believe that about the twenty-second?"

"Gordon does."

"Do you?"

"I don't know, but he's been right so far. He usually is."

"Nevertheless, I need you to go."

There was a long pause as Freek thought about this order. Eventually, there was nothing left to say but "Yes, sir."

Something in Freek's tone failed to satisfy the commissioner. "Listen, Jordaan, I know you're a good officer. That's why I moved you up when I got rid of your colleagues from the old regime. But I want you to think about this: what does it look like when communities in the new South Africa riot? What is the message it sends to the rest of the world? I need a man there who will calm things down without killing people. That's why I want you to go."

"All right, commissioner, I'll leave immediately."

The commissioner was not yet finished. "Another thing. About refusing to take orders from that politician . . ."

"Yes?" Freek said. The commissioner was touching a delicate nerve.

But the other man was not unskilled in handling his senior officers. "You did the right thing. My senior men take orders from me. I don't want my regional commissioners and deputy commissioners taking orders from every member of an executive committee who thinks he's important. If it happens again you tell him to fuck off—in polite language, of course."

"I think that's what I did, sir."

"Good. One other thing . . ."

"Yes."

"Remember I don't want any marks on Bishop. I don't want any bruises left on him. I also don't want your men undressing him. I don't want to hear later that he was naked while being interrogated. I don't want him being kept awake for a hundred hours and more at a time. And I don't want someone squeezing his balls till he screams in agony."

"You're not leaving me with very much," Freek said.

"This is the way it has to be."

"Not even keeping him awake? We have so far."

"Not even that. Do you understand?"

"Yes, I understand."

"Good. Now get out to that township for me."

When Freek replied this time it was with far more conviction. "Yes, sir. I'm on my way."

The twilight was already merging into darkness by the time Freek reached the offending community. He knew township communities like this one almost as well as if he had grown up in one. The people of these communities were not among those who had gained from the country's change of government. Most felt that they were no better off than they had been under the apartheid government. Pension payments, refuse removals, street repairs, the salaries of junior civil servants: all seemed more erratic now to those who had hoped for so much from the new government. The new traffic cops seemed as anxious to find fault with their old and struggling vehicles as the old ones had been, and the banks still saw them as bad risks. Of the jobs and houses promised by the first democratic government, some houses had materialized, but very few jobs. Those who had been poor and uneducated were still as poor, and their children seemed unlikely to achieve better education. Many of the girls who finished high school could still do no better than a position as a domestic worker in the home of a white or Indian family. Many of the young men still gathered in restless groups on street corners, unemployed and no longer looking for employment. The occasional riot was rooted in nothing more than disappointment. Freek knew them well.

A string of policemen and their vehicles, both cars and armored vehicles, were blocking the road, bottling up the riot so that it did not spill out of the township. Beyond them, another barricade prevented the police from entering the township without a fight. This one consisted of piles of burning tires from which dense clouds of black smoke were blowing toward the line of policemen. As Freek drove up, some of the police vehicles were already moving back as their drivers tried to get away from the smoke.

Freek stepped out of his own car and waved an officer closer. He was a young man, perhaps twenty-four or twenty-five, and very earnest about his role in life. "Lieutenant Vilakazi, isn't it?"

"Yes, sir."

Freek pointed to the barricade and the figures behind it that could only be seen dimly through the spasmodic flames from the tires. "Look behind those burning tires. What do you see?"

"People from the community. They look angry."

"And behind them?"

"More tires."

"That's right. If we pull back, they will build another barricade of burning tires in front of the present one. We can't have them driving us back. Tell your men to keep our line where it is. I know this is not pleasant, but we'll have to live with it for now. Perhaps the wind will change."

Lieutenant Vilakazi ordered the police vehicles back to their original positions. The movement caused some shouts of anger from the barricade. As Freek had predicted, some of the men and young boys were already bringing tires forward to set fires closer to the police position. "Put one round of tear gas among them," Freek said.

One of the constables fired the round, and the members of the township community retreated, coughing and spluttering. The tires they had brought remained scattered where they had left them.

"What should we do now, deputy commissioner?" Vilakazi's forehead was wrinkled with indecision.

You're too young to be in charge of this, Freek thought. He hated the fact that he had been forced to leave the interrogation of Bishop, but he was glad for Vilakazi's sake that he had come. "How long has this been going on?"

"All afternoon. They lit the fires at about two."

"Call the nearest fire brigade and tell them we want them to put out piles of burning tires. Then get the roads department to send a front-end loader to stand by in case we need them."

"They will try to stop us."

"Perhaps. I passed a Chicken Licken a few kilometers back. Send a man to bring back burgers for all of us. And coffee."

"Deputy commissioner?"

"I'll authorize the payment."

"But deputy commissioner, what's it for?"

Freek looked seriously at him, then laid a hand on his shoulder. "Listen, son. I just want to make things uncomfortable for them, but I want them to see that we are having a party. When the men eat their burgers, I want them to do it in the light from the vehicles."

"Yes, sir." Lieutenant Vilakazi sounded impressed. "That's very clever, sir."

"Thank you," Freek said. "You have to be clever to be a deputy provincial commissioner."

Before Freek arrived, the lieutenant had made two attempts to negotiate with the protestors at the barricade. Both attempts had been rejected, the second rejection accompanied by a hail of rocks.

"We'll wait," Freek told him. "And while we wait, we'll give them a taste of tear gas every fifteen minutes or so. At the same time, we'll have our burgers and coffee. If they show signs of wanting to negotiate, ignore it. We'll see who gets tired of this game first."

A roadblock at the main intersection leading into the township was turning away cars, the owners of which were unaware of the trouble in the township. Four hours after Freek's arrival, a police car passed through the roadblock and came straight at him. The driver braked hard, stopping within a few meters of the police barricade. Captain Nkobi leaped from the driver's seat, followed by four of his men. Freek had left Nkobi and the men at the Tshwane West police station to support Sergeant Tshabalala and the two on duty with him. He had intended to take no chances with security on this night.

"What in hell are you doing here?" Freek demanded.

"I was told to come. I was told to hurry, that there was a crisis here."

"Who gave that order?"

Before Nkobi could answer, a sheet of flame flared within a few meters of them. A bottle containing liquid fuel had burst against one of the police cars and the burning liquid was spreading under the car. A teenage boy was running back to the shelter of the burning tires. Within moments, a second Molotov cocktail fell short, sending up another burst of flame.

One of the policemen was trying to start the car's engine to get it away from the flames when Nkobi, who had seen the flames reaching up into the engine compartment, pulled him out of the driver's seat. A moment later the car was burning. By the time the fuel tank went, in a far bigger explosion than the Molotov cocktails had produced, the policemen were all clear of it. Freek, who had taken shelter behind an armored vehicle, heard an eruption of cheering from behind the township barricade. The protestors were having a a good time. This was going to take longer than he had anticipated.

A third, fourth and fifth Molotov cocktail burst along the line of police vehicles, one of them landing against a windscreen, cracking the glass, but bouncing into the road and spreading fire as it went. Tshwane West police station and the man being held in the cells there seemed very far away.

36

By the time Abigail arrived home, Robert had been there for some hours. He had fallen asleep in a comfortable armchair, and woke up when Abigail came through the front door. He rose as soon as he saw her. "My God, you look terrible," he said.

Robert too had not slept. "You don't look too great yourself, buddy," she said.

"And Leon?"

"They're getting nowhere with Bishop."

"Any chance they'll find Leon some other way?"

"There's only today and maybe tomorrow." Robert had never heard her sound that desolate.

"You need to sleep."

"But there's so little time."

"You still need to sleep."

"I won't be able to."

"We've got pills."

"I can't sleep. I don't think I'll ever be able to sleep again. I've spent the last week searching for Michael Bishop. We found him and we captured him, and we are still nowhere."

"Look at it this way." Robert reasoned with his wife. "While the police have him, he can't kill Leon."

"But I don't know where he is or how he's being kept. He may be dying of thirst right now."

"Are they still interrogating Bishop?"

"All night. They've been hammering at him all night. Yudel dropped me off. I think he went back there. Oh God, Robert, I don't know what to do."

Robert moved toward her to take her in his arms, but she drew away. "Not now. If I soften, I'll collapse completely."

"I feel so useless that I can't help you. I wish I could," Robert said. "Jesus."

"Just call me Abigail," she said. "Oh, God, that wasn't even funny."

"It's okay, just call me Robert."

This time they both laughed, but it was the helpless laughter of impotence and it lasted only a moment. "Just stay with me, support me tonight and tomorrow."

"I shouldn't even do that."

She was looking at him with desperate, questioning eyes.

"That meeting with the head of the National Prosecuting Authority is tomorrow. The word is that he's going to tell us that he has a prima facie case against the deputy president, but not enough evidence to prosecute. It looks like he wants to try him in the media because he doesn't have enough for the courts."

"Oh, that's so important, but I don't think it's wise," Abigail said.

"Well, it seems that this is what he intends doing."

"You can't come with me, not while this is happening."

"I'll stay away if you ask me to."

"No. You have to go. It's too important."

"I can send my deputy."

"No, never. You must go—a black editor of genuine ability like you." She smiled bleakly at him, but the attempt at a joke was again a feeble one.

For Abigail to remain still was difficult at any time. With midnight approaching, it was impossible. Sleep was not something she had even considered. Robert had tried staying up with her in a gesture of solidarity. He had pointed out that going back to the police station where Bishop was being kept was foolish and unnecessary. The police were doing everything possible, and she was not a trained interrogator. Why not leave it to the professionals? And there was no point in her continually pacing up and down. That also would do no good.

She nodded in apparent agreement with all his arguments. But he had fallen asleep in the chair. Abigail waited only long enough to be sure that he would not wake up with the very gentle opening and closing of the apartment door.

It took her almost thirty minutes from the time she left the building before she stopped in the street outside the police station.

Sergeant William Tshabalala had taken careful note of everything Captain Nkobi had told him before Nkobi left to assist Deputy Commissioner Jordaan at the township riot. The prisoner had been given the last cell in the corner of the small cell block. No one would need to pass his cell. The only cell that shared a common wall with his had been left empty. He was completely isolated and the police officer on duty at the cells had been ordered not even to venture into the passage outside his cell.

For much of the evening, Tshabalala occupied himself with fairly routine tasks. He certified a number of affidavits for members of the public, filled in the log book, gave advice to a woman who said her former husband had stopped paying maintenance for his children, took a statement about a matter he thought might end in civil court, opened a docket for car theft, and booked a drunk found sleeping at the foot of a statue of the leader of the old Boer republic.

By midnight, visits by members of the public had long since ended. Even the sounds of traffic on the artery that passed close by were sporadic now. With his immediate duties over, Tshabalala spent an hour on his plans for the day when he would leave the force. According to his calculations, he would need at least half a million to start a small security company that would specialize in providing guards and dog handlers to protect office parks, warehouses and factories. Inflation and his own spare time renovations had increased the price of his house. He calculated that he could probably get a second mortgage on the family home, of about a quarter of a million. This meant that together with his savings he was still short to the tune of over 200,000 rand. By the time the extra bedroom on the house was finished, that figure should be halved. Another year or two, the sergeant thought, if house prices continued to climb, and he would be able to make his move.

When Abigail came in demanding to know where Deputy Commissioner Jordaan was and why the prisoner was not being interrogated, he rose and tried to explain about the riot and that the deputy commissioner had been called away by the national commissioner himself.

"You can't stop interrogating the prisoner," she almost shouted. "He has to be interrogated every moment. We have to find out what he knows."

Tshabalala tried to defend himself. "The deputy commissioner ordered me to stay away from him."

"How long is he going to be at this riot?" She was suddenly aware that she could probably be heard in the street and perhaps in the buildings on either side. "He shouldn't have gone," she muttered to herself.

But he had gone, and Tshabalala did not know how long Freek was going to be away or exactly why he had found it necessary to go. From the direction of the cells, Abigail heard what she was sure was a humorless chuckle. "Who made that sound?" she demanded.

"Just a prisoner, ma'am. Just a prisoner."

But which prisoner? she almost asked, but managed to suppress the question.

Eventually there was nothing to do but go. The sergeant would not allow her to attempt an interrogation of the prisoner.

And she knew that there was very little point in her trying. From her car she called the number of Freek's mobile, but the answering signal indicated that he was out of range.

By two o'clock, Tshabalala and the officer who had been assisting him in the charge office were playing cards for stakes of twenty cents a hand. The constable in the cells was asleep in a straight-backed chair, snoring softly through his open mouth. There were only three prisoners besides Bishop in the cells. They were all in one cell and they too were asleep. All of them had spent nights in the cells on other occasions and were not bothered by the thinness of the mattresses or the greasiness of blankets that had, over the years, provided warmth for a great many bodies and had not been washed for too many months.

The constable had positioned his chair exactly as Captain Nkobi had told him to. He had also assisted Sergeant Tshabalala in placing the prisoners in the cells that Nkobi had selected. There were only two ways out of Bishop's cell. One was through a heavily barred window set into a wall nearly half a meter thick and so high off the ground that no prisoner had ever been able to reach it. The other was through the barred door of the cell that led into the passage. Before the constable fell asleep, he had inspected the arrangements one last time and been satisfied that he had done as he was told. He had wondered only briefly who this white man was that they had to be so careful with. And why this woman from the Department of Justice was so excited about him. It was not the sort of thing that usually exercised his mind. He was a good cop, whatever this Abigail Bukula might think. He followed the orders that were given to him and did not ask questions. Tonight, only one instruction had been forgotten. Captain Nkobi had told him to leave the cell keys in the charge office. But here they were, dangling from his belt.

The constable was woken by the soft sound of sobbing. It was coming from the cell of this white man in the last cell in the row. Yes, the constable thought, it's too late to cry now. You should have thought of that before you turned to crime.

The constable's instructions were to stay away from the prisoner's cell. He remained seated on his chair, listening to the sobbing. It had a whining, almost animal sound, neither growing nor diminishing in volume. Despite himself, the constable found himself listening to it. Eventually, he reacted: "Hey, keep quiet there. You are not allowed to make a noise in the cells."

The admonishment had no effect. The pathetic keening, an animal in pain, continued as evenly as before. For all the effect it had, the constable might not have spoken at all. He felt that this was not the way to enforce discipline with a prisoner. To call to him in the cell at the end of the passage, where he could not even see you, was no way to do it. If you wanted to enforce discipline with a prisoner you had to have him in front of you, where you could see him and he could see you. Then you could shout orders at him.

The constable pondered briefly the idea of going to Sergeant Tshabalala in the charge office to report the prisoner's behavior, but he resisted the thought. He had been given a job to do and received his instructions. There was no need to bother the sergeant.

There were pauses in the sobbing now, moments of silence broken by periods of crying more intense than before. The constable got up. He would only go far enough down the passage to be able to see into the cell. By staying out of the prisoner's reach, he would still be obeying orders. But it was his duty to see what was happening. It was the job he had been given to do.

The constable went carefully down the passage. Where he stopped he was still almost three meters from the cell door, but he could see the prisoner on the far side of the cell, another three or four meters from him. The prisoner was lying down on one of the thin plastic foam mattresses with his face to the wall. His left arm rested awkwardly against the wall above his head. The constable did not even notice the wristwatch with the mirror face that the prisoner was using to follow his every movement.

A strange gasping for breath joined the sobbing. With the prisoner obviously asleep on the far side of the cell, the constable moved closer until he was almost touching the bars. At that moment the sound of singing reached his ears. Some damned drunk, he thought. The voice was slurred and not holding the tune well, but he could make out some of the words. "Down to the barroom he staggered and fell down by the door, the very last words . . ." The constable only turned in the direction of the singing for a second. It was a reflex that was over almost as quickly as it started. He was already turning back when an arm snapped round his throat, clamping him against the bars. A few seconds later he lost consciousness.

Sergeant Tshabalala had also heard the singing. He was not pleased to have his card game interrupted. The singing had started somewhere behind the building and was coming closer. "Here's another one who wants board and lodging tonight," he told the officer opposite him.

"I'll go and have a look," his colleague said.

The singing wavered a little, paused, then started again in a lower key. ". . . the very last words that he uttered, I'll never love blue eyes no more."

"Drunk as a skunk," Tshabalala said. "Go and get him and he can sleep it off in the cells."

"Beautiful, beautiful brown eyes, beautiful, beautiful brown eyes . . ." the singing continued.

"Get him before he wakes up the people in the flats," Tshabalala said as his fellow officer went through the charge office door into the night.

The singing stopped abruptly. Yes, Tshabalala thought, not so keen on singing now, are you? He waited for the officer and the singer to appear in the doorway. When they did not come immediately he thought that he had better go to help. Perhaps the drunkard was resisting. But it was not the sort of thing his fellow officer usually had a problem with. He waited a moment longer, still watching the door. It turned out to be a moment too long. His back was toward the passage that led to the cells. He had not heard the sobbing from the cells or the scuffle as the constable, who had been left to guard the cells, had died. He had also not heard Michael Bishop's approach.

37

Saturday, October 22

When Abigail returned from the police cells, Robert was still asleep in the same position, just as she had left him. She switched on the kettle to make coffee and sat down in the chair opposite. Sleep was not on her agenda. But Abigail had slept for only a few hours in the previous two days and even the strongest human beings sometimes yield to the weakness of the flesh.

She woke with the day bright outside and the clock's hands showing that the time was already 10:25. She showered and dressed with a desperation driven by guilt that on this day, of all days, she had wasted so much time. Leon, she thought, why couldn't you have sought help from a stronger person?

She tried to remember if Johanna had discovered a time when the other killings had taken place. But she could not recall Johanna saying anything about it. The precision with which Bishop operated gave her some hope. He had always used the exact date of the original event. So surely he would also use the exact time? And that had been long after dark. If it were so, there was still what remained of the day, this one day.

She thought about calling Yudel, but he would almost certainly be down at the police station already.

Abigail was wrong about that. Yudel was in his study. He had not even noticed that the night and much of the day had passed. Rosa had come in a few times with food and coffee, but her years with Yudel had taught her that this was not the time to interrupt him. He had not slept at all that night or the night before. Instead, he had spent most of both nights in his study, allowing the events of the past week to mull over in his mind. He knew that in that jumble of incidents, testimony and assumption, he was missing something. As surely as anything he had ever known, he felt that he was overlooking some fact, probably just a single incident, that he should have noticed. Perhaps if he had seen it, it might all be over by now and Leon Lourens might again be united with his family.

For Yudel, long periods of inaction had never been a trial. His search was internal, and required no outside stimulation. He was sure that no other action was needed, not until his thoughts had reached the conclusion that would guide him in the direction he needed to take. Even at a time like this, the battle that had to be won was with the tangle of impressions that his brain had already stored. All this information, including the unknown missing piece, had been assembled into a coherent order.

It was almost twelve before Abigail called. "We can't just sit around," she said. "We have to do something. We have to find some way."

"Where are you?" Yudel asked.

"In my car, outside your front door."

"You go on," he said. "I'll follow later."

"Jesus, Yudel, what can you be doing that's more important?"

"I have to stay here," he said.

Yudel and Freek had both gone mad. She was sure of it now. Maybe the commissioner of police had been right about them. Maybe they really didn't have what it took to see the thing through.

She drove away, her right foot grinding down far too hard on the accelerator pedal. She had only gone four blocks when a young traffic policeman waved her down. She came to a stop against the curb and he strolled toward her, determined to show that he was the man in charge, one who had no reason to hurry. By the time he reached her, Abigail had her departmental identity card ready. Through gritted teeth she said, "Take a look at this, officer. This is who I am, and I am dealing with an emergency."

"You are still not allowed to exceed the speed limit."

Abigail's immediate impulse was to fight, but some warning signal from deep inside warned her against it. She smiled. "Thank God I wasn't stopped by a rookie. I know that someone of your experience will understand about this being a Department of Justice emergency." The traffic policeman took a while to absorb the thought of how experienced he was and that he would understand. A second Abigail broadside finished him off. "Give me your name. I want to commend you to the national commissioner."

"You know him?"

"Intimately," she said.

"Johnson Mathibela," he said. "I'll give you my number too."

"Write them down for me."

Instead of going back to Tshwane West, Abigail drove to her office. As on every other Saturday morning, the building was empty. The security guards in the lobby, all of whom looking too bored even to attempt conversation, did not even glance at the security card she waved at them. Once in her office, she started phoning. Perhaps she had left it too late. Perhaps she should have done this much earlier, but everyone had told her that she could expect no help, not at this time. And it was Saturday morning. Still, there was nothing else. Bishop was in his cell. Freek was wherever he was, dealing with some riot that, the Lord knew, could surely have taken place at some other time. And Yudel seemed to have entered some strange catatonic state.

Not since she had tried to discover if any official body had arrested Leon had she tried to contact any government agencies about the matter. She found an agent at his desk at the National Intelligence Service. He declared himself interested and promised to take it up on Monday. Even Military Intelligence had someone on duty, but this was definitely not a military matter and he could not help. She spoke to the commanding officers of five of the city's fourteen police stations and three of them promised to keep an eye out for suspicious circumstances and someone answering the description of Leon Lourens. They would also ask some questions in likely parts of the city, wherever those were. The railway police promised to check all the sheds on their property.

She told only as much of the story as she thought was necessary, but she told it too many times. By the time she had exhausted her options she was no longer sure that she believed it herself. Outside her window the street was in deep shadow, the sun only touching the tops of the buildings.

It had taken until late afternoon before Freek felt he could leave. By that time, Captain Nkobi was in consultation with the community leaders. Their weariness and discomfort and a third round of chicken burgers and coffee, which Freek hoped the department would pay for, had at last been decisive in opening negotiations. The captain would stay through to the next night if necessary, in an attempt to have the barricades to the township entrance removed.

Freek could not guess how long it would take before an agreement would be reached. Now that he had left the township, the need to find out why Nkobi had been ordered to back him up was overwhelming. Whatever the motive, the Tshwane West police station was now too vulnerable for his peace of mind. But what could the motive be? Did someone really think he needed help that badly? Or was the aim something altogether different? It could be that the MEC who was behind his leaving the police station had something to answer for. But Freek knew that there were some answers that he would never be allowed to pursue—and he suspected this may be one of them.

The piles of tires that blocked the entrance to the township were just smoking mounds by the time he left. The local fire brigade had arrived and put out the flames. The front-end loaders were also ready to go in as soon as the heat from the tires was such that it was safe to start work.

It was some fifty hours since Freek had last slept, but he was still as alert as ever. He felt his weariness only as a tension in the shoulders and a dryness in the eyes. He was driving quickly, but well within his own capabilities and those of the car. He was old enough to realize that he no longer possessed the immortality of youth. After the length of time he had spent without sleep, driving faster would have been less than wise.

He had covered half the distance back to the city, when his mobile phone rang for the first time. A CID officer had gone to Tshwane West in answer to a panicky call from the morning shift that came on at nine. He had summoned medics and armed support. He had tried twice to contact Freek by mobile phone, but had not been successful. At that point he gave up, not thinking it necessary to interrupt the deputy commissioner in the important work he was doing. Only in the last five minutes had someone called a disbelieving Captain Nkobi, who was, for the moment, in a patch of good reception. It was Nkobi who now called Freek.

Freek's right foot pressed heavily down on the accelerator. For the moment, wisdom was forgotten.

38

Yudel came slowly out of his study and wandered into the kitchen. From where she was seated at the television set, Rosa saw him go and followed. "Coffee?" she offered.

Yudel nodded and sat down slowly, resting his hands on the edge of the table for support. After the coffee percolated and Rosa had poured two mugs, he looked at her for the first time. "I have to go out," he said. "There is a prison psychologist by the name of Patrick Lesela in the department's employ. He is said to have been on the staff at UPE, lecturing in criminology, no doubt. Could you try to find out if that is true and call me on the mobile?"

It had been said almost matter-of-factly, but very seriously. "Is this important, Yudel?"

"Very."

"Are you going to shower first?"

Rosa would not have asked if he had not looked in need of it. "No," he said.

"A change of clothes?"

"No. I must go now. Please try to find the information and call me."

"You know I will."

Thinking about it afterward, Abigail would never know where the thought had come from. But suddenly there was a new outlet for the seemingly endless nervous energy that was bursting inside her.

In the telephone directory, she found a number of entries under the name Hamid. None of them had the initial L, but Lou-Anne's was the third one she tried. "Lou-Anne, it's Abigail Bukula here."

"Oh, Johanna's boss."

"Can you go to your office now?"

"It's Saturday afternoon," Lou-Anne said plaintively. This was not the sort of sacrifice usually expected of civil servants.

"I know what day it is. Can you come immediately?"

"I suppose, if it's important." The tone suggested a hope that it may not be important.

"It's vital. It's literally a matter of life and death."

"Literally?"

"Somebody's life depends on it."

Lou-Anne Hamid was a tiny woman, the kind that is often described as petite. She arrived in the foyer only moments after Abigail. Whatever reluctance she had about being called out on a Saturday had disappeared. There was an eagerness in her that went with something more exciting than her usual day. "I'm glad you waited. Security wouldn't have let you in," she explained.

The archive to which she led Abigail was a mixture of new and old. Rows of computers held the databases with every property in the greater Tshwane area, of which Pretoria was a part. The plans for all the newer properties were also to be found in the computer system. In an adjoining room, on big photocopied sheets, were the plans of the older properties.

"Another Vyefontein?" she asked. "I don't believe so. If it had been there, I would have noticed it the first time you asked me."

"Let's just look, please."

Lou-Anne called up the database that carried the names of the properties on that side of town. "No, just the one," she told Abigail. "Does someone's life really depend on it?"

"Yes, it does. Are you sure that there is just the one?"

"There's just the one. You can see for yourself." She sounded disappointed that she was not able to play a bigger part in whatever it was that was happening. "What's it for?" she asked.

"A man has been abducted."

"No? You and Johanna work on the most amazing stuff."

Abigail had Lou-Anne by the arm. "Listen, are you absolutely certain?"

"Yes. Let's draw the plans. I'll show you."

"I don't think that will help."

"You might as well, while you're here." Lou-Anne's eyes were gleaming. "Is he being held there?"

"Frankly, it doesn't look like it."

"But maybe. You'd better come and look. Who knows?"

Abigail, walking slowly with the lack of purpose of one who has just seen a last hope disappear, followed Lou-Anne down one of the rows of filing cabinets that held the town's older building plans. It took Lou-Anne less than a minute to find the Vyefontein plans. There were perhaps twelve of them, the entire history of a large property's evolution from bushveld shack to rural manor house.

Lou-Anne spread them on a table that had been placed there for that purpose. As the wad of plans struck the surface of the table, they fell open toward the back of the file. There, in front of Abigail, was the one image she had not expected to see. Slightly faded, on one-hundred-year-old yellowing paper, was the design of a handsome gabled mansion in the Cape Dutch style, the house that Jones Ndlovu had told her to expect. It was also the house that she knew was not there.

"This is not right," Abigail said. "The house doesn't look like that."

The little town planner had her head cocked to one side as she studied the drawing. "It must have at one point."

"No, the walls are all still standing. The style is quite different."

"Here. Let's look at this." She turned to the front of the file.

"What are we looking at?" Abigail asked.

"The plan of the property. You see, here's the dwelling."

The dwelling was shown as a simple block. The scale at the side of the plan revealed that the house was set well back from the fence, some distance from the gate she had climbed when she first visited the place. That seemed right. The property was long and relatively narrow, but it ran to the top of the squat mountain range behind.

There was something else on the plan—a larger block higher up the hill. "What's that?" Abigail's voice was almost accusing in its sharpness.

"Well, if you've seen the lower house and it's not the one in the plan we saw, that must be it."

"You mean there're two?"

"It looks like it."

A moment later Lou-Anne had the file open at the diagram of the house that Abigail recognized as the one she had already searched twice. "But if there were two houses, I would have seen the second one."

"The property's under brush, isn't it?"

"Most of it."

"Well, according to the scale, it's at least one hundred and fifty meters beyond the lower house. You wouldn't see it from there."

Abigail paused only a moment, staring at Lou-Anne with an intensity that made her uneasy. The town planner was about to ask if there was something wrong when Abigail turned and, pulling off her shoes, ran as fast as she could, her bare feet steady on the tiled surface.

Waiting for the lift was out of the question. With her shoes in one hand, she bounded down the stairs. When she reached the car, her hands were shaking so that it was difficult to find the right buttons on the mobile phone. The phone on the other end of the connection rang one time. "Yudel," she gasped into the microphone. "Yudel, what are you doing?"

39

Freek Jordaan walked slowly through the offices of Tshwane West police station. He had driven from the township barricade and through the suburbs at a speed that, under other conditions, he would have described as irresponsible. From more than a hundred meters away he had seen the police vehicles that had already arrived, and that the street around the station was already cordoned off.

Until that moment he had been a believer in the idea that small organizations of any kind were more effective than big ones. That was the very reason that he had chosen Tshwane West as the place to hold Bishop. He had known all three men of the duty policemen personally and that they could be trusted without reserve. Very few, including those who had been part of the trap they had set on Saturday night, knew where they had taken Bishop. The staff of the station had not even known their prisoner's identity.

One of the bodies was in the cell that Bishop had occupied, the door locked behind him. The key, too, had disappeared and they had not yet been able to gain access to the cell. As Freek stopped outside the cell, a sergeant from a nearby station came running down the passage, waving a key. "Deputy commissioner, I've got the master." His voice was breathless with the effort of locating it.

Superficially, there were no marks on the policeman's body. The eyes were open and bulging slightly, but there were no obvious wounds. Freek was certain that the autopsy would indicate that the brain had been starved of blood. He had already examined the body of the constable who had gone outside to find the source of the drunken singing. His body was lying on its side, pushed against the wall of the building. In his case, the wound was obvious. A very thin wire, probably a piano wire, had cut deeply into his neck, almost from ear to ear. In its very neatness the wound was different from the cut left by a knife, but it was at least as effective.

Only Tshabalala was missing. Freek had known him, both as a law enforcement officer and as a colleague, for more than ten years and he could not believe the sergeant would have been involved in Bishop's escape.

"He must have been," the sergeant said. "He's not here."

A constable, one of four blocking the passage from the cells to the charge office, had his own opinion. "Unless he was abducted."

"Get out of the way," Freek shouted at the constables. "And out of the building if you're not doing any good." He pointed at the sergeant. "You, have you seen to it that they searched everywhere?"

"Everywhere, deputy commissioner."

A new officer was coming through the door of the charge office. "There's a small storeroom under the building," he said.

"Who the hell are you?" Freek wanted to know.

"Lieutenant van Tonder from Wonderboom, sir. I was stationed here last year."

"Show me this store."

"You get into it from outside," van Tonder said.

"Move, man, move." Freek was pushing him through the charge office door.

Van Tonder led the way to the side of the building and down a short flight of stairs that led to the storeroom door. The door was ajar and he pushed it open. "There's a ceiling-mounted light switch with a cord," he said. "Give me a moment."

As the light came on a faint groan reached them from deeper in the room. "He's here," van Tonder said. Then, after the slightest pause, "He's alive."

Sergeant William Tshabalala was on his back, partly obscured by one of the shelves that had collapsed. The state of the storeroom reflected what had happened there. Few shelves were still mounted, cardboard boxes that had been neatly piled had come crashing down and were either blocking the space between the shelves or simply scattered across the floor. Clearly, he had fought for his life with more than ordinary determination. The wound caused by the wire was not as complete as the one that had killed the constable.

"Has someone called the medics?" Freek heard himself shouting.

"No, sir. We didn't know he was here. The others are dead." The voice behind him sounded like that of the man who had found the spare key to the cell.

"Call them now, for Christ's sake. Call them immediately. I want this man in hospital in ten minutes."

Freek knelt next to Tshabalala. Immediately the sergeant's eyes widened. Freek thought he saw anguish there that had nothing to do with the sergeant's pain. His lips were moving. He was trying to speak, but the faintness of his whispering was drowned by the voices of the men in other parts of the station. "Shut the fuck up, all of you," Freek shouted, turning his head toward the men behind him." He pointed to a man who was blocking the door behind him. "You, go and shut them all up."

The man disappeared and Freek bent over Tshabalala, bringing his face to within a few centimeters of the sergeant's. As the sounds behind him died down, Freek could make out a ragged whisper. "I'm sorry, sir. I'm sorry I let him get away." Duty had never been a small thing to the sergeant. His failure was a more pressing matter than his pain. "I'm sorry."

"It's all right, William. You'd better not talk." Freek had been relieved to find the sergeant alive, even in his present condition. He would never have admitted it, even to himself, but he would rather see one of his good men killed in the line of duty than go bad and take money to help a prisoner escape.

"I made a mistake," Tshabalala whispered painfully. "You know the way you always tell us to . . ." But the voice faded. "You always tell us . . ." he tried again.

"Don't talk, William. The medics are coming."

But Tshabalala had to explain himself. "You always tell us to do the important things first, but I let a drunk interfere . . ." His voice was fading again. "I let a drunk man interfere with the important thing you gave me to do."

"William, quiet now. It's all right." One of Freek's large hands was holding him by a shoulder, a steadying pressure to show him that he was not alone.

"I don't know how the prisoner got free, but I was concentrate . . . concentrating on a drunk man. He was singing . . ." The voice faded unevenly, for the last time now. Sergeant Tshabalala's eyes closed slowly.

Something caused Freek to turn his head. Yudel was at his shoulder, his eyes bright with an intensity Freek had seldom seen in them. "Listen to me," Yudel said. "You must listen." He led Freek away from the sergeant's body. Freek glanced back only once. "Listen to me." Yudel's voice held an urgency that forbade discussion. He led Freek out of the storeroom, then out of the charge office and into the gathering twilight. "You know the place Abigail heard about where she thought Bishop may be holding Lourens."

"Yes, you searched it with her and there was nothing."

"There's a second house farther up the hill. It's hidden in the trees. We didn't even know about it."

Freek's eyes hardened. "Are you telling me this?"

"Abigail's on her way there."

"My God, that woman." He turned and shouted at a nearby officer. "How many flying squad men are here?"

"Six, deputy commissioner," the answer came back.

"I want all of them with me. Get to your cars and follow me."

"I need to explain to you how to get there," Yudel was saying.

Freek seemed to have difficulty believing what he was hearing. "You can tell me on the way."

"No. I need to explain. I can't come with you."

To Freek, this was simply another inexplicable Yudel Gordon moment. "Christ, Yudel. Tell me then. Tell me fast."

40

The road that skirted the lower slopes of the little mountain range had even less traffic than on Abigail's other visits. A few cars and pickup trucks from the small farms that surrounded the city, and the village at Hartebeespoort dam, were on their way into town seeking the evening's entertainment. Almost all the traffic was from the opposite direction, headlights flashing past in the gloomy twilight.

She had told Yudel, so she knew he would be coming, probably with Freek, but waiting for them was out of the question. That this was the last day was the thought that drove all others from her mind. It was the only thought possible.

The brush came right down to the fence line on most properties. Vyefontein was on the right-hand side on the steep slope of the Magaliesberg mountains. Here and there a farm gate punctuated the fence line, usually guarding a rocky farm track that was almost immediately lost in the scrub.

Today, Vyefontein seemed farther from town. Perhaps I've passed it, she thought. I know I've passed it. I've been traveling too fast. It's behind me. Oh, Lord, it's behind me and I've wasted this precious time.

She had lifted her foot from the accelerator and was about to press it down hard on the brake, when her mobile phone rang. The car was slowing without her braking as she used her left hand to get the phone out of her bag. Freek was on the other end. "Abigail?"

"Yes."

"Don't go in. Wait for me at the gate." He was asking the impossible. "Do you hear me?"

"Yes, you said I shouldn't go in."

"Wait for me at the gate. We're on our way."

"Where are you now?"

"In the last suburbs. We'll be out of town in a minute or two." Over the connection she could hear the sirens of the police cars. That meant that they were not waiting for traffic lights.

"Yudel will show you the place. He's been there twice."

"He's not with me."

"Where is he? I thought he was on his way to fetch you."

"He said he couldn't come."

"Couldn't come?" Abigail found the idea as disturbing as any other part of the Leon Lourens matter. "He must have gone crazy. What could possibly be more important?"

"I don't know, but I'm coming and I've got men with me. Just don't enter the property till I get there."

"I hear you."

"It could be a trap. Bishop is free. He may have a trap waiting for you."

"Free? How."

"Never mind how. He's very dangerous."

I know him better than you ever will, she thought, as she switched off the phone. With the call finished, her foot came down hard on the brake. The car slid to a stop directly opposite the gate of Vyefontein.

The old, rusted padlock still held the chain in place. Abigail left the car in front of the steel and wire farm gate. With one foot on a cross-member, she swung the other leg over. In a moment she was inside the property and stumbling up the track. Apart from the remains of some attempt at a driveway, paving stones that broke through the surface of the ground at odd intervals, the earth was deeply rutted as if a truck had tra-versed it after it had been softened by heavy rain.

It was too dark to see the ground's uneven surface clearly. Abigail stumbled on a paving stone that had settled at an angle and went down on her hands and knees. As she got up, she could see the house against what little light was left in the sky. It was the same house she had already searched twice.

Her hands were stinging and she was aware of small stones clinging to them. Without thinking, she wiped them on her trousers. It took a second and third wipe to get rid of them. Now she did look down. She could just make out the smears where she had wiped her hands.

She reached what had once been the garden of the house and stumbled again, this time in loose sand. The track from the road so far had been uneven, but she could see that beyond this point the slope became steeper. There was still no sign of a second house. Could it be that there *was* no house? All she had to go on was a couple of old and faded drawings in a file that had probably not been opened for thirty years. Perhaps there was nothing. Perhaps Bishop did want her to come, but that he knew there was nothing, that this was just his idea of a joke. No, that was impossible. Humor was not something he was capable of. That was not it.

On the far side of the house she found an opening in the brush that could have been an extension of the driveway. It was still longer since this one had been in use. It was densely overgrown in places by hard veld grass. She moved forward, looking down. Even in this light, she was again seeing the occasional paving stone in the grass.

It was another driveway and it was going in the direction the plan had indicated. If the second block on the plan was the gabled house, this would take her there.

But, as Freek had told her, there was the possibility of a trap. She knew that. And how could they have let him go? Bishop was what he was, but what was he? Whatever he was, she be-lieved he was capable of causing death and destruction for its own sake. Even Yudel had not used a scientific term to describe him.

She stopped for a moment to listen. Perhaps Freek and his men had arrived. Faintly, filtered by the scrub, she heard the sound of an internal combustion engine. But it was too deep and too rough—either a farm truck or a tractor, something with a large diesel engine.

With her breath roaring through her open mouth and her legs shaking with the effort, she brushed past an overhanging branch. Ahead she caught the briefest glimpse of a wall that had once been white and was now gray with age. As she drew closer, she saw that it was streaked by the many summer rains since it had last been painted.

She pressed forward, looking up now. She stumbled on another uneven place and went down on her hands and knees again. This time, as she rose, she saw the Cape Dutch gables through the branches. Now she did stop. She stood completely still and listened. There was still no sound from the road.

The house was large and single-storied. A broad flight of stairs in the center led up to the dark hole that the front door had once filled. Like the door, the window frames along the front had long since been removed. They were sought-after items by the region's endless homeless. The two high gables that dominated the façade stood on either end of the house with perhaps forty meters of decaying roofing in between. Some roof beams had collapsed, taking patches of slate tiles with them and leaving ragged holes in the tiled surface. The signs of what must once have been a wonderful garden were still visible. A wooden pergola was still standing, its paint peeling and discolored. The remaining plants in an ancient rose garden had not been pruned for many years and now formed an untidy tangle down one side of the house. On either side of the drive, broad lawns had been overtaken by rough thatching grass that was more than waist high. Despite the decay, something grand remained, a lingering memory of the property's glory days. A hundred years before, the house must have been as fine a dwelling as any in the country.

The last ten or fifteen meters to the house were open, except for the long grass that had overtaken the lawns. She briefly considered the possibility of crawling through the grass, but that would take too long. She wondered about Freek. Considering where he and his men were when he phoned, he should have arrived by now. They would have torches and would surely make better time up the hill than she had. But what if he missed the gate? There were few landmarks in this bush country. She had almost turned back too soon, and she had been there twice before. No, the car was there. They would see the car.

The driveway was in better shape over the last few meters than it was lower down the slope. It was the only way to approach the building, and Abigail had come too far and too single-mindedly to pause now. She walked up the middle of the drive. Had it not been for the weariness in her legs, she would have run up the front steps. The steps were made of heavy wooden beams, something like the railway sleepers of bygone years. They were still as sturdy as ever as she climbed them slowly and entered what remained of the hallway.

Half of the roof had collapsed and she could see the sky in places. There was enough light for her to make out three doorways leading off the hall, one on either side and another at the back. She went right first, down a broad passage, stumbling over material from collapsed roof sections. In places the floor had rotted and she had to be careful to avoid holes. The passage led to a row of rooms that had probably been bedrooms. Even in the gathering darkness it was clear that none of them had been used recently for human habitation.

Back in the hall, she looked out over the scrub but could discern no movement other than a gentle rustling of leaves in the slight evening breeze. The passage on the left of the hall led to what had probably been living and dining rooms, one of them large enough to have seated fifty or more people. But here too there was no sign of recent habitation.

For the first time since she had left the town planning office, Abigail felt some doubt. From the moment Lou-Anne Hamid had shown her Vyefontein's plans she had been certain that this was where she would find Leon. But there was no sign of human presence. If he was not here, she had made no progress at all. And Bishop was free. And she would not find Leon, at least not today and not alive.

She had been so sure. Could she possibly have been wrong? Yudel too believed that Leon was here.

The door at the back of the hall led into another passage and a kitchen that had a floor area bigger than most suburban houses. The equipment and shelving were gone, but the sinks and a single marble work-surface remained. Here too there was no sign of recent occupation.

She stepped out of the kitchen's back door. In front of her was a cutting into the steep bank that had been necessary to make a level site for the house. It was covered in grass and scrub with just a few bare patches that had eroded into shallow *dongas*. Without thinking, Abigail turned and walked along the back of the house, stepping carefully through the long grass. For the first time she considered the possibility of snakes. She tried to see where she was stepping, but there was too little light to see through the grass.

She reached the corner of the house and turned back, walking more quickly. Halfway back to the kitchen door she stopped again. Level with the ground, and hidden by vegetation if you were coming from the other direction, she could just make out a trapdoor and, next to it, what looked like footprints in the sand.

The trapdoor opened easily and a steep flight of stairs led into the basement. Abigail realized that she was looking into what had been the wine cellar. She stumbled down the stairs too hurriedly and had to reach for the side wall to steady herself. It took a while before her eyes became accustomed to the deeper darkness in a small room where only the faintest light came from the trapdoor. A scrambling sound and a sudden movement to her right caused her to turn and crouch in readiness. Something small dashed to a corner and disappeared into a crack, probably a rat. The room was empty, except for a small pile in a corner. She took something that felt like cardboard from the top of the pile and brought it close to her face. It looked like fast-food packaging. And this time it was not a hundred years old.

Another door led deeper under the house. Abigail entered a vault that disappeared into almost total darkness, seeming to run the length of the house. She touched wooden shelving, empty wine racks that had somehow survived. She almost called Leon's name, but stopped herself. There was no knowing who else might be listening. Another scrambling movement reached her.

The impulse to call for Leon rose within her again and now there was no stopping it. "Leon," she called, keeping her voice low. "Leon, Leon."

The muffled, scuffling response was, to Abigail, unmistakeably the sound of someone who was tied and gagged. Holding back was impossible. "Leon!"

Abigail found herself stumbling in the direction of the sound, down a narrow corridor between the wine racks. She bumped into a rack and was thrown across the corridor and into a second rack. The darkness had become impenetrable and she knew she was going too fast, but slowing was impossible. She cannoned off a rack and fell, landing on the relative softness of a human form. The force of her landing threw Abigail off Leon and onto the concrete floor beyond. Her fingers found the tape that was gagging him. She worked her nails under the end and tore it free.

"Abigail," he whispered. "I knew it would be you."

Abigail led Leon out of the house and onto the front steps. They moved slowly, picking their way in the darkness. At almost the same moment Freek and the six men from the flying squad broke cover, the beams of their torches shining through the stiff thatching grass. Seven torch beams found Abigail and Leon. Freek could see Leon turning repeatedly to look at her. "That woman," he muttered. "Giving her instructions is a waste of breath." He came slowly up the steps of the house to meet them. "Mr. Lourens, I presume," he said. The members of the flying squad were all applauding. "I think that's for you," he told Abigail. "Take a bow." He shook Leon's hand. "Glad to see you, friend."

Leon shook his hand, then turned again to look at Abigail.

"Thank you for coming," Abigail said to Freek.

41

Yudel Gordon had started the drive back to C-Max as soon as Freek and his men left for Vyefontein. In a few moments at the Tshwane West police station the many uncertainties of the last week had disappeared.

For the first time, he understood it all. He did not believe that the core of the matter was going to be decided on a smallholding on the side of the Magaliesberg hills. But that was where Abigail had to go and she had Freek and his men to back her up.

He had the C-Max number in the memory of his mobile and called it up as he drove. The dull-sounding voice of the warder, who had been given charge of the switchboard, answered. "Yes, corrections."

"Give me Head Warder Bogopa," Yudel said.

"He's not here," the bored voice told him. "He works day duty."

"Who's in charge now?"

"Who's calling?"

"Yudel Gordon."

"Who?"

"Yudel Gordon. I'm the prison psychologist."

"Oh." It seemed that a moment of recognition had dawned. "But you were retrenched. I'm not allowed to give that information to . . ."

"For God's sake, man, I'm under contract now. I just want to speak to whoever's in charge." Yudel was entering a main artery and the Saturday evening traffic required his attention. Speaking on the mobile was becoming a bad idea.

"Hold on." Before Yudel could respond, the man was gone. His voice came on again some thirty seconds later. "You're not on the list."

"What list?"

"You're not on the list for access. Sorry, Gordon."

"Listen, I just want to speak to the man in charge tonight."

"I don't know where he is. Phone back later."

"But . . ."

The connection went dead and Yudel dropped the phone onto the seat next to him. Since when do they have a list? he asked himself.

Almost immediately the phone rang again. It was Rosa. "I'm sorry it took me so long, but it was hard to find anyone to ask. They did have a Patrick Lesela, but he left in August without giving proper notice."

Prison psychologist Patrick Lesela was seated primly at the desk in his office, his knees touching each other and his hands flat on the desk's surface. His head was tilted slightly to one side, as if he were listening for something. His face seemed to be at rest and devoid of expression.

A few doors down the passage, he heard the sound of voices as the members of the changing shifts compared notes or discussed the weekend's football or the possibility of a pay rise. He looked at his watch. It was almost seven forty. He waited until the hands showed exactly that time, then he rose and moved unhurriedly toward the door.

He paused for only a moment in the doorway, saw that the passage was empty and then turned in the direction of D Block.

From where he was sitting on his bunk, Marinus van Jaarsveld heard the key turn in the cell door. He knew that it would be unlocked for some sixty seconds. That was the time it took the duty warder to walk to the end of the row and back. After that it would be locked again, and if the cell was found empty it would be the night shift man, who was now going off duty, who would have to explain.

He knew also that the changing of shifts in C–Max took some fifteen minutes. The night shift had all arrived by seven forty-five and were waiting in the outer staff office. The senior warder of the new shift would be studying the log book and would be pleased to find that the night had passed without incident.

This was the time when there were the fewest warders on the cell blocks, most of them congregating around the duty room. With the arrangements that had been made, he would have a clear run out of D block and into the passage that led down to the inner gate and then through it. The only possible problem would be at the outer gate itself. If he had to, he would use the Makarov then. The bribe, split between three warders . . . the Makarov and a little care would get him right out of the prison. And Annette, who looked so innocent that no one would suspect her of anything, would be waiting in the parking area in a vehicle that carried the Department of Correctional Services logo.

Van Jaarsveld had already changed into the white T-shirt and jeans that had been smuggled in with the Makarov. He left the cell and walked unhurriedly as far as the first gate. Behind him a murmuring had started as some of the prisoners saw him go and took note of what he was wearing and the Makarov in his right hand. He was carrying the gun loosely behind his right thigh, his arm extended, just out of sight of anyone coming from the front.

In the main control room, warder Ephraim Nkosi was studying the lights on the control panel. He had been on all day. His eyes were tired and he knew that his attention was wavering. But he was sure that the light that indicated that the main gate to D Block was open had flashed on for a moment. Perhaps it was his weariness playing tricks on him, but he doubted it. Tired or not, he had seen the light come on for just a moment.

This was only Nkosi's second shift in the control room and he was determined to do everything right. He called the sentry box at the gate to D Block. There was no answer. The warder should have been there. If he had gone for a leak he should have let Nkosi know.

Nkosi's next move was to call the duty room. The first ring went unanswered. As in most gatherings, no one held himself responsible for answering the phone. All the warders were either too involved in what they were saying, or waiting too eagerly for a chance to say something.

Nkosi tried a second time. Again there was no immediate answer, but he let it ring. After almost a minute a voice came on. "Ja?"

"Nkosi here. Someone just came through the gate to D Block."

"Who?" The voice sounded irritated.

"It's Nkosi here, from the control room."

"Who passed through the gate?"

"I don't know. The gate opened and closed again."

"Phone the gate."

"I did. Nobody's answering."

"Well, I'm going off duty."

"Get me someone from night shift then."

Without answering Nkosi's request, the warder on the other end of the connection could be heard, facing away from the phone, shouting for anyone on night duty.

All the time he had been speaking, Nkosi's eyes had been fixed on the light that monitored the position of the gate to D Block. Now it stayed dark. Unless he was hallucinating, someone had passed through the gate, either going in or out at a time when it should have been closed. Using his second phone, he called the sentry box at the gate to D Block again. There was still no answer. He let it ring, but there was nothing.

"Yes, what's happening?" The voice was coming from the group in the duty room. The noise he heard in the background, the many assertive voices, sounded more like a party than a changing of shifts. Nkosi recognized the voice as belonging to one of the older sergeants, Sergeant Malgas.

"Nkosi here . . ."

"Yes, my bro'."

"The gate light at D Block came on a moment ago."

"Have you called the gate?"

"There's no answer."

"Try again."

"I've tried twice, sergeant, and it's still ringing there now."

It took a moment for the sergeant to digest this piece of information. "Where's that bastard?" he said.

"I think we should send someone up," Nkosi said.

"I'll go myself."

"Sergeant."

"Yes?"

"I don't think you should go alone."

"Do you know what's happening there?" Now the sergeant's voice carried the sharp edges of both authority and suspicion.

"No, sir. I just think you should take someone."

"I know what I'm doing."

"All right, sergeant. Sorry. I just . . ."

"Don't worry, my bro'. I will take Sibiya with me."

Van Jaarsveld felt that he was safely through the gate to D Block. He had had the workings of the monitoring system explained to him. If you went through it quickly and the operator in the control room was not looking directly at the board, he would never know that anything had happened. And most of the time, when they were looking at the board, the operators were three-quarters asleep. There was a ninety percent chance that he would make it though undetected, they had said.

Now that he was through, he was certain that no one had noticed. From where he stopped, he had a clear view down the main passage almost as far as the duty room, but the passage was empty. No one was coming up to investigate and the daily chores, the floor scrubbing, the removal of plates, the laundry, were long past.

He could see the gate that cut off the cell blocks from the administration offices. That too was deserted, just as he had been promised. He knew it was also monitored in the control room, but he would pass through it with as little trouble.

As van Jaarsveld watched, the gate at the bottom of the passage opened, then closed again. It was a moment before he recognized the figure coming slowly up the passage in his direction. It was that snot-nose of a psychologist, Lesela. What was the useless little cunt doing in the cell blocks at this time of night?

The city traffic was at its densest as Yudel passed through the western suburbs on his way to C-Max. This was the side of the city that was least favored by the residents and where growth was slowest. It was no more than a fifteen-minute drive after eight at night on most nights, but on Saturday nights it took twice that long.

He ran a few traffic lights, but at most intersections traffic from the side streets interfered with his progress. Only when he reached the inner city, and the direction of the traffic was largely against him, did he make better time.

Much had become clear to Yudel in the last hour. The fact that there was a second house at Vyefontein built in the Cape Dutch style clarified where Lourens was being held. Yudel had little doubt that Abigail and Freek would find him there. He also had little doubt that Lourens would be unguarded and unharmed. There was enough reason to believe that this had always been Bishop's intention.

Despite his capture, Bishop had successfully led them down the path that he wanted them to follow. The show he had put on for Abigail's benefit, face twitching and hands shaking, were all aimed at giving Lourens to her. Yudel was sure that he had never been the target. Then there was the drunken singing just before Bishop escaped, too much like the singing just before the prisoners were freed in Ficksburg. An identical diversion was not the sort of coincidence Yudel could believe in. Quite possibly the similarity of the two incidents rested not only in the same song, but in the same singer. If Bishop had an associate, this would explain a great deal about his effectiveness. In Yudel's mind, it also explained something about an academic and prison psychologist who knew little about prisons and less about psychology and who would be working in C-Max where Marinus van Jaarsveld was being held. Mr. Lesela's credentials needed examining and his actions needed monitoring. And both needed to happen soon. Lesela was no psychologist. The department would have checked his credentials and been satisfied with them. If the qualifications were real—and they probably were—the man who now presented them as his own was not Patrick Lesela.

And Leon Lourens was not the only member of that raiding party still alive. Van Jaarsveld would always be a far more satisfying target than Lourens.

He took the zigzag at the top of Schubart Street and went under the train bridge. A few hundred meters ahead on his right he could see the main Pretoria Central Prison. Immediately beyond the prison was the street that led past the warder's houses and recreational facilities. Yudel paused for oncoming traffic, swung the car into the side street and stopped at the barrier of the security checkpoint. A prison officer, wearing an expression that reflected the mixture of arrogance and suspicion that was an integral part of the job, approached him from the guard box. "Yes?" The single word held a question and was accompanied by a little upward jerk of the chin.

Yudel had never seen the guard before. Christ, he thought, where did they find you? And you've probably got the same list. "My name is . . ." he started. At that moment he saw a sergeant in the guard box whom he had known for most of his years in the department. He got out of the car and started toward the guard box.

The guard grabbed at Yudel's arm, but only managed to get hold of his sleeve. "Hey, where you going?" Yudel shook himself free and reached the barrier. "You can't just walk past me," the guard was shouting.

"Piss off," Yudel said over his shoulder. "Sergeant Maake," he shouted.

Maake appeared from the guard box, peering at Yudel over a pair of reading glasses. "Mr. Gordon?"

"I'm under contract now. I need to get into C-Max immediately."

"Is his name on the list?" The guard, suffering the indignity of being ignored by a white man whose name was probably not on the list, sounded determined to keep Yudel out. "If he's not on the list, he's not allowed in."

Sergeant Maake looked from Yudel to his junior and considered the matter for only a second. "Mr. Gordon may go in."

"Is his name on the list?"

"Open the boom," Sergeant Maake said.

Yudel was already getting back into his car.

"You should check the list."

"Open the boom."

The boom slid open and Yudel drove through. There were a few more twists in the road before he reached the parking lot in front of C-Max.

42

Warder Nkosi was studying the lights on the control console as if hypnotized by them. He had heard nothing more from the sergeant who had said that he would investigate what was happening at the gate to D Block. He had wanted to phone the duty room again to check, but in the civil service you did not check up on your seniors to make sure that they were doing their jobs properly.

He did call the gate at D Block again, for the third time now, but there was still no answer. A fourth and fifth call had the same result. He reached for the button that would call the duty room, but withdrew his hand. They were probably up there by now. Everything was probably fine up there.

Almost as he withdrew his hand the light that monitored the gate to D Block came on again. This time it stayed on. That meant the gate was open. The sergeant had probably arrived there, he thought. When he entered, he may have left the gate open.

But no, that was supposed never to happen. The standing orders laid out clearly that the gates to the cell blocks had to be closed at all times. In fact, all gates throughout the prison had to be closed, locked and guarded all the time.

Nkosi got up and went to the door. From the doorway he could see most of the main passage that led up to the cell blocks. The gate into D Block and the passage beyond was just out of sight. He could hear the sounds of utensils clanking in the kitchen and the voices from the duty room, but both were some distance away. He could see that the door to the duty room was open, but the doorway was empty. The sounds from the cell blocks themselves were no more than a distant murmur. Other than that, the prison was silent and the passage itself was empty.

He looked toward the duty room again and saw Warder Sibiya appear in the doorway. He was smoking a cigarette and, as Nkosi watched, he leaned against the doorpost, obviously in conversation with someone inside.

They haven't left yet, he realized. How could they not have left yet?

He ran back to the control console and this time he did call the duty room. Sergeant Malgas, whom he had spoken to earlier, answered. "Ja, duty room."

"Sergeant, that gate is standing open now. The light is on all the time."

"Standing open? Are you sure?"

"I'm looking at the light and it's on."

"I'll check."

"I think you should go now, sergeant."

"Don't give me orders, my man."

"The light's on all the time and standing orders say . . ."

"I know the standing orders better than you do. I'm going." Before Sergeant Malgas hung up, Nkosi heard him shout. "You, Sibiya, come."

The day shift men at the outer gate all knew Yudel well and had been on duty when he was invited by the commissioner the week before. They let him in, although his name was not on the list.

Once inside, he ran down the passage toward the duty room. As he reached its door, Sergeant Malgas and Warder Sibiya were coming out. Yudel recognized them both. "Have you seen Lesela?" he asked the sergeant. "The psychologist?"

"No, sir. But I can't help now. Something is wrong at the gate in D Block. It seems to be open."

"D Block?" Yudel said. "I'm coming with you. But take your firearms."

The sergeant stared at Yudel. What he was seeing was a wild-haired and wild-eyed little man who looked as if he had not slept for a week. "Why?" the sergeant asked.

"I'll take responsibility. Just do it." Yudel took a step down the passage in the direction of D Block. "I'll go on ahead."

"No, sir. You come with me." The sergeant's manner was decisive this time. "If I have to take firearms, you are not going on ahead."

Even Yudel could not deny that Malgas had a point. Moments later, Warder Nkosi tore himself away from the console to see Yudel, the sergeant and Warder Sibiya running down the passage toward D Block. He saw that both the sergeant and the warder were wearing sidearms.

The passage to the entrance to D Block had never seemed so long to Yudel. The other two men, both at least ten years younger, were ahead of him. He wished they were carrying their firearms in their hands, instead of in their holsters. He saw Nkosi's head appear in the doorway of the control room for a moment, and then disappear as he quickly withdrew it. Up ahead, the phone at the gate to D Block was ringing in short bursts, interrupted by half-second pauses.

By the time he turned the corner, the two younger men were at the open gate. The warder responsible for the gate was not there. The passage to the D Block cells turned sharply to the left. As far as Yudel could see it, it was empty. That damned phone was still ringing. The sergeant answered. "All right, Nkosi. You can stop now. I'll let you know when I know what's happening." Then the sergeant was speaking to Yudel. "Before we go farther, just what do you expect to see around that corner, Mr. Gordon?"

"Sergeant, I expect to see Mr. Lesela endangering one of the prisoners. I believe he will be armed."

Malgas nodded. Without speaking, he and the warder removed their firearms from their holsters. "Now, Mr. Gordon. You walk five paces behind us. No closer than that."

The two walked slowly, staying close to the inside of the corner and passing just beyond arm's length of the cells. Yudel followed a little less than five paces behind, doing his best to follow the sergeant's instructions. As they came around the bend, he walked in a wider arc than the two warders. The need to see what was in the rest of the passage was simply too great.

As they rounded the corner, they could see van Jaarsveld. He was seated with his back to the door of his cell, his legs stretched out in front of him, his arms resting loosely at his sides. He could have been a man sleeping next to the family swimming pool on a Sunday afternoon. Sergeant Malgas and Warder Sibiya continued at the same pace as before. Both were glancing from side to side, looking for the possibility of an open cell door.

From the distance at which Yudel first saw him, van Jaarsveld seemed to be wearing a sweater that was colored red down the left hand side and white down the right. He had covered half the distance to the prisoner before he realized that the red was blood, and van Jaarsveld was sitting in a pool of blood that spread almost to his feet. It was only when he got within arm's length of the dead man that Yudel could see how deeply the piano wire had cut and where it had severed the carotid artery.

43

Nkosi answered the phone at the first ring. "Put me through to the main gate," Yudel said. "Immediately."

"Yes," an alert sounding voice answered from the main gate. Clearly, word had got round that something was happening.

"It's Gordon here. I think Mr. Lesela, the new psychologist, may be leaving the prison. You have to stop him and hold him."

"He's just left."

"Are you sure? How long ago?"

"Yes, he's gone. Maybe a minute, maybe less."

Yudel rang off and called the control room again. "How do I get through to the security barrier?" he demanded.

"Putting you through," Nkosi said.

A moment later Sergeant Maake answered from the guard box at the security barrier. "Perimeter gate."

"Sergeant, it's Yudel Gordon here. Has this Lesela, the psychologist, come through there?"

"I think that's him here now."

"Stop him. I think he's killed a prisoner."

Yudel pulled his head away as the handset of the telephone in the guard box crashed to the ground. He heard Maake shouting, but he was not speaking English and Yudel could not follow the words.

The man who went by the name Patrick Lesela knew that the security barrier was the last hurdle to cross. He knew also that he had little time before van Jaarsveld's body would be discovered. And finally, he knew that he dared not hurry. Anything that looked like desperation would arouse suspicion.

As he rounded one of the bends in the road a bicycle, ridden by a child from one of the warders' houses, swerved in front of him. He swung the car wide to avoid the child, but a look of distaste crossed his face. After all these years, he still hated bicycles. The memory of the shattered bicycle that he had saved so hard to buy, lying in the dust at the gate of the Bishop farm, had cured him of that means of transport.

At the security barrier he realized immediately what was happening. He heard the excited shouting from the guard box and saw the other guard turn toward him and reach for his firearm.

He had already assessed the strength of the barrier. Originally, it consisted of a light plastic tube that would easily be swept aside by any vehicle, but some alert senior officer had replaced it with a heavy steel gate.

He knew that his chances of smashing through the gate were slight, but it was clear that by this time they had found the old killer's body. He pressed hard down on the accelerator pedal as he engaged the clutch. The car leaped forward at almost the same moment that the guard stepped onto the pavement and drew his firearm.

The force of the car hitting it lifted the gate off its railing. It rose and bent with the weight of the car, but settled on the bonnet, steel shafts puncturing the bodywork and shattering the windscreen. Stunned by a blow he had taken on the car's door frame and partially blinded by shattered glass, the man called Lesela found the door handle and rolled out onto the pavement. He ran for the pedestrian gate, his right shoulder digging into Sergeant Maake's stomach as the sergeant tried to block the way. By the time he was through the gate, the other guard was already firing. Yudel had put the guard in just the right frame of mind for dealing with someone trying to run the barrier, especially a psychologist. For the moment the car provided some cover.

The first bullet from the guard's gun shattered the back window. The second, as he adjusted his aim, ricocheted off the prison wall, landing in Potgieter Street, the traffic artery some twenty meters away.

Lesela was trying to run, but he could only see partially out of one eye, and was trailing a hand along the prison wall to guide him. He went down hard when the guard's fourth bullet hit him in the back. He tried to rise, but the fifth bullet took him in the back of the head.

By the time Yudel reached the security barrier, the man known to the Department of Correctional Services as Patrick Lesela was dead. His face was bruised and perforated by tiny shards of glass, but the cause of his death was apparent in the two bullet wounds, one in his left shoulder blade, where the bullet had been deflected off the bone and entered his heart, and the other that had entered his brain at the base of his skull. The guard looked altogether pleased with his evening's work. "Five shots," he was telling Sergeant Maake, "and I hit a moving target twice. And I had to dodge his car."

No one at the scene of the incident noticed a second car, driven by a single white man, pull away from the curb a hundred meters up Potgieter Street and come slowly past the intersection. The car stopped for a moment to give the driver a view of the body on the pavement and the barrier, now distorted by the crash, before he pulled away smoothly to be absorbed into the traffic.

44

Yudel was still at the security barrier when Abigail arrived. She was alone, having handed Leon over to Freek and his men.

"And this?"

"Bishop's colleague."

Abigail had tried to approach the body, but was stopped by police who were already erecting barriers to keep the public out. "Are you sure?"

"He went under the name Patrick Lesela. He's just killed van Jaarsveld."

Her eyes were wide at this new enlightenment. "My God. Were they aiming at him all the time?"

"Remember that I told you Bishop wanted us to go to the house, but I didn't know why?"

"I remember."

"He wanted us to find Leon. Your friend was always just a decoy, a diversion to keep us busy while he went after the real prize. The truth is that Bishop gave us Leon."

"He played us," Abigail said. "That we were just players in his game may be the most disturbing element of the whole thing."

"It's not quite like that. You still had to find Leon. Bishop didn't exactly hand you a map. And the way we captured him at the concert was not part of his plan."

"You didn't see Bishop here today?"

"No."

"Will the police search for him?"

"Yes. Freek would never be able to let matters rest as they are."

"The government will want him out of the way too," Abigail said. "He's a potential embarrassment. And what about Leon? Will he be safe a year from now?"

"I don't know," Yudel said. "I hope they find him before the year is up."

Abigail and Yudel were standing next to the plastic tape the police used to cordon off the crash scene. They could see the body of Lesela where it had fallen, face downward on the pavement. A detective, who had been bending over the body, straightened up and came over to Yudel. "He had an old ID book in his inside pocket. It gives his name as Matthew Baloyi."

"Perhaps another alias," Yudel said.

"Perhaps," the detective said, "but I don't think so."

"Why not?"

"It's an old book. A forgery would be new."

Yudel nodded. "Good thinking, detective. You'll need to look into it."

"I will."

When they were alone again, Abigail asked, "Where are you going?"

"Home, to sleep, perhaps to listen to a little music."

"Handel's *Samson*?"

"Maybe." He looked searchingly at Abigail, this surprising woman. It seemed that there was nothing left to say. He shook her hand before starting toward his car. "We'll probably see each other around."

"Yudel, wait." She took him by the arm and drew him away from the police attending to the crime scene. "You remember what you said to me about Bishop and Robert and how I should not confuse them?"

He had to think back before he remembered. "It was up at the house, I think."

"Yes."

"I remember saying something."

"Thank you for that. I've been thinking about it." He nodded and again tried to leave, but she stopped him. "You also need some advice," she said.

Yudel looked sharply at her. There was something almost startled in the look. "Come again?"

"Things are not going that well between you and Rosa. When did you last tell her you loved her?"

"Rosa knows I love her."

"When did you last tell her?"

"I don't know. It's got nothing to do with you though."

"It does. You gave me advice. Now I'm giving you some."

"That's different. I'm a psychologist."

"Don't give me that. You're not my psychologist. When you go home now, tell Rosa you love her."

"Might there be anything else?" He was trying, without success, to sound sarcastic.

"Yes, just one thing. Kiss her and make love to her after that."

"You've got a damned cheek," Yudel said.

"And you had a damned cheek discussing my love life with me, but I needed to hear it. And you need to hear this."

Yudel frowned deeply at her. She was definitely an unusual woman. "Would it be in order for me to go home now, do you think?" The sarcasm was still not working.

"Sure. I'll see you around." He started turning away, but Abigail had not yet released her grip on his arm. "Wait. That handshake doesn't do it." Before he could move any further, she had her arms around him and was hugging him. He felt a quick kiss on his left cheek. "Thanks for everything. You're also an African hero."

Why does she always say things that I am unable to answer? he wondered. He was halfway to his car, taking a detour around the crash scene, when Abigail called after him. "Don't forget now. Tell her as soon as you get home."

Damned woman, Yudel thought. He kept going toward his car. He saw no reason to reply.

Abigail was still not finished. "Then, when you've told her, do what I said you should," she yelled after him.

45

The opening evening of the Department of Justice conference on the role of gender diversity in expanding developing national economies in Africa had been planned as a brief affair, but the program had been delayed. The delegates had all been traveling, some of them for more than a day. Johanna's plan was for them to register, have a drink, enjoy a finger supper and listen to two five-minute welcoming speeches from the minister and the director-general.

That had been the plan. But in just a few minutes, it started to go sadly awry. She had come across the minister and the DG comparing notes. And their notes were copious. It had immediately become clear that neither of them were going to pay any attention to the five-minute limit.

Johanna stood in the foyer, on the steps leading up to the auditorium, looking across the sea of moving, chattering humanity. Most of the people in the gathering were tired from the travels that had brought them here. An hour-long program, most of which was devoted to socializing, was about all they could take this evening. But for her to try giving instructions to the minister and the DG was beyond the scope of her imagination.

The voices in the gathering rose suddenly in excitement. The glass doors through which they had all entered had opened, and people were moving aside to make a path for someone who was coming in. "It's Madiba," an excited female voice reached her.

"I didn't know he was on the program," someone else was saying.

Ordinarily Johanna would have always have been delighted to see the great man who had led the country through its years of transition, but now she wondered if he was just going to add to her problems. She wondered if she would have to fit him into the program as well.

The minister had rushed forward to meet the unexpected guest. The great man shook the minister's hand briefly, then continued toward the auditorium, taking small steps on his stiff, old-man's legs. Close behind, two members of his staff followed, in case he needed help.

To reach the auditorium he had to pass within a few steps of Johanna. As he drew abreast, he noticed her for the first time. Stopping opposite her, he turned and smiled. "My dear, you look troubled," he said.

"Oh, President Mandela, I . . ."

"Former president," he corrected her.

"Former President Mandela . . ." Speaking was suddenly a problem. Johanna could barely breathe.

"What seems to be troubling you?"

"I'm the program organizer, and the guests are all tired . . . and I'm afraid some of the speeches . . ."

"May be too long?"

"Yes, sir."

He reached out and squeezed one of her shoulders gently. "Never mind, my dear. I'll deal with it."

A few minutes later the delegates had assembled in the auditorium. The former president had told the master of ceremonies that he had something to say before the speakers who were on the program, and that all introductions were to be kept brief.

Moments later, he had the microphone. His welcome to the delegates took less than a minute. "But I have especially good news for all of you," he went on. "Tonight, none of the speeches are going to be longer than three minutes." A vigorous round of applause followed. He turned his head to look at the speakers seated on the podium behind him, but spoke loudly enough for the audience to hear. "And I'll be timing you."

This time the applause was mingled with laughter and it continued for some time. No one applauded harder or laughed louder than Johanna.

The police car was being driven by one of the flying squad men who, a few hours earlier, had accompanied Freek to the old ruin in the Magaliesberg hills. Leon Lourens sat in the passenger seat next to him. He was massaging both hands. It felt as if their circulation would never be normal again.

The house where the flying squad driver stopped the car was a nondescript suburban dwelling, set back perhaps ten paces from the road. A straight concrete path led from a simple steel and wire gate to the front door. Fewer security measures were visible than at the homes of Abigail or Yudel. There was less worth stealing, and those who lived in the house would be less able to afford elaborate security arrangements.

The driver had called ahead as they entered the Kempton Park municipality and there was a gathering of people, adults and children, around the front door of the house. Susanna Lourens formed the center of the group, the others all hanging back behind her. This was her moment.

Leon got slowly out of the car. His joints and muscles were still stiff. It took him a moment to straighten up. Susanna stared at him, unblinking and seemingly unable to move.

He walked slowly to the gate, pushed it open and stepped onto the path. "Hello, Susanna," he said.

The sound of his voice broke the chains that were holding her to the spot. She would never be able to remember at what point she had moved or how she had traveled the length of the path, but in an instant she was in his arms and they were holding each other. "Leon," she heard herself saying, "I thought I was never going to see you again."

"It was Abigail," he said. "She found me."

"Thank the Lord," Susanna said. "Why did she do it for us? I don't understand why she did it."

The security guard at the entrance to the parking garage had been told what to expect. As each expensive sedan arrived, he directed it to the block of parking spaces that had been reserved for the purpose. A second security guard directed the new arrivals to the lift, where a third accompanied them to the top floor.

Of the country's eight top black newspaper editors, Robert was the seventh to arrive. The state television service was also present. The six editors who had gotten there before him were gathered in a group in the ante room, waiting to be summoned into the presence of the head of public prosecutions. Since his briefing by the chairman of the company he worked for, Robert had assumed that the other editors would also have known what the meeting was about. It surprised him that they all seemed to be puzzled.

"If he's resigning to move into the corporate world," one was saying as Robert entered the room, "I don't know why we had to come."

"Robert, my man," someone else said, as he joined the group. "So what about this?"

"Good afternoon, gentlemen," Robert said. "I have it on good authority that the purpose of this is to invite us to tea with the president."

"Oh, sure. The head of prosecutions doubles as the president's social secretary now?" There was some laughter at the idea.

One of the others, who had been the first beneficiary of an empowerment deal with a major media company, moved in front of Robert, trying to cut him off from the others. "My man, I heard about your deal. That was a biggie." The tone of voice and slightly chagrined expression suggested some envy. His deal had not been nearly as lucrative.

Robert stepped aside to see round him. "I intend to be worth it," he said.

"Quite right. The way we've been moving up in recent years just shows why they had to hold us back. We would have been running all the top businesses in the country long ago, if they had not discriminated against us."

Robert said nothing. He had heard too much of this kind of talk to want to listen to more of it. The last of the editors was coming through the door. His arrival presented an escape opportunity. Robert walked toward the new arrival with his right hand outstretched. "Long time no see."

"Hi, Robert," the new arrival said. "You know what this is about?"

"I've got an idea, but I may be wrong."

The head of public prosecutions kept the editors waiting another thirty minutes. Senior government people felt the need to impress on others just where it was that real power lay. A young woman from his staff invited the editors into the board-room and showed them to seats that were marked with their names. The single television camera was aimed at a brightly lit chair reserved for the man who had invited the editors. When he entered, it was to take a slow tour of the table, shaking hands with each of his guests in turn.

Once he was seated at the head of the table, he looked up from a pile of paper in front of him. "Thank you for coming, gentlemen," he said. "The matter for which I have summoned you is of national importance."

During the next half hour he outlined the prima facie case of corruption that he felt he had against the deputy president. "But the evidence is not such that I am able to prosecute . . ."

So you want us to do it for you, Robert thought. He's not one of my favorite people, but I won't be doing this for you, not a chance. Not ever.

As it turned out, all Robert's colleagues felt the same way about running the story. It was only on the third day that a senior staffer in the office of the head of public prosecutions started phoning the editors to find out when the story would run. It took another two weeks before one of them yielded to the pressure and splashed it across the front page of his paper. With the dam wall broken, the other papers, including Robert's, and all the electronic media, carried the story the next day. Within another month the deputy president had been relieved of his position.

When Yudel Gordon arrived home, Rosa was sitting in the living room, reading a book about the Aztecs. She rose immediately. "Is it all over at last?" she asked.

"I believe so," he said.

"Thank God."

It was only then that she noticed the young man who was following Yudel, a little uncertainly and a few steps behind. "Rosa, this is David Mabuza. He has something to show you."

Rosa looked with some puzzlement at the young man with his red tie and dark suit. "How do you do?" she said, glancing at Yudel for an explanation.

"David's from Union Appliances," Yudel said. "He had his mobile number on his card." To explain further, he added, "He gave it to me earlier this week. I asked him over."

If that had been Yudel's idea of an explanation, Rosa understood no part of it. "I'm pleased to meet you," she said to Mabuza.

David needed no further assistance. In a moment, he was next to Rosa and opening a colorful catalog. "Mr. Gordon explained that you need a new stove," he said. "He insisted that I show you only top-of-the-range models."

"Did he indeed?" Rosa asked.

"Yes, he did—indeed," David said.

"You are a very dedicated young man," she said, "coming out at this time of night."

"Yes, ma'am. I just got married and my wife's pregnant."

After Rosa had chosen what she wanted and Mabuza had left, having filled another page in his order book, Yudel started toward the kitchen with Rosa following. "I need some coffee."

"I'll do it," she said. "You must be exhausted."

Yudel sat down on one of the kitchen chairs while Rosa switched on the kettle. "That was very nice, Yudel," she said. "Thank you."

He looked at her. She was watching him. He could see in her face both the pleasure brought about by the new stove, and some anxiety that had to do with concern for his well-being. Yudel remembered how, as a child, his mother had told him that the most important thing for a man was to marry a good woman. Why this memory came back to him now he could not say, but, looking at Rosa, he realized that he had achieved that one thing. He had married a good woman.

At almost the same moment, Abigail's advice came to him. Advice? he thought. It was an order, not advice. Although she was more than twenty years younger than he was, it was almost like a new instruction from his mother.

Rosa was pouring the coffee. Yudel struggled to frame the words that would reflect his intentions. "Rosa," he started.

"Yes, Yudel."

"There's something I've been wanting to mention."

"Yes, dear. What is it?"

Fuck it, Yudel thought. Why does that damned woman have this effect on me? I won't do it. Why should I embarrass myself this way?

"Yes, Yudel. What did you want to say?"

"I just thought I should mention . . ." Damn that Abigail, he thought.

"Yes, Yudel, what did you want to mention?"

"I think I have been remiss in some way."

"Oh?" She was handing him his coffee. The last remark had got her attention. "What have you been up to?"

"I . . ."

"It can't be too serious," she assured him, "or I would have noticed."

"Rosa, I've been meaning to remind you . . ." He paused again, building his courage. ". . . that I love you," he finished, studying her face for a reaction.

"I beg your pardon," she said.

"I love you."

"I thought that's what you said, but I wasn't sure."

"Well, that is what I said."

She had started sitting down. Now she rose slowly, assuming perhaps that Yudel's declaration heralded some other action on his part. "What brought this on?"

He considered briefly telling her that it was Abigail's idea, but rejected the thought. It might be better, he reasoned, simply to take the credit. "It just came to me," he said. "I hope you don't mind."

"I don't mind at all, Yudel." She was on her feet now, obviously expecting that there would be more to this that just the bland statement of his affection.

Yudel also rose. The kitchen table was between them and he had to circle it in order to reach her. On the way he stumbled over a chair. By the time he reached her, her eyes were closed and her lips were being held up to him. He kissed them, just as Abigail had told him to.

That night there was a full moon over Pretoria and the surrounding veld. It threw a clean, white light over buildings, trees and hills bright enough to cast sharp shadows, and even to compete with the city's artificial lighting.

In the apartment block where Abigail and Robert lived, it seemed brighter than anywhere else. There was only one street light near the building, a few muted lights in the next-door garden and, tonight, only scattered lights from the apartments. The grounds were partly in the moon's bright light and partly in deep shadow.

If their building felt the effect of the full moon more than others, their apartment felt it most of all. No lights were on and the curtains in their bedroom window were open, allowing the moonlight to flow unhindered into the room.

If the moon itself had been able to see and to follow its own light into Robert and Abigail's bedroom, it would have seen that Abigail had been gathered, unresisting, into Robert's arms. It would also have seen a slow, rhythmical movement from the bed. It was a movement that restarted a number of times during the night, long after the moon had set and the room was in darkness.

46

Freek Jordaan had gone straight to bed when he got home. The last few days without sleep and the capture and interrogation of Michael Bishop had left him near exhaustion. As he fell asleep, he had reflected sadly that he no longer had the stamina of earlier years. The last thing he said to Magda was that he felt that he was going to sleep for a week.

In fact, the week lasted less than an hour. He sat up suddenly and swung his legs over the edge of the bed. The thought that woke him had emerged, unbidden, from some deep recess in his mind. How is it that I was called away to that riot at just that moment? If that was just bad luck, it was the worst possible luck.

Magda had not yet come to bed. Freek could see that the lights in the living room were still on. She was probably sitting in her favorite chair, reading. He went to his cupboard and, feeling in the top pocket of his tunic, found the piece of paper where he had written down the number of the minister's mobile phone. An old mechanical clock on the bedroom bookcase told him that it was still a few minutes before eleven.

Sitting down on the room's only chair, Freek called the number from the bedroom telephone and heard the minister answer. He announced himself, then said, "We did manage to save the building."

"This is very late, deputy commissioner, to be reporting on

something that happened twenty-four hours ago," the minister said.

"I also wanted to apologize for seeming reluctant to attend to it myself," Freek told him.

"That's quite all right. I understand fully. I'm sure you were operating under orders." He was the senior man, showing himself to be deeply and self-consciously magnanimous. "And I was sorry to hear about the problem that developed in that police station while you were away."

Were you? Freek thought. "That's all right. We caught up with the suspects. Unfortunately we had to kill them."

There was a long moment before the minister spoke. "I understood one got away."

"No. They're both dead." Freek lied well, with the off-handedness of someone who was not even considering the possibility that he may not be believed.

"Michael Bishop?" The minister was no longer able to hide the surprise in his voice.

"Who?" Freek asked.

"I thought that was the name . . ." His voice trailed away.

"Michael somebody, you say?"

"You had him in custody," the minister said. "Are you telling me you didn't know his name?"

"Perhaps you can tell me about him, Mr. Minister," Freek said.

"I barely know him. I didn't know him. I heard about him."

"You wouldn't have heard how that riot started?"

This time the pause was longer as the minister considered the implications of all possible answers. Eventually, he resorted to his rank. "What are you implying, deputy commissioner?"

"I wasn't implying anything, Mr. Minister. I simply wondered if you knew how that riot started."

The minister thought about that and made his decision. "Of course I don't. It's very late. You have no business phoning me this late."

Freek apologized again and hung up. What was I implying? he mused. What indeed?

He hung up and went back to bed. Before he fell asleep he wondered if Yudel and Abigail were sleeping well. He hoped so. It seemed possible that the events of the last week may yet reecho in all their lives.

47

The car was late and the pilot of the light aircraft had been kept waiting for an extra thirty minutes. The driver got out of the car and made his way across the sun-scorched dirt surface of a runway surrounded by dense bushveld.

Apart from the moon and the last remnants of daylight, the runway had no lighting of any sort. Neither that nor his passenger's lateness bothered the pilot. He had known that this was going to be a night run and that there was a fair chance his passenger would not be on time. He had done this sort of thing before and schedules were always approximate at best.

The pilot had been a member of the armed forces of the apartheid regime, and had some success at dropping bombs on the forces of liberation. After the change of government he had been one of the first to be told that his services were no longer required. He had found this new line of work, shuttling the kind of people across the country's borders who, for their own reasons, would rather keep their passage secret. It was only marginally less hazardous than his old occupation had been, but it paid much better.

What did surprise him was that only one man got out of the car and was now approaching the aircraft on foot. In the moonlight he could watch his passenger all the way from the car. The pilot had flown this man on other occasions. He knew him to be a strange one. He said little, but he paid without quibbling and that was not something to ignore. The pilot did not know what his passenger's game was, but that did not matter. He would do the job and, as long as he got his money, nothing else mattered.

The man arrived at the aircraft and climbed into the seat next to him without saying anything. "I thought there were going to be two," the pilot said. "Is the other one still coming?"

"He won't be coming. It's just me tonight."

"You realize the price is the same. It doesn't change my expenses if there's one or two passengers."

"I realize that."

"I'm sorry, but my time . . . and it hardly uses any less fuel . . ."

"It's all right."

The pilot started the engine, gave it time to warm up and took off, facing north, the direction in which they would be traveling. "Your people know what to do with the car?" his passenger asked.

"Yes. It has already been taken away. By tomorrow night it will be a collection of spares in four different Jo'burg scrap-yards."

"Good."

For the first few minutes the pilot flew no more than fifty meters above the tangled African scrub that covered the landscape below. Later, he would have to climb a few hundred meters to get above the Waterberg range, and still later the process would be repeated for the Soutpansberg range. But, for the entire trip, he would stay out of the reach of any South African radar system.

It was after ten when they crossed the Zimbabwe border and another half hour before they found the runway they were looking for. It was not unlike the one from which they had taken off—a strip of dry veld grass surrounded by bushveld. To guide the aircraft in, it had been marked by four brush fires made in old oil drums and positioned at the edges of the runway.

The landing was smoother than Michael Bishop had expected, and the pilot brought the aircraft to a halt not far from two parked cars where, if you looked carefully, two men could be seen waiting in the moonlight. Bishop paid first the pilot, then the men who had brought the car, both payments being in South African folding money. An hour later he was driving down a little-used dirt road off the national road between Bulawayo and Victoria Falls.

The full moon, the same one that flooded Abigail's bedroom with its light, was still overhead. He switched off the headlights and drove by the moonlight for a while. Even after the events of the last few days, the risk was invigorating.

He was alone. It was the first time in his adult life that he had been altogether alone. That Matthew was gone was bad enough, but the way he had been taken made it worse. And he had sat there, just down the road, and watched it. He could still see the face of the prison guard who had pulled the trigger. He would never forget it.

When Bishop finally reached his destination and brought the car to a halt, he looked at his watch by the light from the dashboard. Matthew had died only hours before; but it was already the twenty-third.